THE LAST GATHERING

KENDRA HENDERSON

Cover Design: Key International Designs

Published by: Kendra Henderson

Copyright © 2025 by Kendra Henderson

First Edition, November 2025

Printed in The United States

ISBN: 979-8-9935811-0-1

I dedicate this book to all the Behavioral Therapists out there. Keep up the good work—working in the mental health field demands a unique kind of person.

"I am not a product of my circumstances. I am a product of my decisions." —**Stephan Covey**

PROLOGUE

They all appear to be so happy, strolling around town with smiles on their faces. Ugh pathetic. Sarah owns a donut shop, and Alice runs a tech company. What's so special about them? Now they're cozying up to the Mayor, while I remain the black sheep of the family. I'm nothing but garbage, discarded and forgotten.

These two are so oblivious that they don't even realize someone is following them. I've learned their everyday patterns. I know when Alice gets her coffee and when Sarah checks on her horses. I've learned the kids' habits and how often Kandice and her little friend practice these stupid TikTok dances. I can thank Adam for how I've gotten here because he live-streams all his games. Maybe in another life, I'd be a good uncle to him; he actually seems like a cool kid.

I can't let myself get off track, though. I've spent years putting this plan into motion. I've used every penny to make sure I reclaim what's mine. These two have no idea what hell I'm about to unleash on them. People might tell me to forget it because I'm a grown man, but little do they know I've lost a lot, and I'm here for blood, not a family reunion.

As I sit in my car, watching them cross the street in downtown Shelly Grove, preparing to address the town, I feel a surge of anger building inside me. I'm tempted to floor it and run them down. I

1

put my hand to my head and bang it, trying to shake off those dark thoughts, because I need to stay calm. I remind myself that now isn't the time. This isn't a sprint; it's a marathon, and I need to control my rage.

"Oh my sisters, if only you knew what's coming to you," I say to myself. "I'm getting ready to wipe those smiles right off your faces."

I'm going to kill them all. Every last one of them.

CHAPTER 1

— · —

If someone had asked me two years ago what I was doing on a Saturday morning, I probably would have told them I was preparing for one of my mother's outrageous parties, which she was hosting. I might have said I was shopping for the finest dress, as our mother always prioritized appearances. But fast forward two years, and I can honestly say I'm sitting in the best donut shop in town, enjoying a cup of coffee with a warm chocolate-frosted donut while chatting with my sister.

Many might think this is something normal people would do on a Saturday morning, but there's nothing normal about my sister Sarah and me. We couldn't breathe the wrong way without facing beatings or scoldings as kids. I can still taste the metallic in my mouth from being hit hard enough until I bled. As adults, Lily-Ann would try to manipulate us or make us feel less than a person if we didn't do as she said. But this was it; we no longer had to look over our shoulders, worried that our mother would pop up out of nowhere. *I still can't wrap my head around how that woman was always everywhere at once.*

A chime sounds, and I'm instantly startled. I look behind me and notice it's just a customer entering the donut shop. Maybe I lied a little bit. I still get a little jumpy occasionally, but I'm quickly reminded that we no longer have to worry about our brothers. No more telling Mommy Dear about their sisters when we aren't doing as Mother says.

We were finally free. Free to wear what we wanted. We were free to speak our minds. No more grammatically correcting every word that comes out of my mouth. *For goodness' sake, I'm an adult.* I don't need to be reminded that the word "ain't" isn't in the dictionary. Our mother wanted us to be perfect. I no longer had to get my hair silk-pressed to hide my natural curls. I could finally walk around with my natural afro and a bonnet if I wanted to.

Out of everything, my favorite part is that I was finally free to leave the house in sweatpants if I wanted to, and today, that's precisely what I'm wearing: grey sweatpants, a white t-shirt, and my black and white Nike 270s. There's no one to impress. It's time for me to get to know myself, and this version of me loves to be comfortable. I no longer have to put on a full face of makeup to go to the gas station. Our mother used to tell my sister and me, "You'll never find a good-looking man dressed like you just got out of bed."

"Hey, Mom! Jenny and I wanted to ask if it's okay if we go see a movie tonight with some kids from school," Kandice asks as she enters the donut shop.

I smile, and at this point, I can tell Kandice thinks I'm nuts because I haven't answered her question.

"Mom?"

"Sorry, sweetie," I say.

"Are you okay, sis?" Sarah asks.

"Yes," I sigh. "I'm just taking this all in."

"Taking what all in?" Sarah asks.

4

I gaze into my sister's eyes, tears of joy forming in my own, as I whisper, "Our freedom."

Sarah smiles and gives my hand a light squeeze.

"Mom?"

"Sorry, sweetie. Yes, you can go, but you're only sixteen. I want you in by nine." I demand.

"Mom," Kandice whines. "Everyone else's parents are letting them come home at ten. We were going to see the new Blood Suckers movies. Can I please come home at ten?"

"Fine, ten and no later. Just because you can drive now doesn't mean you get to stay out late. You're only sixteen, young lady," I explain.

"Yes, ma'am, I'll be home on time," Kandice says, drawing an invisible cross across her chest. "I promise."

I smile at Kandice as I watch her and Jenny go to a corner in the donut shop to practice one of the latest TikTok dance trends. It's crazy how time has flown. I actually have a teenager who can drive. I can't say that I'm disappointed, though. It's nice to sit on the passenger side of the car now and then.

"Can you believe it, sis?" Sarah asks, smiling.

"Believe what?" I ask.

"We did this. Who would have thought Kandice would be learning a dance with a friend in a donut shop on a social media platform?" she points out. "Lily-Ann would have freaked if she saw this."

I chuckle. We can do that now that she's not around. We can laugh at the awful things our mother would have said or done in these situations.

5

"What kind of mother lets her teenage daughter dance in public?" I jokingly say as if I were Lily-Ann. "A lady with class doesn't act like a fool in public."

We will probably be scarred for life because of the things our mother has put us through, but Sarah and I are survivors, and we're finally free.

CHAPTER 2

— · —

O ne thing Lily-Ann was right about was that the town of Shallow Hale brought terrible memories. The last night I thought I spent in Shallow Hale reminded me of how awful the town is. My mother wanted to keep me confined so badly that she had to hypnotize me to do it.

It was time for a change in our town. Not only did Lily-Ann hypnotize me, but she did the same thing to everyone in our town. She wanted total control over all of us, and it was time we reassured the people in town that something like this would never happen again. Once everyone emerged from their hypnosis, we were able to meet the actual mayor of this town. Surprisingly, he is a very kind man who genuinely cares for the residents. It took some time to explain to him what had occurred, but with Mr. Gerald's help, we were finally able to convince him that hypnosis was real.

We informed the mayor that the people in town had the right to know what had been happening around here for all these years, so he agreed to let Sarah and me hold a meeting to gain the town's trust. We knew this would be challenging because who could believe the one person everyone adored the most would hypnotize them?

"Are you ready?" Sarah asks.

"Ready as I can be," I say after taking the last bite of my chocolate-frosted donut.

"Are you nervous?" she asks.

"Definitely," I say.

For weeks, Sarah and I had been telling people around town to meet at the city park, where all the significant meetings were held. We wanted to show everyone that Lily-Ann would no longer be over this town. We also wanted to ensure everyone was okay and knew they didn't have to continue living here. I mean, who could blame them?

If I'm being honest, I didn't want to spend another night in this hellhole. Sarah reminded me that we were no longer under our mother's control. She believed we could turn this place around and show everyone our town could be the tight-knit community our mother supposedly wanted us all to have.

Lily-Ann always pretended to care about our community. She made people think she wanted the best for Shallow Hale. But in truth, she tried to manipulate us and keep us under her control. That's all behind her now. She's trapped in a small room, lost and without a sense of self.

She is no longer that mysterious woman. She is no longer the keeper of this town. She will not hurt anyone again as long as I live. I now control her, and she is under my hypnosis, destined to spend her days with dementia.

Luckily, the donut shop is downtown, and the park is within walking distance. I chug the rest of my coffee and toss the cup in the trash as we make our way out the door.

CHAPTER 3

—·—

After everyone is assembled at the park, the mayor delivers a brief speech about his vision for the town. He shares his thoughts on what needs to change and how he plans to draw in new businesses. He's teamed up with some Atlanta government officials to bring more jobs to our town, which would help build more communities. His goal for this town was never to remain so small that only the elderly would stay. He informed Sarah and me that after his speech, he would invite us on stage to explain what had happened to us all.

"If you all could give a warm welcome to two of our very own, Ms. Alice and Ms. Sarah," he says, gesturing for us to come on the stage to join him. "These two ladies would like to talk to you about some things that have unfolded right under our noses."

Sarah and I link arms, and we slowly take the stage.

"Thank you, sir, for this opportunity," I say, taking the microphone from him.

In my mind, the first thing I want to address is what happened to all of us. Before I can get a word out, one person asks, "What was the cause of death for your neighbor?"

Another person asks, "Was the person who murdered Dr. Bryant's receptionist caught?"

The questions asked were valid. I had never led a meeting like this before, so perhaps I was over my head by taking on this challenge. I pause momentarily, staring at the crowd like a deer caught in headlights. People began asking questions simultaneously, making the atmosphere feel more like a zoo than a town meeting.

This situation was overwhelming for Sarah and me, but we understood that we were the only ones who could explain what had happened. Mr. Gerald stayed right next to us the entire time; he never left our side, even after what we all discovered.

I guess you can say Lily-Ann did get another thing right, surprisingly. She made it possible for us to meet a good person who was more of a father figure to us than our father. It felt good to have a sane person around here. You know what they say: Blood doesn't always make you family. Mr. Gerald did not share the same DNA as Sarah and me, but he was more of a parent to us than our mother could ever be.

My kids, Kandice and Adam, continued to call Mr. Gerald "Grandpa." They loved him just as much as Sarah and I did. We spent several days with him and enjoyed many family dinners together. We always look forward to the holidays to create genuine family memories together. Our mother wouldn't know anything about that. She always paid a photographer to take photos of our family and made us stand and smile how she wanted.

While Sarah and I silently observe the townspeople, Mr. Gerald notices our nervousness. He looks at us, takes our hands, and says, "You girls got this."

Right now, I understand precisely what these people need. They don't need someone to control them; they need a genuine explanation. They need someone who cares about them and wants the best for this town. They are frightened and want to hear some truth for once.

I take a deep breath and raise the microphone to carry my voice across the park. I start explaining everything that happened to them from the beginning, informing everyone that the person they thought they loved and adored was a murderer—a psychopath, if you ask me.

Silence filled the park as the people in town listened to what I told them. At this point, I could see the confusion on each of their faces. To help them understand better, I explain how Mr. Cramer, as everyone knew him, was really our brother Cameron, and the so-called good Dr. Bryant was really our brother James. I told them that both were our mother's accomplices and that Cameron was responsible for the detective's murder. To this day, we remain uncertain about what she did with his body.

Questions begin to arise, and chatter starts to circulate. At this point, people are scared and unsure whether they can trust us. I can't blame them for their doubts; I wouldn't trust myself either if I were in their position. After all, look at who our mother is.

I continue to explain to them how Lily-Ann hypnotized each of us so we would all remain here. I explain how she wanted to control us all and turn this town into what she wanted it to be. At this point, more questions came, and the chatter grew louder.

It's hard to believe something like this could actually happen. It's clear to me that talk is cheap, and I needed to earn their trust. I raise the microphone to my lips and say, "Listen, we were all victims in this situation. My own mother even tried to kill my sister and me."

The crowd falls silent, fixated on me in disbelief. The loving, God-fearing woman, they all knew, was nothing but a wolf in sheep's clothing.

CHAPTER 4

— · —

C hatter fills the air, and I hear someone ask, "If your mother really tried to kill you, how do we know you two won't try to kill us? It was your neighbor after all who turned up dead," an elderly woman says in the crowd.

Everyone is safe now, I assure them. I remind them that my family went through the same thing they did. I explain that our mom wasn't capable of hurting anyone else after what happened to her. But there's one thing I can't share with them—we actually hypnotized her into believing she had dementia. If I told them the truth, they wouldn't trust us. So, I stick with the story everyone else thinks: our mom was diagnosed with dementia, and she will stay at the facility for the rest of her life.

Is it wrong that I don't want to tell them the truth? Does that make me like her? I thought to myself. The people here didn't need to know how she developed dementia; they only needed reassurance that she was no longer free to walk around our town.

Before I can say another word, a random guy in the crowd raises his hand like a kid in the classroom waiting for the teacher to acknowledge him.

"Hi, yes, sir. Do you have a question?" I ask.

"Hi, ma'am. My name is Jimmy Wilkes. I live in the Whispering Meadows community. I was a few houses down from Mr. Cramer or Cameron, as you said." He explains.

I nod.

"You're telling us all about what your mother has done to us here and how you girls want to make this a better place..." he pauses.

"Yes, that's correct," I say, not quite understanding where he is going with his question.

"Well, in my opinion, none of us want to stay in Shallow Hale anymore..." he pauses as the crowd starts speaking simultaneously.

People become enraged, insisting they want to leave town. Some even threaten to harm Lily-Ann if they can find her in the facility. The meeting starts to spin out of control, and Jimmy Wilkes quickly moves to the front of the crowd, signaling for me to hand him the microphone.

I hesitate briefly because he had incited the crowd's fury. While I was speaking, it appeared that everyone was beginning to sympathize with me. But something inside me told me I could trust where he was going with this. So, I cautiously pass him the microphone and allow him to continue, praying internally that he won't say anything else to stir up the crowd.

"I'm not suggesting that we all leave this town. I mean, we all have lives here. Most of us have raised our children here. What I'm suggesting is, what if we officially vote to change the town's name? Shallow Hale is a sad reminder of what that woman has stolen from each of us." Jimmy Wilkes suggests as he passes the microphone back to me.

The crowd falls silent, and their expressions shift from fiery to contemplative. Perhaps this is what the town truly needs. Renaming our town might be the fresh start that we all need. Glancing at the mayor, he gives me a nod, indicating that he also likes the idea of a name change. He steps closer to me and places his hand over the microphone so no one can hear what he says next.

"Hey, all the true leaders are present," he whispers.

I glance around and notice a few people who look official, all dressed in business attire. "Yes, I see."

"Well, let's hear the people out. The entire community is here today; it seems like the perfect time to initiate a vote on a new town name. Don't you think?" he asks.

I nod my head in agreement.

The mayor grabs the microphone, "Does anyone have any ideas? We are open for suggestions."

Random name ideas are thrown out from every direction of the crowd. None of the ideas stand out to me, and as I glance at the mayor, I notice nothing seems to catch his interest either.

A lightbulb moment hits me like a ton of bricks: "What if we stick with Shelly Grove?" I suggest leaning into the microphone so my voice will project across the park.

Once again, the entire park falls silent, and everyone's staring at me in shock, as if they're wondering how I could suggest such a thing. I glance over at the mayor, and he looks just as bewildered.

"Hear me out, please. Our mother hypnotized us into thinking this town was called Shelly Grove, but in reality, it was still Shallow Hale. Why not leave it, Shelly Grove? Why not leave it, so it can be a reminder of how we overcame her hold over us? And when we enter our town and see the new sign with Shelly Grove plastered across it, we can see it as more of a victory than a defeat."

Once more, silence settles over the park, and all I can hear now is the sound of birds chirping. Everyone is staring at me. Then, out of nowhere, the unthinkable happens. The mayor puts his hand on my shoulder, leaning in close to the microphone so his voice can carry across the crowd. "Honey, I think that sounds like a great idea."

My mind is still reeling from the shock. Sarah and I are on the verge of a huge change, and I'm at a loss for words. It's hard to believe what just happened. We truly outdid our mother. As I take in everyone's smiling faces, I realize the mayor and the other town leaders are voting in agreement to officially name the town Shelly Grove.

Just as the meeting is about to adjourn, a woman in the crowd raises her hand to ask one more question. "Yes, hi, my name is Joan Marshall, and I live in the Whispering Meadows community," she says with a strong Southern accent. "What are y'all's plans with your mother's house? Even though we are trying to move forward and recover from what she's done to us all, her house sticks out like a sore thumb. It's a little creepy if you ask me. It sits at the top of the hill as if someone is still up there."

She has a point. I never would have thought about setting foot in that house. The town's name was terrible and brought back awful memories, but the thought of her house was horrifying. I couldn't imagine stepping back in that place. She almost killed my kids in that house, and she was willing to murder her own daughters there. Just thinking about setting foot in Lily-Ann's house has become my biggest nightmare.

CHAPTER 5

— · —

As months went by, Sarah and I kept our promises. We truly wanted this town to be better. Working closely with the mayor, we engaged with everyone in town and took the time to get to know each of them. We heard their concerns and took into consideration their wants.

Sarah and I reached out to as many people as we could to spread the word about Shelly Grove. Thanks to my tech-savvy son and my book-loving daughter, we were able to connect with people in bigger cities. We were determined to make Shelly Grove more than just another small town. This was our home, and we deserved better, and we wanted to share our story with the world.

With all our hard work, our town was finally going to get a bigger store that would be a one-stop shop. You would have all you needed in one place. Shelly Grove was undergoing a positive transformation. We were all coming together as the community Lily-Ann pretended to create. I guess we finally gave her something she wanted. Our community was more like a family than a town.

Oh God, did I just agree with her on something?

As we walked by, we all waved at each other. The mayor and his council had decided to build a new playground in the park for the kids to enjoy. They'd signed a contract with three companies from Atlanta to come in and cut down some trees in the area, making the space brighter. Shelly Grove was now becoming a town where people could escape the big city and enjoy some peace and quiet. This was a place where you could take in the small-town vibe and visit unique mom-and-pop shops.

It felt good walking around town now. People no longer had those painful smiles. The people here were full of life, and we were all free to be who we wanted to be.

The donut shop Sarah ran remained the best in town. Although she wanted to continue running it, she decided not to put all her efforts into one thing. To keep the shop going, she brought in more help to manage it, as she had bigger goals in mind. Thanks to her, Shelly Grove got its first horse stable: Grove Stables. I was so proud of her because she'd always dreamed of working with horses, and now she's made it a reality. She spent most of her time taking care of them, and she even convinced Kandice to help after school, promising to pay her since she now has her own car.

I took over my brother's business and kept the "jeans on Fridays" policy. Cameron was right: people really do enjoy wearing jeans on Fridays. My aim was to improve the workplace and manage it more efficiently. I wanted my employees to feel supported and know that I genuinely cared about their well-being.

The Psychiatrist's office, James ran, was shut down. One of the people in town took over the suite and turned it into a yoga studio. We all suffered enough in Shelly Grove and didn't need the reminder that our minds were being controlled. So, if anyone needed to speak with a Psychiatrist, they had to travel to the next biggest city, Atlanta, to talk with someone. No one complained about that.

I told myself I wouldn't let the receptionist and my neighbor's deaths go in vain. I believe I stayed true to them, and I pray that their souls can now rest in peace. I thought it would make me feel better knowing that, but looking at that suite was still a painful reminder of what they did to the receptionist. I'll never be able to get the image of her tied to the chair, beaten, and strangled to death out of my mind.

Even though this is supposed to be a fresh start for Shelly Grove, some memories still haunt me. I'll never forget the terrified look on my neighbor's face the night she came to warn me, and I'll never forget how Cameron dug the knife into the detective's stomach. Each of them died trying to help me, and for that, I'll always remember them. I'll never let this place go back to the way it was. I'll never take my eyes off Lily-Ann until the day she leaves this earth.

My neighbor's house didn't remain empty. Mr. Gerald was kind enough to move in, allowing him to be close to us. I honestly don't blame him for moving out of that big house. There were too many secrets, and we all wanted to stay close to each other, so Sarah bought a house in my subdivision as well. We felt safer knowing we were close to each other. It also made it easier to have family dinners. We didn't have to drive; we could walk.

My son, Adam, remained the same kid he had always been. He loved playing video games. Now that everyone was no longer hypno-tized, he was no longer the center of attention at school. He was able to experience school the way it should be. He was also able to form real friendships. I had several kids playing video games at my house every weekend with Adam. It didn't bother me at all. As long as he was happy, I was even happier.

My kids had been through enough, and seeing them smile meant the world to me. Our lives flashed before our eyes the night my mother tried to kill us. We don't take each day lightly. So, seeing them smile and having fun means more to me than controlling how many hours a day Adam spends playing video games.

As Adam always says, this was definitely the life. Something terrible happened to all of us, but in a twisted way, it has also brought us closer. I've gained a father, and the kids have gained a Grandfather. Sarah and I are closer, and my mother is no longer in control. We couldn't ask for anything more.

CHAPTER 6

— · —

As I lie in bed, gazing up at the ceiling and reflecting on all we've accomplished, a loud alarm suddenly blares. I'm not sure where the sound is coming from, but it's close enough that it might be my own car alarm. Out of curiosity, I peek out the window to see whose alarm it is. To my surprise, it's my car. *Great.* Jumping out of bed, I grab my robe and pick up my keys from the entryway table. I'm not worried about robbers, but I'm more concerned about waking up the neighbors.

Approaching the front door, my mind takes me back to what I did to my brother, Cameron, the night I broke into his house. I needed to create a distraction to get him out of the house. So I pulled on his car's door handle, which caused the alarm to go off. I shake my head to clear my thoughts. *We're safe, Alice, calm down.* Cameron is dead, James is long gone, and Lily-Ann is stuck in a facility for the rest of her life.

Chuckling at the silly thought of it being one of them, I step outside and observe my surroundings. Something still didn't sit right with me. What would cause my car alarm to go off? I mean, there were no heavy winds to shake the car. Looking over at Mr. Gerald's house, I start to feel that unsettling feeling again—the feeling that my neighbor is here. I couldn't blame her spirit for wanting to return and haunt this place. She was hypnotized and then murdered. If I were her, I would visit Lily-Ann every night, torturing her.

Approaching my car, I press the unlock button on the key fob to turn off the alarm. I place my head against the passenger side window to peek inside. It's dark, but I'm still able to see that it doesn't look like anything has been tampered with. Unsure of the state of the rest of the car, I decide to do a walk-around and check the outside of the car: *just as I left it,* I think to myself when I realize that no windows have been broken and there is no sign of forced entry. *Why did the alarm go off then?*

The only plausible explanation is that a stray animal might have been circling the car. Shelly Grove does have some stray dogs and cats in the area. It's possible that the animal could have brushed up against the car somehow.

Just as I'm about to accept that it's an animal and decide to head back inside, I stop dead in my tracks at the sound of something coming from the side of the house. "Was that a banging sound?" I ask myself. It sounds like something just hit the trash cans, and I'm not sure if it's an animal, but I know I have to find out what's back there.

As I slowly walk to the side of my house, I glance over my shoulder to make sure I'm alone. The night is eerily quiet and dark, and you could hear a pin drop if you listened closely. There's something unsettling about walking in the dark; the silence is always creepy, and your eyes play tricks on you. The trash can on the side of Mr. Gerald's house could easily be mistaken for a person lurking in the shadows. And the light pole could pass for a ghost—if I were the type to believe in those sorts of things. As I head to the back of the house, a sudden chill runs down my spine, and that gut feeling I get when something's off kicks in.

"Come on, Alice. Pull yourself together. This is a safe town, and your mother is no longer in control," I remind myself as I approach the trash cans.

I slowly lift the lid, and suddenly—bam! A raccoon leaps out of the trash can, making me jump back in shock. My heart races, pounding hard in my chest. I had no clue this little guy was hiding in there—definitely not what I was expecting!

I gather myself and start laughing so hard that tears form in the corner of my eyes. It felt like I was in a horror movie, and one of the freakishly muscular killers was about to jump out and get me. I just knew I was done for. Shaking my head at the idea, I place the lid back on the trash can and head towards the front of the house.

Approaching the front of my lawn, I find myself still tickled at what I just experienced; I remind myself that this town is not a part of a horror movie. I remind myself that my neighbor is resting peacefully and has not returned from the dead to haunt the place. We have all been through a lot, so I also remind myself that things will take a while to feel completely normal.

Before going back inside, I decide it's probably best to recheck the car. At this point, it's clear to me that it was a raccoon, but you can never be too careful. I pull on the handle to ensure all the doors are locked, and I click the lock button on the key fob for extra reassurance that the car is definitely locked.

As I turn around to head for the front door, I'm suddenly confronted by my brother James. He's standing on my front lawn, wearing a dark ball cap and all-black clothes. It's clear to me in that moment why I had that uneasy feeling—someone had been watching me, and that someone was James.

"You thought you could run me away, didn't you, sis?" he asks through his teeth, his eyes wide, and I can no longer see the shade of brown in them; they had gone entirely black just before hitting me on the side of my head with a crowbar.

CHAPTER 7

— · —

Gasping for air, my chest heaving and heart racing, I slowly open my eyes to see Kandice standing over me, her expression a mix of concern and alarm. The dim light filters through the room, casting eerie shadows on the walls, and I blink several times, trying to figure out where I am. My head throbs with a dull, pulsating ache as if someone had swung a crowbar straight into my skull, and I can hardly believe it. *What just happened?*

I feel my head, and I don't feel any wet spots, which tells me I can't be bleeding. I bring my hand in front of me, and I blink several times to reassure myself that there is no blood on my hand. I feel my clothes, and I realize I'm still in my pajamas. *Is this possible? Was it all just a dream?* I wonder.

"What's going on?" I mumble.

"Mom, your car alarm is going off," Kandice tells me.

I'd be lying if I said chills didn't roll down my spine at her very words. I was frozen. It was clear that I had just had a horrible dream, but what were the odds that my car alarm was going off just as it had in my dream?

"Well, are you going to shut it off before it wakes up the whole neighborhood?" she asks.

Gathering myself, I sit up, clearing my throat, "Can you give me my robe so I can go check it out?"

Right now, a wave of nervousness overwhelmed me. My stomach clenched with anticipation, and my mind raced through endless possibilities of what might happen once I stepped outside. I was completely unsure of what to expect. Despite my fears, I told myself that James couldn't possibly be foolish enough to come back. After all, he had seen firsthand what I did to our mother, and I doubt he would risk returning. *Would he?*

Carefully opening the door, I reach for my keys on the entryway table. A wave of déjà vu hits me as I look at my keys. I step onto the front porch, trying to stay silent. I survey my surroundings, and just like in my dream, it is unusually dark outside. I make my way down the two porch steps, keeping a close eye on my car as I approach. As I reach for the door handle, my gaze drifts over to Mr. Gerald's house. *It was just a dream,* I remind myself, because as I look at his house, I feel a sense of calm. There's no sense of being watched, and I don't hear any crazy raccoons messing with my trash cans.

Clicking the lock button on my key fob, I begin to head back inside when I notice the front door of Mr. Gerald's house opens, and I see him running out. *What they—*

"Hey, is everything okay?" he asks.

I chuckle.

"Yes, everything is okay. The alarm on my car just randomly went off," I explain. "I'm sure it was just a stray running around."

Exhausted and still reeling from the worst nightmare I'd ever had, I was more than ready for this night to be over. I said goodnight to Mr. Gerald, who stayed to make sure I got into the house safely. Just as he was about to close the door, a mysterious black sedan with tinted windows crept by. It slowed down a few houses away and came to a stop.

For a moment, the car sat still in the middle of the road. Mr. Gerald and I locked eyes, our disbelief evident. *Who could that be at this hour?* Shelly Grove doesn't have bars or clubs. All the local businesses close early. Who would be out this late?

I wasn't going to sit there and wait to find out. It was already a long night for me. I was startled by James haunting my dreams. I was uneasy with the thought of my neighbor coming back to haunt Shelly Grove, so I did what any curious person would do: I ran towards the car to figure out who was in it. But someone didn't want to be seen. As I got close, it sped off. Leaving nothing but tire marks behind.

I stood there in the middle of the street, scratching my head. Mr. Gerald finally caught up to me and wondered if I was able to get a good look at who was in the car, but I couldn't give him an answer. I was lost for words.

Who was in the car, and what were they doing creeping down our street? I wondered as I kept staring at the faint dust the car had left behind.

CHAPTER 8

—·—

The entire night, I sat awake, unable to sleep because my mind was racing. I kept pondering why I had that dream about James, feeling uneasy about the strange presence from my neighbor's house. The biggest mystery of all was identifying who was in that black car.

I hadn't visited Lily-Ann since we placed her in the facility, and I felt it was time I went. Something strange was happening; I could sense it. I needed to make sure she was still confined to her room, wasting away like a prune.

As soon as morning hit, I lay in bed for a second, feeling restless. I must have drifted off to sleep after my adrenaline settled. It was clear to me last night that I would be going to visit Lily-Ann at the facility today, but for some reason, this morning, my anxiety level is off the charts. I reach over to my nightstand and unplug my cell phone from the charger. It's six in the morning, and I'm wondering if my sister is awake yet. I scroll down to Sarah's name and press the green call button.

"Alice?" Sarah answers, confusion in her voice. She's probably trying to figure out why I'm calling her so early in the morning. "Is everything okay?"

"Hey sis!" I say overjoyed. Forgetting that it is early in the morning. "So what do you have planned today?"

"Other than going to check on the donut shop and feed my horses?" she says sarcastically.

"You know what I mean," I say with a chuckle.

"Nothing really, what's up?" she asks.

I begin to tell her about what Mr. Gerald and I experienced last night. Before I go too much into detail, I first tell her about the dream I had about James being back. From what I can tell, that freaked her out as well.

"Some dreams can be warnings," she says.

I agree with her and tell her that's what freaks me out the most. *Was my dream a warning?* Not forgetting what happened the rest of my night, I tell her about the mysterious black car that stopped in the middle of the street. I tell her how I ran after the car, trying to get a better look at the person.

Sarah sits up from what I can hear and gets closer to the speaker. "Are you crazy? You could have been killed?"

She's not wrong. Something just came over me, and I was fed up with being afraid, I guess. I also needed to know if it was James. What are the odds that I dream about him and then this car shows up out of nowhere? That has to mean something, right?

"I'm getting up now, try not to run after any more mysterious vehicles until I get there," she says.

I agree, but honestly, Sarah knows me better than anyone. I can't let things go. If something doesn't seem right or look right to me, it's in my nature to go check it out. I'm the person in those scary movies who goes towards the noise when I know good and well my black behind should be running away from it. But if the car shows up again, I'd definitely be the first one out the door.

"Got it, sis, I won't," I lie.

CHAPTER 9

—·—

Waiting for my sister to arrive, I decide to take care of my motherly duties and make the kids some breakfast before they head out for school. Both my kids are in the kitchen with me, giving me a hand with breakfast. "Why aren't you wearing your work clothes?" Kandice asks.

"What are you up to today, Mom?" Adam asks.

"Yeah, where do you think you are going, young lady?" Kandice asks jokingly.

I don't want to startle them, so I do what any good parent would do in my situation.

"Your aunt and I are having breakfast this morning. We wanted to talk about a new project for the town," I lie. The last thing I want is for them to think their grandmother might be out of the facility.

Kandice gives me a look that tells me she isn't buying what I'm telling them. Someone once told me a little lie isn't bad when you're doing it to protect the ones you love. I can't let them relive that nightmare. We're finally making progress and getting over the past, but I can tell my mother has traumatized them because they startle easily when there's a loud noise.

31

The doorbell rings, and I jump, a little shaken up from last night's events and knowing where I'm headed today.

Adam rushes to the door, "Mom, it's Aunt Sarah!"

Now I understand how the kids feel every time they hear something unexpected. Lily-Ann has traumatized all of us. But this is why I can't leave this town. If I weren't here, she'd be able to get out of the facility and possibly hurt more innocent people in this community.

Shaking off those thoughts, I quickly grab my purse and plant a kiss on both my kids' foreheads. I hurry out the door and give my sister a quick hug. "Alright, let's get going before these two start asking more questions," I say jokingly to Sarah.

"Well, you're in a hurry to see our mother dearest," she says sarcastically.

I purse my lips, giving her a girl, please look and click my seatbelt in place. "Just drive."

Driving through town, I glance out the window and let my mind wander. I can't shake off that dream. James' face looked like pure evil—his eyes were dark and full of hatred, and his face was twisted in rage. He was ready to kill me, and now I'm starting to wonder if my dream was actually a warning.

"We're here," Sarah says, interrupting my thoughts. "I wonder if Sharon is up front; she could be assisting with passing out breakfast to all the patients?"

I shrug my shoulders.

After hypnotizing our mom, we met Sharon, one of the nurses at the facility. We all became close when she found out our mom had something to do with her grandmother's death. It turned out that the little old lady next door was actually her grandmother, so she was on board with giving Lily-Ann her pill daily. We had found a large enough supply in our mom's house to last for years—at least until she died, I hoped. It was clear to us, though, that one day they would run out. For now, we're just hoping for more or at least figuring out how our grandparents made them.

We step out of the car, and I pull my sunglasses down slightly, instinctively glancing at the building with an uneasy feeling. It's all dark, weathered brick, the kind that has long since decayed, with black mold creeping across its surface and weeds strangling the foundations. The windows are barred, giving it a prison-like feel, and there's a battered statue in front of a naked man with half of his face shattered, as if time and neglect have eroded him. The statue is probably as old as the facility itself, which only adds to the eeriness. The statue's figure has huge, sprawling wings, and its arms are stretched skyward, as if pleading or reaching for something just out of reach. There's an unsettling silence here—something about this place feels wrong.

I glance at Sarah, "Ready?"

Sarah reaches out her hand and grabs mine, "Ready as I can be."

Walking towards the front entrance, it felt like bats were flying around in my stomach. Although we trust Sharon, we know our mother is cunning and manipulative—she was a con artist at heart. I wouldn't put it past her to persuade someone at the facility to help her escape. We hadn't seen Lily-Ann since we put her in this facility, so you can see why I am a little nervous to see our mother. *I've never hypnotized anyone before, so is it possible that it only works for a little while?* I wonder. There are no written instructions on how to hypnotize a person other than what we've researched online.

Stepping inside feels just as creepy as being outside. An overwhelming, rotten smell hits me, reminding me of a discarded, filthy mop left in the bucket for too long. The walls are a light brown color, cracked and bare, showing signs of neglect. The lobby is eerily silent, with no television or signs of life. The chairs in the lobby appear disgusting, as if they were infested with bed bugs, making it possible to bring them home if someone were to sit in them. I've never been inside a prison before, but if I had to imagine it, this would be it—haunting, abandoned, and oppressive.

"Something seems off, don't you think?" I ask my sister.

"Maybe—" she starts to say something, but is interrupted.

A man pops up from under the check-in desk. He has smooth chocolate skin that makes me think he spends hours on a skincare routine every morning. He's built like he's played sports, and his muscles are straining against the tight fabric of his scrubs. For a moment, I'm convinced my eyes are deceiving me, and I have to do a double-take. I'm rooted to the spot, standing in front of him, because for a second, I think it's James. He has a neatly trimmed beard, and his hair is jet-black with waves. But then I catch sight of the black mole on the side of his eye, and I realize my mind is playing tricks on me—James doesn't have that. I also have to remind myself of my dream. Right now, anyone could resemble my brother. He's clearly haunting me. *Does that mean he's dead?*

My gaze falls on Sarah, and I give her a look that says my instinct was probably on target. We haven't been back to the facility since we dropped our mom off, but Sharon's always been the one at the front desk. She made sure to keep track of who came and went from the building, treating our mother like a high-profile inmate.

Right now, I'm at a loss for words because he's staring at us with that unsettling look, the same way we're all looking at him—like he doesn't belong here. There's something about this guy that doesn't sit right with me. My stomach tightens with that familiar, jittery feeling—like bats fluttering around—and that tells me everything I need to know: we can't trust him.

CHAPTER 10

— · —

"Hi, checking in?" he asks, standing to his feet, revealing he has to be close to six feet tall.

"Um, may I ask who you are?" My curiosity begins to take hold.

"Sorry, my apologies. My name is Aaron," he says with his hand stretched out to shake ours. "I'm the new assistant here."

Sarah and I scrunch our eyebrows, confused as to why the facility has hired an assistant. We have never seen this Aaron guy around Shelly Grove before. For a small town, it's hard to believe we hadn't crossed paths with him before.

"So, Aaron, when did you move here? Where did you come from? Where are you living now?" I bombard him with questions.

He chuckles, "You must be the detective around here?"

I give a fake laugh.

Maybe I'm coming across too strong, but with this town's history, you can never be too careful. My sister and I have met with a lot of the locals and never once seen this Aaron guy anywhere. *Oh God, am I turning into my mother by meddling in people's business?*

We always talked to Sharon, and she's never mentioned a new guy. She also knows how much I've wanted to get Sarah hooked up with someone. She would have definitely told us about Aaron.

He still hasn't answered any of my questions, which makes me even more suspicious of him.

"Well, considering you're new here, our town really values making newcomers feel at home. It would have been nice to know you were in town," I say, preparing to do something that will make me feel like Lily-Ann to the core. "Our mother started this tradition where we have a welcome party for newcomers in town. It's kind of our way of saying welcome to Shelly Grove."

Sarah's eyes widen in shock as she looks at me, clearly not understanding what I'm doing. I gently nudge her to let her know she's being obvious.

"Y'all are sweet, thank you." He says with a smile, but he still hasn't answered my questions.

This isn't easy. I don't know how our mother managed to keep up the charade for so long.

"How do you like the town?" I ask, trying to pry a little. "Do you live close?"

As Aaron shares the name of his neighborhood and starts describing the house he's renting, my smile slowly fades away. The house he's talking about sounds incredibly familiar. Then it hit me—he's moved into our brother Cameron's house. Sarah and I catch each other's gaze. Warning bells go off in my head—something about this guy doesn't feel right.

At this point, Lily-Ann and her whereabouts were the least of my worries. I recall the mysterious black sedan roaming through my neighborhood and how it sped off as I tried to approach the vehicle. Now this Aaron guy drops in out of nowhere.

"You know the person who used to live there died recently," I say, trying to get something out of him, but he's too good at beating around the bush.

"Oh yes, it's unfortunate. The rental agency informed me of that. They said the guy who owned the home didn't die inside. Thank God, right?" he says as he places his hand on his chest as if he were sorrowful.

Little did he know that the man who used to live there was also a psychopath, much like his mother, who had killed two innocent women and a detective. What he didn't realize was that I was the one who killed that man, but I couldn't reveal that to him. I was still trying to figure him out. I'd feel terrible if it turns out that he's a good person. I wouldn't want anyone to leave this town on my watch.

Fortunately, our town hasn't expanded much, so there is still only one real estate company that manages all the rental properties. If anyone can tell us more about Aaron, it would be them. It seems a little suspicious that the new guy in town has moved into our dead brother's house. *I mean, who moves into a dead person's house?* Then it hits me like a ton of bricks—Mr. Gerald moved into a house where someone had died. *Maybe I'm overthinking this.*

Sarah can tell the wheels in my head are spinning and quickly changes the subject. "We're here to see our mother. Lily-Ann is her name."

"Um, you said Lily-Ann? Is that right?" he asks..

"Yes! She's in room 334," I say, snapping out of my intrusive thoughts.

"Got it," he says, starting to look up the information on the computer. "Is her name spelled with a 'Y' or an 'I'?"

"Y!" Sarah says quickly.

Aaron continues searching the system. It appears that he is struggling to find her. At this point, I'm starting to get anxious and start biting my nails. *Lily-Ann has to be here; there is no way he shouldn't be able to find her. She is a top-level psychopath. She should be listed first, in bold letters.*

"Aha! Here she is," he says as if he just accomplished something great, but not realizing he almost gave me a heart attack.

I exhale a long breath that I had been holding, bracing myself for him to tell us that she had been checked out. A wave of relief washes over me as if a heavy weight had been lifted from my chest. The suspense was tearing me apart.

Sarah notices my hands trembling, so she reaches over and gives my hand a light squeeze, silently telling me to relax.

I knew Sarah was right, I did need to relax, but I was nervous—hell, I was terrified after the dream I had. Then, all of a sudden, a random black car crept through my neighborhood and stopped in the middle of the road. At this point, I had never wanted to see my mother as much as I did in that moment.

Behind the check-in desk is a board with keys labeled with numbers. Aaron points to something on the screen with his finger, saying "33...334" as if he's just had an "aha" moment. He turns around to grab a key. I'm guessing this is the key to Lily-Ann's room.

"Follow me," he says as he unlocks a gate, allowing us access to the back.

We take the elevator to the third floor and walk down the hallway at a slow pace. This moment almost feels like Deja Vu, reminding me of the day we visited our mother in the hospital. We pass several rooms, counting each room number, until we reach room 334.

This was going to be the first time in months that we've laid eyes on her. Sarah grabs my hand just as Aaron begins to open the door. The suspense is killing me. The scene felt just right: the hallway is dark, and the door slowly creaks open. It was the perfect setup. I could almost imagine Lily-Ann standing in front of the door, ready to jump out and attack us like a crazy person.

Surprisingly, it's the complete opposite. As we enter her room, we see Lily-Ann lying in bed, still unaware of who she is. She glances at us, and for a moment, you can almost feel sorry for her—the fact that she's in this state because of us. *Mommy dear, you brought this on yourself.* I can't let my heart manipulate my emotions. This woman is far from a saint.

With a sigh of relief, I turn and face Aaron, thanking him for taking us back to see our mom. We tell him that it's been a while since we last saw her—*more like months.* In my opinion, this is not the best way to welcome someone to Shelly Grove, but at least he's able to see firsthand what the town's psychopath looks like.

Aaron escorts us back to the lobby and assures us she's in good hands. I guess, with all that built-up emotion, he assumed it was because we missed her.

"Hey, so what happened to her?" he asks. "If you don't mind me asking," he says quickly.

I'm at a loss for words. How do you explain to someone that you hypnotized your mother because she tried to kill you and her grandkids?

The best I can say is, "Yeah, it's sad, but at least she's in such a fine place as this."

Aaron scrunches his eyebrows. Maybe I shouldn't have said that. First, it is clear this place isn't all that great, and second, I didn't answer his question at all. I guess it's payback for him not answering any of mine, but in my opinion, he didn't need to know anything else about her. I'm sure her files tell him all that he needs to know, which is that she has dementia and that she will be here for the rest of her life. If you ask me, that's better than being in prison for the rest of her life. At least she doesn't have to fight some muscular woman who goes by Big Bertha.

Before walking out the door, something else hits me: "Hey, have you seen Sharon today?"

He scrunches his eyebrows as if he doesn't know who I'm talking about.

"You know, Sharon, the head nurse here?" I say, trying to help him figure out who I'm referring to.

"I'm sorry that name doesn't ring a bell," he says, leaving us confused. Sharon pretty much runs this building. There's no way on this planet he wouldn't know her. That jittery feeling returns, and I can't say anything. Sarah and I catch each other's gaze in disbelief.

Something is really off about this guy.

CHAPTER 11

— · —

On the way home, Sarah and I drove in silence. I felt bad for dragging my sister to the facility. Staring at her, I could see that something was bothering her. She never once looked at me. She kept her eyes laser-focused on the road in front of us. I could see visiting our mother hurt her a little more than it did me. She is the youngest of us all. I'm sure that for her, she imagined growing up with a loving mother who would braid her hair and could one day be the wonderful grandma to love her future children.

Unfortunately, this is our reality. Our mom is locked up in a facility. I know it's tough, but one day Lily-Ann has to pass away. Once she's gone, she'll be a memory to us. She'll be a photo on the wall and dust six feet underground. I long for that day when I won't have to deal with these mixed emotions anymore.

Before my sister dropped me off at home, she asked if it was okay for her to stop by the donut shop to check on things. While I waited in the car for her to come out, my mind began to wander, thinking about the new guy at the facility. It seemed strange that he said he didn't know Sharon, since there's no way he would've been hired without her help.

I'm lost in my thoughts when I notice a familiar face walking down the sidewalk—*Sharon?* I jump out of the car and hurry after her.

"Hey Sharon!" I yell, trying to get her attention, but oddly enough, she doesn't budge. She doesn't even flinch at the sound of her name. I assumed I was saying her name loud enough for her to hear me.

Picking up the pace, I catch up to her and grab her arm to get her attention. "Hey, did you hear me calling you?"

Sharon turns around, looking a bit startled. Once she notices who grabbed her arm, her expression shifts. She takes out her earbuds and says, "Hey, girl. Sorry, I was listening to something."

I'm eager to ask her about Aaron. It was unusual to me that he didn't know who she was. But it was also odd that Sharon was not at work. She is always at work. She wanted to keep a close eye on Lily-Ann just as badly as I did.

"Hey, so I ran into some guy not too long ago at the facility. He said his name is Aaron." I explain.

"Oh yes, Aaron!" she responds in a high-pitched voice. "He's such a nice guy. He's our newest employee at the facility."

"Oh, okay." I'm a little lost for words at this point. I don't know why this seems odd to me. I mean, this is real life. People get hired for jobs all the time. I just hired a new employee the other day. So why am I freaking out about this?

"He is well put together if you ask me," she says, winking at me. "From my understanding, he just moved here, and like most of the newbies, he just wanted a change from city life."

Hearing that from Sharon made me feel better about him. But it is interesting how she knew so much about him, and he did not seem to know anything about her.

"Sounds like y'all hit the lottery then with him," I say with a chuckle. "I just...I just don't understand something?"

She slightly tilts her head. "What's wrong?"

"Well, we asked him where you were earlier, and he acted as if he's never met you," I say.

"Oh, girl, please don't worry about that. This guy is not good with names. He's called me Shannon, Sherry, and oh goodness, he's even called me Sarah." Sharon chuckles.

Right now, I'm probably looking concerned, because Sharon puts her hands on my shoulders and gives them a gentle squeeze. "Don't worry, Lily-Ann is in good hands."

I guess if Sharon is telling me everything is okay, then I should believe it. Maybe I'm just being paranoid. My mom is still around here, and James is still alive. I should have just killed him that night. I could probably sleep more peacefully if I knew he was dead. *I wish I had killed them both that night.*

"These last two days have been a little rough," I explain, shaking my head, trying to clear my thoughts. "Well, anyway, I won't hold you up any longer. I have to get back home. I hope you have a good day."

As I walk back to the car, my mind drifts to what Sharon was telling me about Aaron. The sun hits me square in the face, so I put my hand over my eyebrows to shield my eyes. A flock of birds flies by, making me glance up. Birds don't usually fly together like that unless something's coming. When I look up, there it is—Lily-Ann's house, right in front of me. It stands out like a sore thumb, just like the lady at the town meeting said. The locals want to tear it down, and honestly, it's easy to see why. The house brings back some pretty bad memories. I have to agree, it's probably for the best.

44

It no longer looks like that beautiful painting that hung on the walls of all the businesses here in town. Now, when I look at it, the house looks haunted. You can tell when something bad has happened to a place. The innocence is gone, and it just seems creepy.

"Alice! Alice!" Sarah shook me as she tried to get my attention. "Are you alright? Seems like you were daydreaming."

I look at her, confused, "Yes, of course. Why do you ask?"

"Well, for one, you're standing in the middle of the road staring into outer space," she says, looking at me like I've lost my mind.

I chuckle.

"I was just looking at something," I say.

"Oh yeah, what's that?" she asks.

I look towards the hill, extending my arm, and point in the direction of our mother's house.

She traces my arm with her gaze, taking in the haunted-looking house we used to call home. For a moment, she stands frozen, her eyes fixed on the house on the hill.

"Look, sis, I know today was not easy for either of us. I also understand that last night was scary for you. I also want you to know that I know it's hard for you to continue living in this town." She says as she reaches for my hand. "I just want you to know that we will get through this together."

For once, I didn't have to be the strong one. I start blinking rapidly to hold back my tears, but the weight that had been on me since the day we placed our mother in the facility, along with everything else that has happened, overwhelmed me. My sister wraps her arms around my neck, and we hug each other for what feels like an eternity.

"So guess who I just saw," I say as we walk back to the car.

"Who?" she asks, grabbing for the handle to open the car door.

"Sharon," I sit down and buckle my seatbelt.

Sarah cranks the car and glances over at me, "Sharon? What did she say? Did she mention anything about Aaron?"

I tell her how our conversation went and how she mentioned nothing but good things about him. Sarah seems relieved, as if a weight has been lifted from her shoulders.

"Maybe we should try something new," she suggests.

"Like what?" I ask.

"Can we maybe try to give people real chances around here? Not everyone is Lily-Ann, Cameron, or James. I know it's hard for you to trust anyone at the moment, but can we please try to move on and start living life to its fullest? I'm so tired of looking over my shoulder every five seconds."

She does make a good point. Perhaps we should give Aaron a chance and let him see what our town is really about. This is a town of people who've been through the worst, and together, we're strong. That's when it hits me—when I have a light bulb moment.

I look at Sarah, "How do you feel about putting together a cookout for Aaron? Lily-Ann might have been on to something when having all those welcome parties. It doesn't hurt to keep those going." I say matter-of-factly.

"Well, let's get to planning," she says.

As we drive back to my house, I gaze out the window and take in the town's scenery. Never in a million years would I want to be like my mother. She's never had good intentions, but does that mean I have to be like her to take an idea of hers?

46

CHAPTER 12

—·—

O ne thing I've realized about myself is that I am extremely paranoid. I've also learned that to move forward in life, I must leave
the past behind. The longer I stay in this mindset, the longer I remain
Lily-Ann's prisoner. So, the next day, I decide the best way to start
living is to try to build genuine friendships. Everyone around me has
some connection to my mother. Dinners with Mr. Gerald are nice, but
we are only connected because of our mother. Sharon is great too, but
we've never had a girls' day together; we're only connected because my
brother killed her grandmother.

It's a Saturday morning, and the house is quiet because the kids
prefer to sleep in on the weekends. I head to the kitchen and whip
up a cup of coffee. I take a seat at the table to let my mind drift. I
start thinking about the cookout and begin making plans in my head.
*What food will we have? Mr. Gerald can put something on the grill.
Maybe flyers would be a good idea to pass out.* Then that's when it hit
me: I was acting just like my mother. I hadn't even discussed any of
this with Aaron. I need to check if he would be okay with us having a
cookout for him. He might be an introvert and may not want to deal
with large groups of people.

Because I did not want to wake the kids, I send them a quick text telling them I was stepping out for a bit and I'll be back later. I also make sure they know to clean their rooms, specifically Adam, because he will wake up and go straight to the game.

Approaching the facility, I quickly park the car and run inside, ignoring the creepy statue in front and the bars on all the windows. I have a one-track mind at the moment, and right now, all I want to know is how Aaron will feel about this cookout.

"Checking in?" he asks, not realizing I was coming through the door.

"I just want to apologize for being short with you the other day," I say quickly, ignoring his offer for me to check in. Little does he know I'm not here to see my mother. He will learn soon that we are probably the only people he will not see often.

"You don't have to apologize to me for that," Aaron says, brushing off my apology. "I understand why you were being cautious. I would feel the same if I had a loved one in a facility like this."

I laugh a little on the inside because little does he know I'm the one who put her in this place.

"Speaking of our mother, she started something in this town that my sister and I thought would be a good idea to continue," I explain.

"Oh yeah, what's that?" he asks.

I remind him of our conversation when I told him about the welcome parties our mother used to have for newcomers. When I first said it, it was kind of my way of trying to figure him out, but this time it's genuine. I tell him it was her way of getting the community together and a way to build friendships. *It doesn't hurt to tell a little white lie as long as it's for a good reason, right?* Aaron seems to think this is a cool

48

idea, but doesn't care so much about the lavish party idea. Little did he know I agreed with him; this is why I assured him we wanted to do something a little more laidback.

"How do you feel about a good old-fashioned cookout?" I ask. "You know, maybe a little line dance here and there," I say with a chuckle.

"A little dance, huh?" he says with a smile so big that I can see all thirty-two bright white teeth.

"Yup, that's right. You can't have a cookout without a line dance. I know you know the electric slide?" I ask jokingly.

"Do I know it? Girl, I'm the king of line dances. You gotta hit me with that cupid shuffle, and a party isn't a party without the wobble," he says jokingly.

I was surprised at how cool Aaron was. After our back-and-forth conversation about the different line dances, he informed me he was a master of the grill. I couldn't let him be the chef at his own party. Mr. Gerald had that under control. I wanted to assure him this party was to welcome him, not to put him to work.

We reviewed the details of the cookout and decided on which games we could all play to get people involved. I can honestly say my sister was right about opening up and giving people real chances. It was nice getting to know him. I was able to see a side of him that we hadn't seen the first day we met. He could really be a fun guy friend to have around. I know Sarah would love him because he is extremely funny and seems to know how to have a good time. *Just what we need at a time like this.*

"Well, it was great talking to you, but I know my kids are up by now and I need to get home before they kill each other," I say with a chuckle.

"Touché," he says, causing me to blush because at this point, I know he's trying to be charming.

As soon as I get in the car, the first thing I do is call my sister.

"Hey, sis!" Sarah answers excitedly.

"It's on," I say quickly.

"What's on?" she asks.

"The cookout," I remind her.

"No freaking way! He agreed to it," she asks. "That's what's up, well, I need to get with some people from the donut shop and see who wants to make some extra money helping me prepare a large batch of donuts.

I'm unsure how Lily-Ann managed to do all of this, but she pulled it together just fine. This party will be smaller than the one they had for me. But it will have one thing mine did not: good intentions. My party was a cover-up and a fake. It was just another scheme my mother had to keep me under her wing. However, this party is not that; it's simply a gathering of friends welcoming a newcomer to our town.

As soon as I got off the phone with Sarah, I called Mr. Gerald and told him what we had in mind. He wasn't too fond of us following our mothers' footsteps, but he was happy to see us opening up to new people. He was also excited that it was a guy friend I was talking to him about, because he keeps telling me and Sarah that he's not going to be around forever to help hang fans and change lightbulbs.

I lean back and rest my head against the headrest, taking in everything we've done in this town. Sadness starts to creep in because, in another life, I would call my mom and share this news with her. In another life, I would tell her the guy seems really cool, and my imaginary mom probably would have tried to convince me to make a move on him because sometimes men can be a little shy about making the first move. I would tell her that he isn't my type, but I definitely planned to hook him up with Sarah. We would laugh about it and say our I love you goodbyes. But in reality, the mother I have is sitting behind these barred windows in this facility, with a statue of a man with half a face and large wings, lifting his arms—to whom I have no idea, but it sure as hell is creepy if you ask me.

CHAPTER 13

—·—

We decided to give everyone a week's notice and thought it'd be best to hold the first cookout in the park the following Saturday. All week, I stopped by the facility a few times to discuss food, games, and music with Aaron. This was the most I'd been there, and the creepy statue started to seem less intimidating. I even gave it a name: Big John. I'm not sure where the name came from, but it was fitting—the statue was big, and the name was catchy in my head. So, I'd give Big John a salute every time I walked past him.

By Thursday, I had everything planned out, and honestly, I needed a mental break.

"Hey, do you like food and board games?" I prop my elbows on the check-in counter and rest my head on my hands. "I mean, a lot of people like food, but how about the board games?"

Aaron laughs.

"Are you asking me out?" he asks jokingly, placing his hand on his chest. "I'd be honored."

I give him a playful slap on the shoulder, "You're funny, but I hate to break it to you, you're kind of not my type."

Aaron gives a playful sad face puckering out his bottom lip.

"It's cool, I'm just messing with you. I'm only here for friends. I don't really have time for dating," he says and then slaps my shoulder playfully. "Besides, you're kind of like one of the guys to me."

On one hand, I feel a little bummed because I really wanted to set him up with Sarah, but on the other hand, I think that having a good friend is what we need right now. Love can wait.

"Well, I'm honored," I say jokingly, placing my hand now on my chest. "Anyway, does six work for you tonight?"

Aaron shakes his head in agreement.

"Great, I'll see you later. It's a not date, date," I smile, waving as I head out the door.

Before heading home, I decide to stop by the park to assess the area and see if there's a lot of cleaning we need to get done before the cookout. To my surprise, the park was clean, and the grass was the same vibrant green it has always been. While standing under the gazebo, I happened to glance up at the clock tower, and my mind instantly drifted. I can recall meeting David at this very park, thinking he may be one of Lily-Ann's accomplices. Shelly Grove is really a beautiful town; it is just unfortunate that the lasting impression our mother has left on this town is so negative.

My thoughts are quickly interrupted at the sight of Sharon walking through town. Strangely, she hasn't been to the facility consistently like she usually is. *Perhaps I should ask her if everything is okay.* It does concern me a little because she is the only one who is in charge of giving our mother her pill each day.

Quickly hurrying over to Sharon, I notice she has her earbuds in. So, calling her name, I realize it was a waste of time, and her back is to me, so she wouldn't even see me if I waved her down. Shuffling out of the park, I approach Sharon and extend my arm to get her attention, but something stops me in my tracks: she's singing the same song again.

I swear I have heard that song somewhere, but it's driving me crazy that I cannot figure it out. I don't recall the lyrics so much, but the humming sounds she makes is what sounds familiar to me. It *almost sounds like something from a nursery rhyme. Like something a mother would hum to a baby.* Brushing off the idea of the song, I approach Sharon and ask her if everything is okay.

"Of course it is. What makes you think something is wrong?" she says, taking one of the earbuds out of her ear.

"What song are you listening to if you don't mind me asking?" It's something about this song that I can't get out of my head.

"Rockabye, bye Sean Paul," she says. "Do you want to listen?" she asks, holding one of her earbuds out to me.

For a minute, I want to break out laughing, but I don't because she will think I've lost my mind. She may even suggest I get admitted right along with Lily-Ann. Little does she know I'm thinking she's listening to nursery rhymes when she's really listening to Sean Paul.

I wave her off, suggesting I don't want to hear the song.

I wasn't sure how to ask her my real question because, in reality, it was none of my business why she was not at work. I am neither her boss nor a coworker of hers. So, how do you ask someone why they aren't at work every time you see them?

"When will you be returning to work because you're the only one who gives our mother her medicine?" I go straight for it. If I'm being honest, there's no beating around the bush with that question.

Sharon seems off for a minute. She tilts her head as if trying to figure out what to say. Finally, she holds my gaze with a somewhat creepy smile. "We hired a new guy, remember, he will be assisting with administering all medications, even to your mom."

"Aaron? Are you sure?" I ask.

For a moment, I feel a sense of betrayal, which is weird because we barely know him, but for some reason, I feel like he should have told me that. I've seen him almost every day this week, and he never once mentioned that he'd be giving Lily-Ann her medication.

I try not to get frustrated with Sharon, because at the end of the day, she's doing us a favor. Her grandmother is gone, and she could easily move on, but she knows what our mother has done to all these innocent people. Why would she want to leave her in someone else's care?

"You know what I actually need to get home," I lie, pretending to look at the time on my cell. In reality, I really need to make a pit stop. Sarah wanted me to let my guard down and start trusting people, but look what that has done: a stranger is now looking over our mother.

I was furious. *What was he really doing here in Shelly Grove?* "How is it that he got a job at the facility so quickly?" I ask myself. I had all these questions, and the only person who could answer them was Aaron.

Hurrying across the street to my car, one thing is on my mind and one thing only: Aaron. I press the unlock button on my key fob before reaching my car so I don't waste any time. I open the car door and toss my purse onto the front passenger seat. As I prepare to get in, I'm caught off guard by something that makes me forget why I was leaving the park in the first place: the black sedan sitting in the parking lot facing me. I can tell someone is inside because the daytime running lights are on, and even though the windows are jet black, my gut tells me someone's inside.

The car pulls out of its parking space, leaving me wondering who's behind the wheel. I'd bet my life that it's my brother James, and he's toying with me.

CHAPTER 14

—.—

R ushing through traffic, I had no idea what to think. Was Aaron trustworthy? Does he know what Lily-Ann did to the people in this town? Has Sharon told him what medicine she is supposed to have?

I'm unsure what to expect, but I knew my car was not moving fast enough to reach the facility. I thought about calling Sarah to tell her what I had just found out, but the last thing I needed was my sister having a nervous breakdown. It would be best to keep this information to myself until I talk to Aaron.

Finally, I make it to the facility, and my heart is pounding. I'm not sure if it's from being upset that we didn't know Aaron was now giving our mother her medication, or if it's the fact that this black car has popped up now twice. I'm not sure if I should even be worried just yet. Many people own black vehicles. It's a standard color.

I grab my purse and quickly hop out of my car, hitting the button on the door to lock it. I give Big John his usual salute—because let's be honest, he's probably my only true friend at this point. There's just something about a guy who stays in the same spot all the time; at least

I can trust him. He'll never lie to me because I can always count on him to be exactly where I left him.

I approach the check-in desk, and like clockwork, Aaron comes from around back.

"Hey!" He is excited to see me, but little does he know this is not going to be a pleasant conversation. "I'm not supposed to see you until later on."

You have to forgive me, but I have a low tolerance for liars at this point in my life. So, I did not bother with the small talk. "Why didn't you tell Sarah and me that you would be assisting with taking care of our mother here in the facility?"

Aaron pauses for a minute, and I can see he is trying to come up with an answer. I hate liars. I could tell that the next word that was going to come out of his mouth would be a bunch of lies.

"Alice, I can explain," he says with his hands in the air as if he were surrendering. "Sharon asked me to assist her with taking care of Lily-Ann. She's pulled from every direction around here. I feel bad for her, if I'm being honest. She couldn't ask me fast enough to assist her with giving medications, not just to your mom, but to all the patients here."

I nod my head slowly, "I see."

"I'm sorry I didn't tell you girls when we first met," he says.

I understood what he was saying, but it didn't make sense to me. He's been employed here for all of two seconds and is already being trusted to administer medications to these people. *He also knows she is our mother; why would he keep this from us?*

"Aaron, that's our mother," I say softly.

"Alice, I know, and I'm very sorry. I didn't..." he hesitates to finish his sentence.

"You didn't what?"

"I didn't want to worry you and Sarah by telling you both that I would be the one caring for your mom. I mean... I've only been here for a little while, and I didn't want you both to think I couldn't take care of her," he explains.

Little did Aaron know, I didn't care whether he could care for her. All I cared about was knowing she would be getting her freaking pill every day. Lily-Ann is evil; if she were to escape from this place, she would come after us, no questions asked.

Either Aaron is an excellent liar, or he genuinely has good intentions.

Holding Aaron's gaze, I try to gauge my feelings about him, but that's when it hit me—Lily-Ann has messed with my head. She has tortured us so severely that it's hard to trust anyone. Maybe Sarah is right; perhaps I should start learning to trust others. Aaron isn't my mother or my brother. He seems like a genuinely nice guy and has been nothing but kind to me. Our mother has been living rent-free for far too long, and it's time I evict her.

"You know what? I'm really sorry. I have this issue with trusting people," I explain. This isn't the welcome he deserves. I feel horrible for my sudden reaction and jumping to conclusions about him.

Aaron smiles, showing all thirty-two white teeth. "Well, it looks like we're going to need to change that then, aren't we?"

I chuckle.

"Hey, do you mind taking me back to see my mother?" I ask, figuring I needed to get something off my chest to her, even though she doesn't even know who I am. Lily-Ann has controlled my life for far too long, and at this point, it's time I put an end to this once and for all. Enough is enough. I need to say my final goodbyes. If I'm going to move on with my life, I figured today would be the last day I step foot in this place. As for Aaron, he will just have to see us outside of work.

Deep down, it felt as if Aaron knew this would be my last visit. He gave me a look of remorse. I could tell by his eyes that he had several questions, but I think he was a little afraid to ask, so he kindly grabbed the key to Lily-Ann's room and did as I wished.

Walking down the hall this time, I notice that several patients have their doors open. We make it to a dimly lit hallway, and here I'm reminded that we are close to my mother's rooms. A wave of remorse suddenly washes over me. Perhaps it was simply the realization of how many patients were housed in this facility. People place their loved ones in places like this because they either cannot take care of them or do not want to deal with the challenges of caregiving. In my case, it was neither. Lily-Ann was here because she is a psychopath—a danger to society.

As we approach her room, I find myself drawn to the small window set into the door. Peering through the glass, I notice Lily-Ann nestled in her bed, her frail figure sprawled across the sheets. Looking at her, something happened that hadn't happened to me in a long time; I had a flashback. This flashback took me back to the night Lily-Ann was going to kill my kids and my sister. I had a choice that night. I could have killed her, but then that left the possibility of James killing our sister.

I wasn't sure why I had that flashback, but maybe it was a reminder or a warning. Whatever the reason for the flashback, it did show me one thing: I am capable of killing Lily-Ann. A choice had to be made that night, and I chose to save us all. But we are not in danger now. What is stopping me from murdering her right here?

Aaron unlocks the door, and I slowly walk in. Deep down, I felt I was no longer there to say goodbye; it felt like I was there for revenge.

"Hey, do you mind giving me some privacy with mom?" I ask.

"Are you sure? Patients with dementia tend to have outbursts and hurt anyone in their sight," he explains.

I chuckle, "Yes, I will be just fine; I just want to speak to my mother in private."

"Okay, but if you need anything, there is a remote next to her bed with a big red call button," he reassures me.

This was the perfect time to get rid of her for good. I would no longer have to worry about sleeping with one eye open. I no longer would have to worry about her coming out of her hypnosis. This was my only chance to end all this pain and suffering—not just for me, but for Sarah, for Mr. Gerald, for all the innocent people here in Shelly Grove, and especially for my kids.

"Lily-Ann!" I call out her name as I approach her bed, but she doesn't move. I slowly kneel next to her bed to see if she is awake, but she is out cold.

Slowly lifting her head, I slide the pillow from underneath her. I've never intentionally harmed anyone before, but I figured I was going about this the right way. I stand next to her bed, staring at her frail body, and watch as her chest rises and falls with her breathing. Anger begins to stir up inside of me. *Maybe this is what real murderers feel before they take a life.*

Anger takes over me as I grip the cotton-filled pillow as tightly as I can, thinking about everything my mother has done. This was my moment—I was ready to end it all. I was prepared to take this woman's life. I'd become just like my mother, a murderer.

I lift the pillow in an attempt to suffocate her by placing the pillow over her face. I'm startled when her hand quickly grips my arm, digging her nails into my skin. This is all too familiar to me because it is typical of her to dig her nails into your skin when she squeezes you. I don't let this stop me; I continue to press the pillow over her face as hard as possible. I can feel her trying to fight back, until finally her grip loosens. Life was leaving her body, and for some reason, this didn't feel wrong at all. She gave me no choice; I should have done this years ago instead of trying to run from her.

"ALICE! WHAT ARE YOU DOING?" A voice shouts from behind me. I look towards the doorway, and it's my sister. She dashes over to me and grabs my arms.

"I can't do this anymore," I tell her. "I can't go another day knowing she is still alive. She consumes my mind and appears in all my dreams. She's turning me into a crazy person. She is turning me into her," I cry.

"You will be just like her if you kill her, Alice," Sarah says softly as she carefully grabs the pillow out of my hands.

What she says is true and hits me like a load of bricks. Lily-Ann is the last person I want to be like. I wrap my arms around my sister's neck, squeezing her tightly. "I hate what she has done to us. I just want her dead."

Sarah reassures me that our mother's death should be the least of our concerns at this point. With her getting the pill daily, she will stay in this place for the rest of her life.

I already knew this to be true, but there was something about it coming from my sister that allowed it to sink in. I take the pillow back from Sarah and assure her I won't do anything stupid. I lean over my mother, lifting her head, and place the pillow back underneath her head. I plant a soft kiss on her forehead and remind her, "You will die in here."

Sarah gives me a smile that tells me she is concerned about me. We lock arms and head for the door when we are suddenly startled by Aaron's appearance.

"Sorry, ladies. I was coming to give my friend here her medication," he says with a smile.

I nod. Not sure if he would ever want Lily-Ann as a friend. *If she were in her right mind, she'd probably hypnotize him to be her friend.*

In that moment, something quite intriguing happens. Aaron's smile suddenly disappears, replaced by an expression that shows shock—his eyes wide and mouth slightly open. Sarah and I exchange curious looks, our brows crease in confusion as we try to figure out what caused his sudden change.

"Oh wow! This is something new," Aaron says as if something surprising just happened.

"What? What's wrong?" I ask.

Aaron extended his arm, pointing his finger. He wasn't pointing at either of us, *so what is it?*

"Um, ladies..." he hesitates.

"What's wrong?" I ask.

"You may want to turn around," he instructs us.

We slowly turn our heads, unsure of what Aaron wanted us to look at. We were not prepared for what our eyes had in store for us.

Our mother is sitting upright, her head tilted forward, her chin pressed against her chest, and her gaze fixed on us with an intensity that sends chills down our spines. The fury burning in her eyes was tangible; she resembled one of the nightmarish figures from those haunting exorcism films. It felt as though her glare could slice through the air, particularly targeting Sarah and me. Though she remained deathly silent, the oppressive weight of her stare was suffocating, wrapping around us like a cold fog. We both knew that if looks could kill, we would have already become shadows, lost in the darkness of her wrath.

Sarah and I instantly met each other's gaze. I didn't know if I should be afraid at this moment. *Was the hypnosis wearing off? Was she going to tell Aaron what I was doing in here?* All these thoughts ran through my head, but the most crucial question remained: why was she sitting up in bed staring at us as if she was ready to rip us apart?

CHAPTER 15

—·—

After seeing Lily-Ann sitting up in bed, a moment that caught us all off guard, Sarah and I quickly told Aaron to give our mother her medication without delay. I could sense the confusion swirling in his mind; he had many questions about our suspicious reaction to Lily-Ann's movements. However, he remained unaware of the dark history that followed her. I wasn't sure how long we could keep up the act of being grieving daughters. Something inside me told me it was time to reveal the truth to him—it was time he understood the real nature of the woman he was caring for, a woman whose actions had deeply impacted many lives in our community.

I'm also beginning to suspect that Aaron has a negative perception of both Sarah and me. From his perspective, it probably seems like we are the kind of daughters who don't want to take on the responsibility of caring for our mother. This must be particularly concerning for him, especially given his position. He probably thinks that we were devastated to witness our mother managing to sit up on her own, and while I can understand his concern, he's not entirely wrong. The sight indeed stirred a complicated mix of emotions within us. She hypnotized a whole freaking town, for god's sake; of course, we were devastated.

I decided tonight wasn't a good night after all to have Aaron over for food and games after what we witnessed, but it was clear he had a lot of questions. As I lay in bed, the thought of Aaron having negative thoughts about us didn't sit well with me. It was time for me to reveal to him who Lily-Ann really is. It was time he knew what she was capable of. I also don't want him to think he's not welcome over for food and games another night.

My mind is racing, making me feel restless. I reach over and unplug my cell from the charger, then scroll through my contacts until I find Aaron's name. Right now, I have no idea what I'm doing; I take it one second at a time. I take a deep breath and press the green call button. *How am I going to explain all of this?*

"Hello," he answers, his voice sounding a little muffled.

"Hey, Aaron! Sorry to call you so late. Did I wake you?" I ask, knowing he's more than likely already in bed.

"Oh... hey. No problem at all. I was just getting in bed," he says, his voice sounding a lot closer to the speaker now. It also sounds like he sat up in bed.

"I wanted to talk to you about what we witnessed earlier. You know... with my mom," I explain.

"Oh, okay. When do you want to talk? I mean, we're both up now..." he says.

"No," I sigh. "This is one of those conversations where we need to be face-to-face and possibly sitting down. Maybe even having a little alcohol in our system," I say with a chuckle.

He chuckles, completely oblivious to what I'm going to tell him. "Okay, no problem at all. When do you want to meet?"

"If you have some time after work tomorrow, my schedule is pretty open in the evening. Does that work for you?" I ask.

"Sounds good to me," he says excitedly, like we are getting ready to meet for dinner and drinks tomorrow. "I'll see you tomorrow," he says before ending the call.

***

I WAKE UP IN THE MORNING FEELING INCREDIBLY EX-HAUSTED, as if I've barely slept at all, and the last thing I want to do is get out of bed. Instead, I just want to curl up under the blankets and go back to sleep. It's Friday, the last day of the week, and you would think I'd be full of energy. All I have on my mind are the tasks I need to complete today, which really aren't many, but mentally they will drain me—go to work, boss a few people around, and my least favorite, meeting with Aaron to tell him about my crazy mother. "Why me, Lord?" I ask as I look in the mirror, dreading picking up my toothbrush. To me, it's like the ultimate move you make to ensure your day gets started. Once my teeth are brushed and my breath is fresh, I feel like I need to shower, and at that point, it's all downhill from there.

After showering and moisturizing, I put on a pair of black slacks, a white dress shirt, and my black flats. Now that I'm the boss of TelNet, I've learned to wear comfortable shoes.

I head for the kitchen to do my usual morning ritual, which is putting on a pot of coffee because let's be honest, I'm really going to need the caffeine today. As the pot is brewing, I check all the doors, something I've grown to do after James left to ensure they are all locked before I head out for work.

I check the door leading into the garage, and it's as I left it last night: locked. I glance at my cell and notice I have about five minutes left to get out of the house, or I'll be late for work. I quickly walk through the living room, heading for the kitchen, when something catches my eye. I have a small coffee table in the middle of my living room, and on it is a brown wicker bowl with fake fruits, and next to it is a stack of magazines.

As I approach the table, a chill runs down my spine. The magazines aren't where I left them last night, and an unsettling feeling has crept over me. I clearly remember coming home from the facility, sitting on the couch, and replaying the eerie encounter with Lily-Ann in my mind. To distract myself, I grabbed the latest edition of Vogue Magazine that was on top of the stack. After losing myself in its pages, I carefully placed it back on top before going to my room to lie down in bed. Now, the stack is not where I left it.

The stack of magazines is underneath the wicker bowl of fake fruit as if someone had deliberately hidden them. My heart races as I scan my surroundings. Looking closer at the stack, I notice the magazine I read last night was missing entirely. *Did someone come into my home while the kids and I were sleeping?* The disturbing thought lingers, gripping my chest, and I can't shake the feeling that something was very, very wrong.

I rush through the kitchen and head to the back door. My eyes widen, and fear overtakes me—it's unlocked. I was sure I had locked it; this triggers a memory that still haunts me today, reminding me why I started making sure the back door, specifically, always remained locked. My mind drifts back to the day I found the receptionist at her house, only to discover her dead, beaten body in the bedroom. Her back door was also unlocked, and since then, it has become my top priority to keep that door secure. It was also clear to me that intruders typically don't break in through the front; it's always the back. That's why I was absolutely convinced I had locked it. "What in the world is going on?" I question myself.

For a minute, I stand frozen in the kitchen, unsure of what's going on. It's possible that one of the kids simply unlocked the door and forgot to lock it again, but on the other hand, they know how paranoid all this has made me over the years. Suddenly, I'm startled by the sound of an alarm going off. *Shoot, it's mine.* I glance at the time on my cell and realize I'm about to be late for work. I snap out of it and quickly lock the door. My coffee is ready, so I grab a mug from the cabinet and pour myself a to-go cup. I run upstairs, taking the steps two at a time, and remind the kids to get ready so they aren't late for school, just as I am about to be for work.

On my way to work, I drive in silence, recalling some of the weird things that have happened lately. First, a black car stops in the middle of my street, then Sharon is walking around town singing Rockabye, Lily-Ann sits up in bed staring at us like she wants to kill us, and now my back door is unlocked. Sarah is aware of the first two encounters, but I'm not sure whether I should share the others with her. The last thing I want is for her to panic. With everything weighing on my mind, it feels like I'm driving on autopilot; I was moving, but everything around me seemed to be in slow motion.

Parking my car in my designated space, labeled "Boss." (It was not my idea; one of my employees thought it would be cute to give me an assigned spot.) I quickly grab my purse and coffee mug, then jump out of my car to avoid wasting any more time. As I get ready to lock the door, something catches my eye. I freeze in place and forget I'm holding my coffee mug because it completely shatters on the ground. There it is—the black sedan parked at the far end of the lot, its presence unsettling. The limo-tinted windows leave me unable to see who's lurking inside. It leaves an uneasy feeling as if whoever is inside is intensely watching me, waiting. *What is this person doing?*

The only way I was going to find out who was in that car was to pull myself together. I couldn't let fear take over any longer, so I did what any curious person would do—I slammed my car door as I got back in and sped out of my assigned parking space. However, the person in the car was not waiting for me to figure anything out because they also sped off, leading me into a high-speed chase through Shelly Grove.

CHAPTER 16

— · —

Now I understand how cops feel when chasing a suspect. It's an intense and overwhelming experience. You have to be careful not to hit pedestrians, watch out for stray animals, and goodness, those elderly drivers—bless their hearts—are the worst when you're in a rush. I'm doing my best to keep up with this person, even though I've probably broken several laws by now, including running a red light. Thank goodness we don't have those red light cameras.

My pursuit is cut short when I slam on the brakes. "Damn it, damn it, damn it," I shout, pounding on the steering wheel. Just as I'm in the middle of my impromptu high-speed chase, someone decides to cross the road. Now all I see are the car's brake lights as they slowly fade away, and I'm furious at whoever thought it was a good idea to cross the road at that moment.

"Aaron?" I now feel horrible that I was upset at the person trying to cross the road because that person is Aaron. I put my car in park in the middle of the road and jump out of my car. "What in the world are you doing? I could have killed you."

He is a little shaken up and may have seen his life flash before his eyes. Maybe this is why high-speed chases aren't allowed in other countries. I can see now how dangerous and life-threatening they can be. *Why isn't Aaron at work yet?* I wonder.

"Um... sorry, Alice. I was just out for a walk before my shift started. But why were you driving like a maniac in a small town like this?" Aaron asks.

How do I tell him that someone possibly broke into my house and stole my Vogue magazine, of all things? I've also got a stalker who drives a black sedan with limo-tinted windows, and I decided to conduct a high-speed chase to see who that person is. Oh, and let's just go ahead and add that my mother has me on edge because she hypnotized the whole town and killed a few people along the way. This all sounds insane. *How do I tell him what's really going on?*

"Give me a second," I instruct him.

As I pull into the nearest parking spot, I figure it's as good a time as any to spill the truth about our mother's past and this town. I ask Aaron to hop in so we can talk. I'm not sure if telling him this will scare him away from Shelly Grove, but to be honest, I wouldn't blame him if it did.

"Are..." he hesitates to finish his question. "Are you okay? You seem a little off this morning."

"Lily-Ann is not a good person, Aaron," I say suddenly, the words spilling out of my mouth without warning.

"Um... okay. Isn't she your mom? Why do you feel your mom isn't a good person?" he asks.

With a deep breath, I lay it all out for him from the beginning. I tell him about my childhood and how our mother was abusive and manipulative. Aaron is stunned to hear this. Considering the frail woman he cares for every day, he can hardly believe she would hurt a fly. I feel bad for shattering his illusions, but I explain how our mother hypnotized the whole town—including Sarah and me.

"Yeah, right, be serious," he says with a chuckle.

I rub my temples. I knew this would sound crazy. Who would believe a story like this?

"Aaron, I am being serious," I say sternly, giving him a look that conveys my seriousness. "Lily-Ann, the woman you are taking care of isn't that old. Think about it; I know you read her reports. She hasn't had any other known medical conditions, and all of a sudden, she wakes up with dementia one day."

His smile begins to fade as if he's actually considering what I'm telling him. "Okay?"

"My mother is a psychopath; no, my mother is a certified psychopath. She tried to hold everyone hostage here in this town," I explain.

"So let's say, theoretically speaking, she did hypnotize this town, including you and Sarah; how did she do it? Also, how did she end up with dementia?" Aaron's curiosity starts to kick in, and he is full of questions.

I explain to him that we believe this goes back to our grandparents, who invented these water filtration tablets, but in reality, they were tablets to keep people under their hypnosis.

It's clear that I now have his undivided attention. He's sat up a little taller, and his eyes are now locked in on my every word.

Going more into detail, I tell him what Mr. Geral and I did to save the people of this town by hypnotizing Lily-Ann into thinking she had dementia. Desperation kicks in, and I need him to understand why she must remain under her hypnosis and why giving her the medication each day is so important.

"I'm not proud of the things I've had to do; you have to believe me. But I'm laying it all out on the table, so you know who and what you are getting yourself into..." I pause briefly, gazing at him, trying to figure out his thoughts. "I also had to kill my brother Cameron and run my brother James out of this town."

My eyes start to water, and I struggle to hold back hot tears from spilling out. Hearing the words come out of my mouth cuts deeper than a two-edged sword. I've actually killed a man... No, I've killed my own brother. My flesh and blood. *Who have I become?*

"I'm sorry, Aaron. I understand if this changes how you feel about us and this town." I say, lowering my gaze. "I wouldn't blame you if you packed up your things tonight and left."

Aaron peers out the window and rubs his chin. His lips form nothing but a straight line. He has no expression.

"I'm sorry for not telling you sooner," I say. "I just really felt you needed to know," I say, fiddling with my fingers in my lap.

Finally, his lips curl into a smile. He grabs one of my hands, and with his other hand, he wipes the tears that have fallen down my cheeks with his thumb.

"I can see now..." he pauses. "I can see now that you girls are going to be a pain in my neck."

I must be dreaming because I can't believe what I'm hearing. *Does he understand what I just told him?*

"..."

"On a serious note, you don't need to apologize for doing what you had to do to protect your family. A strange story about your mom and

74

the town isn't going to scare me off. In fact, it does the opposite; I'm interested in learning more about this place. There's something special about this town, and I can't leave now," he explains, smiling.

For a minute, I hold his gaze, trying to replay what he just said. My mind is trying to process that he finds this town: *special.* Who in their right mind would want to live here? I want to speak up and beg him to leave for some reason because our mother is dangerous, but then it hits me: *Lily-Ann is a prisoner of her own mind now. She can't hurt me anymore.*

"So tell me more about this hypnosis?" Aaron asks.

I chuckle because this guy is really interested in knowing what happened here, but I guess it's not every day that you move to a town with a real-life horror story.

We sit in my car for what feels like hours. I go more into detail about my upbringing. Out of nowhere, Aaron snaps his fingers as if he just remembered something. "Hey, so why were you speeding? You know when you almost took me out of here."

"So about that..." I say hesitantly. "This random black car was parked in the middle of the road in my neighborhood."

"Is something wrong with that? I mean, people park in the streets all the time. You sure that person wasn't visiting anyone?" he asks.

"Well, it was the middle of the night, and when I tried to get closer..." I pause.

"What happened?"

"The car sped off. I keep seeing the same car everywhere now, and every time I try to approach it, it speeds off. So I was tired of being followed, and I took matters into my own hands." I explain.

"So you thought it was a good idea to play detective? I mean, you don't know who could have been in there, Alice." Aaron's is now filled with concern. "You didn't think about calling the police?"

"No, I didn't want to worry the police until I found out who was in the car. I was also tired of being scared. Everywhere I go, I have to look over my shoulder. I mean, what's really keeping my brother James from coming back and finishing us off?" I ask, but really I'm asking myself this same question.

"I get it, but there's something you got that James doesn't know about," he says.

"What's that?" I'm curious because at this point, I really don't know what I have.

"Me. He doesn't know anything about me. I got you girls. If you ever need anything, give me a call and I'll be there," he says, giving my hand a light squeeze.

It felt good getting all this off my chest. Having someone else to talk to in Shelly Grove was like a breath of fresh air. Mr. Gerald is sweet, but Lily-Ann traumatized him as well. We are all broken in some way here. How can we help each other if we are suffering the same trauma from the same person? I desperately needed someone else to talk to who was an outsider, and Aaron was the perfect person to turn to.

CHAPTER 17

— • —

I t's Saturday, and it feels like a weight has been lifted off my chest after talking to Aaron. Today is the cookout and our first official welcome party since our mother was sent to the facility. Sarah, Mr. Gerald, and I had been working tirelessly to prepare for this event. I still have the paper cuts from the flyers I distributed throughout the community during the week.

The clock tower chime was no longer intimidating, but it was louder the closer we got to it, and since this party was being held in the town's park, we were right under it. With Adams' help, I was able to locate DJ Smoke, who appeared to be in his late thirties. He had shoulder-length dreadlocks, and the entire top row of his teeth was covered in gold.

Apparently, he is based in Atlanta and works at some of the city's hottest nightclubs. It's crazy the things these kids can find by searching Instagram and TikTok. Thank goodness he was willing to come this far. *We sure paid him enough.* With his many speakers and talent, he was able to drown out the sound of the clock tower's chime with a vast selection of songs, from the Cha Cha Slide to an old favorite of mine from Nelly, "It's getting hot in here."

"Looking good, Mr. Gerald," I say as I approach the area with the grills. He's wearing an apron I got him for this occasion that says, "Grill Master."

"Thanks, baby girl." He isn't our father at all, but he has been there for us through this crazy, rollercoaster of a journey. He's made it his main goal to make sure my sister and I know he isn't going anywhere. As a result, he's started giving us little nicknames here and there.

Looking around the park, I'm filled with joy at what we've achieved. This town has been through tough times—heck, I have too—but now we're all coming together to make something amazing happen for a complete stranger. It's hard not to be overwhelmed with happiness.

"Y'all ready to get this party started!" DJ Smoke shouts as he holds the mic close to his lips. His voice, projecting through the many speakers throughout the entire park—let's be honest, it was so loud that it probably carried through the whole town—it didn't matter, though. From the look of it, I bet the entire town is here.

Our setup was far from elegant. We weren't rolling out red carpets like Lily-Ann did at my party. We certainly weren't requiring anyone to wear white button-up shirts, tuxedos, and white gloves to serve guests. And we definitely weren't dressing up as if we were preparing to attend a fancy ball, like something out of the show *Bridgerton*.

A cookout is what we planned, and a good old-fashioned cookout is what Aaron was getting. Today's attire was whatever you wanted as long as it was comfortable. The baseball field was packed with residents. It was all fun and games out here.

The music was blasting, and we were all dancing and having a good time. This was the best party I think I have ever been to. There was no drama, just good, wholesome people getting along and having a great time.

"I think we did an outstanding job with this one!" I shout over the music to Sarah as I accompany her in doing the electric slide.

"I agree!" she also shouts.

Scanning the park, I notice Aaron, who has been all smiles since the cookout started. Currently, he is enjoying a dance from an elderly lady trying to show him she's still got it. *Bless her soul, she better stop trying to seduce that man.* I've never seen a grandma get that low to the ground. I'm sure she'll need some pain meds in the morning, but right about now, that doesn't even matter. What matters is everyone is out here cutting up, having a good old time, and that's what this welcome party is supposed to be about.

The kids are next to the grill with Mr. Gerald. He must be telling one of his many jokes because the kids are leaning back, mouths wide open, and cracking up at whatever he's saying. This is a good day, and nothing could change that.

Continuing to scan the party, something catches me by surprise. *I didn't see her out here.* I wonder as I notice Sharon on the other end of the park. Honestly, I thought she would have been at work, especially since Aaron is here.

"Hey, I'll be right back," I say to Sarah before I exit the dance floor.

She nods her head, ensuring she hears me. I quickly exit the dance floor and grab a small cup of water. Believe it or not, I'm no spring chicken; I can't get low on the dance floor and pop back up like I could back in my teenage years. I was out of breath, so a small cup of water was exactly what I needed at this moment.

I make my way through the crowd. For a small town, it's crazy how many people actually live here.

"This is exactly what this town needed," Mr. Jimmy Wilkes from the town meeting says as I walk by.

I nod and raise my cup in agreement. This is exactly what the town needed, but I can't let Mr. Wilkes distract me from my main focus right now. I continue walking, my gaze fixed on Sharon. It's not bothering me that she's here, because this is a cookout for the entire town to enjoy. However, I worry about who's watching over our mother if the only two people who know the truth about her are here.

The closer I get to Sharon, the further away she seems to become. She's walking through the crowd as if she were in a hurry. *Where is she going?* I wonder.

Suddenly, I stop in my tracks, my feet locking me in place. My heart begins to race as disbelief washes over me. I blink frantically, desperately hoping that my eyes are deceiving me, but the shocking sight before me remains unchanged, each heartbeat echoing the intensity of the moment.

Sharon has approached a car—no, not any car. It's the same black car that's been stalking me this entire time. "What is this?" I ask myself in complete and total shock.

From where I'm standing, I notice the limo's tented window on the driver's side slowly roll down. I don't wear glasses, but I need to squint my eyes to get a better view of the person in the driver's seat.

The cup I'm holding drops to the ground because I can't believe what I'm seeing, or rather, who I'm seeing.

It's a man—a black man. Not just a black man, but a black man with a black beard. He's wearing a ballcap, and his sunglasses look pitch black from my vantage point. I doubt she can even see his eyes. My eyes could be playing tricks on me, but that guy almost looks like James.

"That can't be," I say to myself.

You know, in the movies, when someone does something stupid, you start screaming at them as if they can hear you. Well, today, I am that stupid person. I catch my breath and clear my head. There's only one way for me to find out who Sharon is talking to and why.

Pushing through the crowd, I take off running. I don't take my gaze off Sharon. I was a hawk, and I had zeroed in on my target, and of course, everyone got in my way. People were stepping in my path as I ran through the park, and just like the movies, I apologized as I pushed a few of them out of my way.

Who in the world thought it would be a good idea to build a freaking park this big? My feet are moving, but it doesn't seem like they are moving fast enough. Maybe joining one of those military boot camps wouldn't be such a bad idea. Those people can run miles at a time without even trying. I recall watching this Navy SEALs show where they were running through the desert to escape the enemy. I mean, jeez, all they were doing was running. I know it was just a show, but my goodness, not one person needed to stop for a sip of water.

In this situation, it's evident that I'm no military soldier running through the desert. I also realize that I'm completely out of shape, and it's even more apparent to me that I could use a sip of water from the cup I was holding. Instead, that water is now soaking into the lush green grass of Shelly Grove Town Park, and I'm out of breath.

Whoever Sharon's talking to must have seen me coming. As I get closer, the man driving the black sedan quickly rolls up the window and speeds off. At this point, I have a cramp in my stomach, and my breathing is now painful.

"Who...?" I can't finish my question. I'm currently leaning over with my hands on my knees, trying to catch my breath.

"Who?" Sharon repeats.

"Who... were?" I still can't get all the words out at once.

Struggling to speak, I jump at the unexpected touch on my shoulder. *Oh, how delightful! I've gone from having a fantastic time with friends and family in the park to being a paranoid, jumpy mess! Isn't that just perfect? Maybe it's my imagination playing tricks on me—could it be?* I could have sworn I just saw Sharon talking to my brother, and not just any brother, but the charmingly deranged sibling I so wisely chose to let go.

"Alice, are you okay?" a familiar voice asks as I turn around to see who is touching me.

"Yeah, Sarah saw you running through the park and she took off after you," Aaron begins to explain, catching his breath. "Then I saw her running, so I took off after her. You know, back in my younger days, when we saw our friends running, when you already knew what time it was!" he says jokingly.

I'm still completely out of breath, but I feel like I can get a few more words out at this point. "Who... were... you... talking... to?"

"Who me?" Sharon asks, pointing to herself.

At this point, my ribs hurt from sprinting across this ginormous field. My throat is burning because I dropped my cup of water from being in shock, so I didn't have anything to drink after sprinting across the field. And Sharon wants to play dumb. She's got the wrong one today.

"WHO WERE YOU TALKING TO, SHARON?" I scream, grabbing her arms. I must have startled Sarah and Aaron, because they jumped, surprised by my outburst.

"Um—" Sharon looks confused and is also lost for words.

I tighten my grip on her arms, my gaze locked onto hers with an intensity that demands her attention. "I'm serious, Sharon," I say, my voice low and urgent. "I need to know who you were talking to." The weight of my words hangs in the air, thick with tension.

"I really don't know who that was. From what he told me, he was passing through town. He asked what was going on in the park. I told him the town was holding a welcome party. Now, can you please let my arms go?"

I study her eyes, trying to determine if she is telling me the truth. My fingers remain tightly wrapped around her arms. At this point, I can no longer hear the music from DJ Smoke or anything else. It is as if Sharon and I are left locking eyes in a silent staring contest.

"Okay, how about you release her arms, and we all just calm down," Aaron interjects, breaking our focus.

"Thank you, Aaron," Sharon says as she rubs one of her arms in the spot where I was squeezing.

"Look, I'm sorry, I just saw you talking to this man, and this black car has been following me, and I had this dream about James, and I could have sworn that's who was in the car, and I've just been on edge lately," I explain, panicked.

"Alice, calm down," Sarah says. "You're freaking out and talking too fast. Did you even breathe getting all that out?"

"Was it James?" I ask.

Sharon's look raises my suspicion. She looks at me as if she doesn't know who James is. *Do I need to remind her?*

"Are you okay, Alice?" Sharon asks.

I know I'm not losing my mind. That man looked just like my brother. Then again, I could be going a bit crazy; he was wearing a baseball cap and dark sunglasses. Perhaps I'm just overreacting. Maybe my sister is right.

I need to get out of this town.

"Yes, I'm fine, but you still didn't answer my question, Sharon. Was that James?" I hold her gaze, studying her eyes as I wait for her response.

Sharon glances between the three of us. "Look, I'm not sure what's going on with you, Alice, but that guy was definitely not James. He said his name was Mike."

"Mike?"

"..." She looks at me with a blank expression.

"Sharon!" I yell, causing her to jump out of whatever daydream she's in.

"I... I can only tell you what he told me. His name was Mike," she explains.

Sarah and I exchange a concerned glance, sensing that something isn't right with Sharon. She had always been poised and articulate, never one to stumble over her words. In fact, her keen awareness of her surroundings had always set her apart in her line of work, where attention to detail and clear communication were essential. But at this moment, her eyes dart nervously, and her voice wavers as she struggles to find the right words. It's an unsettling feeling, and I can't shake the feeling that something is off with her.

"If there's nothing else you need to ask, I've got to get back to work. I just fed all the patients and handed out their meds. Most of them were already sleeping, and before you ask, your mother was one of them. I know you're probably wondering why I'm here. I just wanted to come get some free food since I was on my lunch break," she explains, likely annoyed at my actions.

Sharon stomps off, periodically glancing back at us over her shoulder. Right now, I don't have the mental capacity to understand why she left the facility. My main focus is on who she was speaking to.

"Why do you think that was James?" Sarah asks as she places her hand on my shoulder.

"I haven't mentioned this before because I didn't want to worry you, but a black car has been following me, and it was parked on the street near my house," I say, keeping my eyes on Sharon as she disappears into the distance.

Sarah chuckles, "Are you sure that was the same car? There are a billion black cars worldwide, and I own one of them."

I know what she is saying is true, but there is something off about this particular car. Deep down, I know it is the same black car that has been following me. I just need to figure out a way to prove it.

Aaron hadn't known me that long, but it's clear he can read my facial expression and can tell that something is bothering me. He can see that something about that particular black car spooked me. "How about we get back to the party, ladies? The car is gone, and Sharon is heading back to the facility."

I stand there for a moment, my gaze fixed on the empty street as if I'm waiting for the car to reappear, but it never does. The road is clear because everyone in Shelly Grove is here at the cookout, and all the cars are lined up along the side of the park. My head is spinning as many thoughts run through my mind: *Am I being followed? Was that James? Why was Sharon acting so weird, and who the hell is Mike?*

"I'm not sure who you saw, sis, but it wasn't James," Sarah says as she grabs my hand and gives it a light squeeze. "Everything is okay, Alice. Remember, we are starting over. This is our life, and no one can control it anymore."

I really wish the words coming out of my sister's mouth were true, but something is leading me to believe one of my questions is valid. Something isn't right; I can feel it.

CHAPTER 18

—·—

After the incident at the party, Aaron and Sarah decided I should go home and rest. Aaron kindly offered to take me home and stay overnight so I could recover while he looked after the kids. The last few days have been mentally draining, and I knew I needed some time to relax. I suspect my sister and Aaron think I'm losing it. It's not long before they might put me in the facility, and I'll be my mother's neighbor. Maybe James's plan all along was to drive me crazy enough so that I would become a patient as well. This all sounds insane; *perhaps I am really losing my mind.*

"Thank you for staying over, Aaron," I say, standing in the doorway to my room. It feels good to have a man around for once. It wasn't anything intimate between us; it was more like a strong friendship. Who made that stupid rule anyway that guys and girls can't be friends?

"No problem, I'll be right here if you need anything," Aaron reassures me as I close the door.

I lay in bed looking up at the ceiling, in deep thought about the cookout. I keep beating myself up because this was supposed to be a party for Aaron. *Leave it to me to mess up an event.* The doorbell rings, and I quietly get out of bed so Aaron doesn't hear me shuffling around in my room. I peer out the window and notice my sister and Mr. Gerald standing on the porch. I can hear Aaron open the door and offer for them to come in.

Mr. Gerald is concerned about me, and he keeps asking Aaron how I'm doing. He also wants to come into my room to check on me, but thankfully, he tells him I'm asleep. *I don't have the energy to entertain anyone right now.*

"Our mother has truly traumatized us, " I hear my sister whisper, not knowing that I have my ear to the door, trying to hear what they're talking about. "To be honest, when we were younger, it seemed like my sister was treated the worst. I also believe she felt she had to protect me, which led her to take on many of my punishments."

Hearing my sister brings my mind back to the day of my high school graduation. I can remember this day so well because I was eighteen and knew that the day I graduated, I was now considered an adult. I was sitting in the auditorium as the valedictorian gave her speech. Sarah was sitting next to a boy named Kenny. She was over the top in love with Kenny. She looked so cute wearing this pretty, strapless, bright pink summer dress. Thank goodness our mother wasn't there because she would have dragged my sister through the mud because it was an abomination to wear anything that showed our shoulders. I bought my sister that dress because it was cute and on sale, and she wanted to wear something to impress Kenny for once.

I remember glancing back at them: his arm around her shoulder, her head resting on his. I smiled and waved at her, but her expression changed suddenly. Lily-Ann had arrived, despite earlier saying she wouldn't. She had told me, "Who would dare show up to watch you walk across the stage?" I should have realized it was a lie—why wouldn't she come? Why would she let the town's people down by skipping her oldest daughter's graduation?

Lily-Ann saw Sarah and Kenny, and her anger was obvious. If she were a cartoon character, there would be smoke coming from her head. She was furious. She quickly moved to them, grabbed Sarah by her ponytail, and led her out of the auditorium. I didn't hesitate; I ran out without looking back. Unfortunately, I missed my chance to walk across the stage—something most teens dream of during their senior year. I didn't get to take those cute graduation photos with my friends, but what I experienced was much worse.

When we got home, Sarah was sitting in the chair, hands tied behind her back. Lily-Ann was slapping her in the face and calling her a whore and slut for the way she was dressed. Sarah cried, apologizing, hoping that she would stop. Our mother didn't care; she got a kick out of it, in my opinion. We were used to being hit, so I think we were numb to the beatings, but the words always cut deeper.

"Mom, stop!" I yelled. "It was my fault, I bought her the dress. I told her to come with Kenny."

Lily-Ann turned around slowly, her gaze piercing into mine, "You did this to my little girl?"

Even though I was eighteen, she still knew how to put fear in me, and just because I was eighteen didn't mean I was free. I still needed a place to live.

"Yes, I did it, so if you want to punish someone, punish me," I demanded.

It was clear what she had in store for Sarah that day because she went into the pocket of her skirt and pulled out five of the biggest rings she had. I knew what was next at that point; she didn't have to say a word.

I rub my face as I think back on that day. Some days I feel my face because that was a sting I will never forget. She hit me multiple times until my face was unrecognizable. *So much for my graduation pictures,* I remember thinking as I looked at myself in the mirror after it was over. I don't regret it, though; Sarah is my baby sister, and I'd retake the beating for her if I had to.

"Damn," Aaron says softly, realizing I wasn't over exaggerating about how awful our mom is. "Do you two think that maybe she needs to get out of this town and start over fresh?"

The room is silent for a moment, and then I hear Mr. Gerald say, "Maybe what she really needs is for us to find another facility for Lily-Ann that's not in this town. Perhaps Atlanta, maybe even Savannah."

Enough is Enough. I am not the type of person to sit here and let others discuss my life. Our mother controlled me for many years, and I will not let anyone start now. I turn back around and yank my room door open, entering the living room. "I know you all are worried about me, but please don't try to plan my life without me present."

The room goes silent, and the three of them are staring at me, speechless.

"Baby girl, we're not trying to plan your life; we're just concerned. I hate seeing you like this. We hate seeing you like this. We care about you," Mr. Gerald says as he approaches me with open arms.

"I understand, and I'm sorry for barking at you guys. I'm exhausted from planning this party and the mental rollercoaster I've been on. I really need some rest," I say.

90

"I understand. Your sister and I are going to head out so you can get some rest," Mr. Gerald says softly. He then reaches out to shake Aaron's hand. "Keep an eye on her, buddy, and don't hesitate to call me if you need anything. I'm right next door."

Aaron nods and escorts them out the door. I'm sitting on the couch, curled up, when Aaron suggests I get in bed. On any other day, I would have looked at him like he was crazy. No one tells me what to do, but as of right now, I have no more fight in me, and if I'm being honest with myself, he's absolutely right. I was exhausted, and the bed was screaming my name.

"Hey..." I hesitate. "Do you mind sitting with me until I fall asleep? I'm still a little freaked out, and I just want to see a friendly face before I close my eyes."

"Sure, no problem at all; you got a blanket I can take with me, just in case I fall asleep?" he asks.

"I got you," I say as we head for my room.

CHAPTER 19

— • —

"A lice!" I'm startled by Aaron shaking me to wake up. I must have been out cold because it seems as if he's been trying to wake me for a while.

I blink several times, trying to clear the blur that clouds my vision and grasp the situation around me. Finally, my eyes adjust, and I focus intently on Aaron's concerned face. With a hint of urgency in my voice, I ask, "What's wrong?"

"Someone is outside the house; do you have a gun?" For a minute, I try to convince myself that he's messing around. "Alice, do you have a gun?"

"Wait, What? What do you mean someone is outside the house?" I believe I'm a bit confused and maybe even a little shocked. I've never thought about purchasing a gun.

"I don't have time to explain; we need a weapon; do you have a gun?"

"No... no, I don't have a gun." At this point, I can see that this is not a game. This is very real. Someone is really outside my house. "I have a metal bat. One of those bats that truckers use to check their tires. Will that help?"

"That will have to do," he says quickly.

I jump out of bed and rush to my closet. I swing open the closet doors, and tucked in the corner is my large metal bat, gifted to me by Mr. Gerald. I've never been one for guns. I especially didn't care for them after seeing my brother point one at my sister's head.

"Here it is. Should I call the police?" My hands are shaking as I hand him the bat. Shelly Grove has been a nice, quiet town since we put our mother away; I can't believe this is happening.

"Yes, call the police, but first, get the kids, and hide in one of the closets," he instructs me.

I don't hesitate, I do exactly what he tells me.

Running upstairs, I take the steps two at a time. I go into Kandice's room, gently shaking her to wake up, then we both head for Adam's room to wake him. Sadly, at this point, my kids are familiar with the drill. I've been one of those parents who prepares her kids for the worst. We were caught off guard last time, and I wanted to ensure they knew what to do if James came back.

"Someone is outside the house, and Aaron is going to check it out," I whisper. "You two know the drill; we hide in Adams' closet."

After my brothers broke into my house and took my kids, I decided it was best to build a hidden wall in one of our closets. We chose Adam's room because he has a larger walk-in closet. To a burglar, it will appear as just a bare wall, making it look like the back of the closet. In reality, it provides enough space for the three of us to hide behind it.

I know this has to be scary for a child. Given what my kids have been through. *Gosh, I hope this hasn't ruined them for life.*

"911, what's your emergency?" the operator asks as I call for help.

I inform the operator that someone is outside my house, and my friend is trying to keep us safe. The operator does the usual and asks a slew of questions, including my address and whether we have a safe place to hide in the house.

I inform the operator that my kids and I are safe, but I'm not sure about Aaron. The operator instructs me to remain quiet until the authorities arrive. Adam and Kandice are scared, and I'm worried about Aaron. *What have I dragged him into?* I can't let anything happen to him while we sit upstairs hiding.

"Kandice, since you're the oldest, I need you to stay on the phone with the operator," I whisper.

"Where are you going, Mom?" she whimpers.

"I'm just going to step out of the closet to see if I hear anything. I need to make sure Aaron is okay. Remember, no one knows about this wall but us, so if you hear a knock, you know it's me," I explain.

I slowly crawl out of the closet, my heart racing as I inch toward Adam's door. With cautious fingers, I push it open, straining to hear any sound from downstairs. But the house is unnervingly silent. The stillness is so profound that I can even hear the air conditioner clicking on, followed by the soft rush of cool air escaping the ceiling vents. I peek my head out, eyes scanning the dimly lit hallway, every instinct on high alert, but there's only darkness. No movement, just an eerie calm that sends chills down my spine.

"Aaron?" I whisper, trying to keep my voice low. "Is everything okay?"

Just as I was about to head back to the closet, a loud gunshot suddenly stopped me in my tracks. I don't own a gun, and when Aaron asked me if I did, it hit me that he probably didn't have one either. That only leaves one person who could possibly have a gun: the burglar.

I head back to the closet, pressing my ear against the wall, with my heart racing. I whisper urgently through the drywall, telling Kandice to alert the operator that a gunshot just went off. With a surge of adrenaline, I bolt for the door and fling it open, breath quickening. As I burst into the hallway, reality slams into me. I suddenly realize I need to be cautious—the last thing I want is for the burglar to hear me coming. My mind races as I consider my next move, the tension tightening with each step toward the stairs.

I grip the rail and slowly descend the stairs, tiptoeing each step one by one. As soon as I can see, I glance around the living room, and it's empty. Where did they—

"NO! NO! NO!" I rush down the last few steps and notice Aaron lying on the floor, not moving. *God, please, not again.*

As I approach him, I kneel on the cold floor beside him, my heart racing in the eerie silence. I shake his body, desperation gripping me, but he doesn't respond. Suddenly, something catches my eye—a chilling sight that freezes me in place. My heart stops beating as I realize what it is. My hands and knees are slick with something warm and thick, something that resembles blood. The dreadful reality sinks in, and I have entirely forgotten all about the burglar. This is far worse than I imagined.

CHAPTER 20

— · —

I slide my hand under Aaron's back and pull it out; my palm is now covered in a crimson substance. *Oh God, please, no. Not blood.* It's definitely blood. Looking around, I notice a large amount of something spreading from underneath him. This can't be good. I'm no doctor, but I don't think the human body is supposed to lose this much blood.

"Aaron, can you hear me? Are you alive?" I whisper as I scan my surroundings. "Aaron, did you see the person's face?"

He doesn't move a muscle, but I sure wasn't about to let another person die on my watch. Reflecting on all the rescue shows I've watched, I recall an episode where a woman is instructed to apply pressure to a person's wound who was bleeding profusely. I scan the living room for anything I can use to cover his wound; then, I notice my fluffy, cream-colored pillows. I glance at the amount of blood still spreading from under Aaron and then back at my cream-colored pillows. *I'm definitely going to have to buy myself more pillows after this.*

I grab the pillow from off the couch to cover the wound. I pray that doing this will slow the bleeding until the ambulance arrives. I place the pillow over the tiny hole in his abdomen from where the bullet must have entered. At this point, my arms and legs are now covered in blood. I lean on the pillow, applying as much of my body weight as possible on top. *I hope this works.*

Moments like this make you feel like it takes the police forever to get here. I swear it feels like hours have passed, and still no one has shown up. I continue to hold the pillow over Aaron's wound, applying as much pressure as possible.

Scanning the room, I'm stunned to see the back door wide open. Panic sets in, and I realize I wasn't overreacting about checking the locks every day. It's clear now that burglars only come through the back door. I turn my gaze toward the living room window, hoping to see flashing red and blue lights. Instead, I'm startled by a figure dressed in black, wearing a mask over their face. For a moment, fear grips me, and my life flashes before my eyes. But then, my protective instincts take over. *I have to protect my kids.* I place Aaron's hand on the pillow and spring up from the floor. Grabbing the bat, I rush out the door.

The burglar must have gotten spooked by the sight of me with the bat. Whoever that was, they ran off the moment they saw me getting off the floor. It's too dark to see which direction the burglar has vanished to. I stand frozen in my yard, my heart racing as disbelief washes over me like a cold wave. This kind of thing doesn't happen in Shelly Grove—not since Lily-Ann was admitted to the facility. I scan the darkness around me, my pulse quickening—*who was that?* A shiver runs down my spine as I begin to question what the burglar really wanted.

Red and blue lights illuminate the entrance of my neighborhood. I can see their reflection in the darkness and on the houses as the lights approach. When they arrive, multiple emergency personnel exit their vehicles with medical bags in hand.

"My friend has been shot," I say quickly, gesturing for them to follow me into the house. I notice another group of emergency personnel pull a stretcher out of the ambulance, and I begin to think the worst. *Oh God, does that mean he's dead?*

"Ma'am, was anyone else hurt?" an officer from the Shelly Grove Police Department asks.

"No, my kids are upstairs hiding in the closet. The burglar was standing outside the window just before you arrived. I tried to chase after the person, but they got away," I say.

"So, you ran after the person..." The officer raises an eyebrow. "Holding the gun?"

As stupid as it sounds, I guess I did run after an armed person. When your adrenaline is pumping, and you're fed up, I don't think you think about the fact that they have the gun and you only have a metal bat.

"I guess I did," I say, realizing I could have been shot.

"Well, it's a good thing you're still standing here to tell us what happened," the officer says as he tugs on his belt.

"What's going on?" Mr. Gerald asks, panting as he enters my house, concern clear on his face. "Where are the kids? Is everyone okay? Where's Aaron?"

"Someone tried to break in," I say with tears forming in my eyes. At this point, I think reality has finally caught up with me. The brave, crazy woman who runs out of doors after armed individuals have officially left the building. *Oh my god, I actually ran out of the house after an armed burglar with a metal bat. What was I thinking?* I wonder as panic takes over.

It only takes Mr. Gerald a few seconds before he finally notices the EMTs sliding Aaron on a board.

"Jesus, Alice, what happened?" he asks.

Tears stream down my cheeks as I stand frozen, biting down on my fist, watching them lift Aaron onto the stretcher. It felt like déjà vu, a haunting reminder of a nightmare I thought I had escaped. At that moment, I have a flashback, taking me back to the day I found the receptionist tied helplessly to a chair. The chaos of police cars and the sound of ambulances filled my mind, a painful reminder of a past I desperately wished to forget.

"Alice, what happened?" Mr. Gerald asks again as he places his hand on my shoulder, interrupting my thoughts.

"Someone attempted to break in, and Aaron told me and the kids to hide. God, I shouldn't have hidden; I should have been here to help him." I cry. "He may die because he was protecting us."

The room is silent, and I've blocked out all the noise around me. I can only see Mr. Gerald. He grabs a blanket off the couch and wraps it around my shoulders, hugging me tightly. I'm thankful for him; he is exactly who I needed at this moment. I need a father to hold me and reassure me that everything will be okay.

"It's going to be okay, baby girl. Aaron is going to be okay," Mr. Gerald says as he wraps his arms around me and softly kisses my forehead.

After getting Aaron on the stretcher, I agree to ride in the ambulance with him. The kids are shaken up, but they would be in good hands. Mr. Gerald was kind enough to stay at my house with them so I could be there for Aaron when he woke up.

As we rush to the hospital, I squeeze Aaron's hand tightly, doing my best to keep him awake by talking to him. It was terrifying being in the back of the ambulance, surrounded by so much chaos in that cramped space. The urgent sounds and bright lights only added to my anxiety. Above all, my heart was heavy with worry, and all I could think about was whether he would be okay.

This was an incredibly overwhelming moment for me, and I couldn't shake the feeling that it was somehow my fault. If I hadn't run through the park thinking I saw James, Aaron wouldn't have been at my house tonight. I know I can't dwell on what could have been, though; right now, what matters most is being strong for him.

Pulling into the hospital, the scene unfolds like something out of one of those medical shows. A crowd of doctors and nurses is gathered outside, their serious expressions signaling the urgency of the situation. When the ambulance doors swing open, it is as if a switch has been flipped; they spring into action with remarkable speed and efficiency.

A medical staff member hurries onto the stretcher, urgently performing CPR and shouting, "We're losing him!" Their frantic voice sends a shiver down my spine. Standing nearby at the entrance, my heart pounds, and fear overwhelms me. I watch helplessly as they wheel him off under the flickering hospital lights.

Even with the chaos, a wave of emotion washes over me, my heart aching for him. I knew I had to muster every ounce of strength to hold it together, not just for myself but for both of us. I refuse to let my fear show, hoping that he could somehow feel my presence as they rush him toward the operating room. The weight of the moment is almost unbearable, but I know I need to stay strong.

Sitting in the dimly lit waiting room, my heart races as I nervously bite my nails. The ticking sound of the clock above me echoes in my ears, each tick seeming to stretch time. Every time I glance at the clock, it appears that the minute hand barely budges, leaving me with the unsettling impression that only moments have passed. A heavy weight of uncertainty creeps in as I contemplate Aaron's condition.

"Sis, any word yet?" Sarah says, holding her arms out for my embrace as tears form in her eyes. "I came as fast as I could. Mr. Gerald told me what happened. Are you okay?"

I nod my head to assure her that I was okay, but to answer her question, I really didn't know what condition Aaron was in. "I don't know how he's doing. They took him back what felt like forever ago, but no one has come out yet."

Sarah clasps her hand over her mouth.

"Are you family or friends of Aaron Shaw?" an older man appears, coming from the same double doors they wheeled Aaron through when we arrived. He's wearing green scrubs and a light blue cover over his head, which lets me know he must be a doctor.

"Yes, we are. Is he okay?" I quickly ask.

He reaches out his hand to shake mine, "I'm Doctor Frazier. Our friend made it through surgery just fine. You have a fighter on your hands."

Tears flow down my cheeks because at this point, I'm overjoyed that another person hasn't died because of me.

The doctor took the time to explain the specifics of his injuries to us. He informed us that the bullet had passed straight through

101

without damaging any major organs. Although I wasn't completely clear on all the medical terminology, the most reassuring part of the conversation was when the doctor assured us that Aaron would make it. That news lifted an enormous weight off my shoulders.

"When can we see him?" Sarah asks.

"Well, he will probably sleep for the rest of the night. He was pumped up with quite a bit of pain meds and anesthesia," the doctor explains. "They're taking him to his room now; we're only allowing two people at a time in the room."

"Got it, we won't be long," I lie, knowing that I will not leave Aaron's side until he's released.

As Sarah and I enter Aaron's room, we find him peacefully sleeping, just as the doctor had predicted. The soft hum of the machines fills the air, creating a somewhat calming environment given the circumstances. I approach his bedside and observe the way his chest rises and falls in sync with the beeping monitors. Taking a moment to examine the web of wires and tubes connected to him, I realize each one is monitoring a vital sign. It's an overwhelming sight, and I can hardly wrap my mind around the reality of the situation.

"Who do you think it was, Alice?" Sarah asks in a soft enough tone that she won't disturb Aaron's rest.

"I don't know, whoever was in that black car that has been following me, is the only thing that makes sense right about now," I whisper.

"Who do you think was in the black car?" she whispers.

"Honestly, I don't know, but the only person my mind keeps going back to is..." I pause because I can't bring myself to say his name.

"Is who?" she asks.

"James."

102

CHAPTER 21

— · —

The hospital has never been my ideal place. If I'm being honest, it creeps me out. Life is lost in here. On the other hand, life is also given here. People are cut open here, and then again, they are sewn back together in this place. The last time I was in the hospital was the day our mother was admitted. Some people come in, while others don't. In our mother's case, she came out, but only to be escorted to the facility for the mentally unstable.

As I walk through the halls, I notice an elderly woman lying in bed in her room, staring at the ceiling. She must be in her eighties, at least, if I had to guess. She looks lost and hopeless. It reminds me of the state of mind that Lily-Ann is currently in. I can't help but feel a sense of sadness for her, knowing that she will be just like this elderly woman for the rest of her life.

Bang!

I'm startled by a man banging on the receptionist's desk and yelling, "I want answers now! What the hell kind of hospital is this?"

"Sir, please calm down. The doctor will be out shortly to talk to you about your wife," the lady sitting at the desk says calmly.

I shake my head at the sight unfolding in front of me. *Some people can't act right*, I think to myself. I turn around to look back at the elderly lady lying in the bed.

"What the..." She's literally standing in front of me with her eyes piercing into mine.

"Lily-Ann, is that you? Oh, honey, how are the babies doing?" the elderly woman says.

I'm unsure of what to do—should I call a nurse or just run away? Her eyes are staring into my soul, but it feels as though she isn't really seeing me at all. I wave my hand in front of her face, but she doesn't blink, not even once. So, I decide to do something else, "Oh, hey! How are you? The kids are doing just fine." *It's worth a short right?*

"Oh, that's good, dear. Please give them my love and tell them Nana loves them," she says.

"Nana? Nana... who? Who is Nana?" I ask repeatedly, but at this point, the woman has snapped out of whatever dimension she was in and is walking back to her bed. "Ma'am, who is Nana, or exactly whose Nana are you?"

She doesn't say another word. She slowly gets back in bed, straightening her nightgown. She pulls the thin hospital covers back over her. She then lays her head on the uncomfortable pillows the hospital provides and stares at the ceiling again. Something feels wrong, and the silence in the room is beginning to creep me out.

What just happened?

CHAPTER 22

— · —

A s I make my way back to Aaron's room, with a heaviness in my heart. Thoughts of the elderly lady weigh on my mind as I enter his room. It doesn't dawn on me that he has woken up until I hear, "Alice, are the kids okay?"

I quickly snap out of it: "Aaron, you're awake! The kids are doing just fine. How are you feeling?"

He coughs, the sound raspy and strained, and winces as a sharp wave of pain floods through him. He instinctively places his hand over his abdomen, where the doctors had removed the bullet, his fingers pressing against the tender skin. I can't help but feel like this is all my fault. Had he not been at my house, he wouldn't be lying in a hospital bed.

"That's good to hear," he murmurs, his voice barely above a whisper, discomfort evident in his tone.

"Look, we can talk about the kids when it doesn't hurt you to speak. I'm just glad you're alive," I say.

He nods his head, and his lips curve up into a smile. "Listen," he coughs once again, struggling to get his words out. "I have to pee. Do you think you can get the nurse to help me?"

"Yes, of course," I say.

While Aaron gets assistance in the bathroom, Sarah must have noticed the look on my face when I first walked into the room. "So, was everything okay out there?"

"Yeah, what do you mean?" I ask.

"Well, you were gone for quite a while, and I know you don't like this place, so I know you weren't just walking around taking a tour."

She knows me so well.

I look back at the bathroom to ensure Aaron is still in there, "I saw an elderly lady out there."

"Okay, what's so special about that? You're in a hospital; I'm sure there are a ton of elderly people in here," she says.

"No, Sarah, there was something about this lady that kind of gave me the creeps," I whisper.

"What do you mean?" she whispers.

"She knew Mom's name?" I say.

"Who doesn't know that psycho's name?" She has a point.

"No, Sarah. She didn't just know her name..." I pause and look back at the bathroom to ensure Aaron is still in there. The last thing he needs is to be overwhelmed with our mommy issues. "She knew mom; she knew she had kids and everything."

Sarah's confused look is now turning into a look of concern: "Okay, so everyone in town knows she has kids."

"I'm not sure, but something about this woman felt different. She referred to herself as Nana."

"Who is Nana?" Sarah asks.

"Exactly, or whose Nana?"

106

"We're back." I'm startled by the sound of the door slamming and the voice coming from behind me, which causes me to jump in my chair.

"I'm so sorry; I was trying to help Aaron and forgot to grab the door," the nurse says as she escorts him to the bed.

This place is starting to freak me out. Not only was my friend shot and could have possibly died in this place, but now a creepy old lady is walking around here, and she seems to know our mother. Better yet, a creepy old lady is walking around here, referring to herself as Nana. *Whose Nana, though?* I wonder as I watch the nurse gently lift Aaron's legs back onto the hospital bed.

CHAPTER 23

— · —

Sitting beside Aaron's bedside, I find myself captivated by the array of monitors around him. Each screen displays fluctuating numbers for his heartbeat and oxygen saturation, rhythmically pulsating like a breath of life. My gaze is fixed on the numerous wires linking different devices to his arms, forming a complex network that both fascinates and horrifies me.

In any other circumstance, the sight of needles piercing skin and tubes entwined with flesh would have sent my stomach into knots. The very thought of medical devices probing the human body is enough to make me queasy; I can barely endure having blood drawn without feeling faint. Yet, at this moment, confronting Aaron's fragile state stirred something within me that was different. I felt a profound sense of urgency and concern that overshadowed my fear, compelling me to remain at his side and hope for a quick recovery.

I cannot imagine what might have happened if Aaron hadn't been at my house. The pain of what he has endured weighs heavily on me, but I am immensely thankful for his presence. He was our guardian angel in a situation where someone was prepared to enter our home and potentially harm me and my children. The intruder who approached my home clearly underestimated the situation; they had no idea that a man was inside, ready to protect us. I have no idea how I can ever repay him for this, but I will be forever grateful.

"So, did they catch the guy who shot me?" he asks softly as he clears his raspy throat.

Sarah and I look at each other because we are both thinking the same thing. "No, they haven't said anything yet."

This is the worst news I've ever had to deliver to anyone. Well, maybe the next best. Telling my kids, Mrs. Sally, well, their grandmother, should I say, was the one who kidnapped them, was probably the worst thing I've ever had to tell anyone. But telling Aaron the person who shot him is still on the run is definitely next in line.

I can see the disappointment wash over him as the news sinks in; it is evident that this wasn't the outcome he had been hoping for. His face, which had held a glimmer of hope just moments earlier, now bore the signs of discouragement. Reaching out, I take his hand, giving it a gentle squeeze. "I know this isn't the news you were wishing for, and I can understand how disappointing this must be for you. I truly believe that the authorities are committed to finding the person responsible for this. Let's hold onto that hope together, okay."

Without saying a word, he nods his head in agreement.

***

SEVERAL HOURS HAVE PASSED, AND AARON IS SOUND ASLEEP. I was starting to feel the fatigue from being up all night, especially after waiting in the lobby for him to undergo surgery. After all the commotion, my body is finally signaling that it is time to get some rest. However, I'm committed at this point; I wasn't going anywhere.

"Do you want some coffee, sis?" Sarah asks as she heads for the door.

"No thanks, I'm good," I say quickly. But was I really? Was I really good? Absolutely not. I was not good, not even a little. On the inside, I was worried like hell. I had no idea who had come to my house. The only person who comes to mind is James. He is, in my opinion, the only person who would have a reason to try something like this.

"Alice, you haven't slept, and you've been going on almost twenty-four hours without sleep. Have you even checked on the kids?" Sarah asks.

I continue to stare into outer space, trying to piece together what happened last night. Everything is a bit foggy, but I need to remember how tall the person who did this was.

"Alice!"

Could the person who did this have been the same height as James? The person was wearing a mask and was completely covered from head to toe, so that I couldn't get a glimpse of their complexion.

"Alice!"

Maybe if I had come down sooner, I would have been able to get close enough to see exactly how tall the person was.

"Alice!"

If only I were close enough, I would have seen their arms as they lifted the gun to shoot at Aaron. Maybe if...

"Alice!" Sarah yells again, finally getting my attention.

"For God's sake, what is it, Sarah?" I snap my head in her direction, only to be startled by a dark-skinned man. He's wearing an all-black suit and has a gun attached to his belt buckle, along with a shiny gold badge engraved with the word "Detective."

"Sorry to interrupt, but my name is Detective Green," the man says with a strong Southern accent. He's holding his hand out to shake ours, but at this moment, I'm completely taken aback by the accent. *He's definitely not from around here.*

"Please tell me you've found the guy who did this?" I ask desperately.

"What makes you think the intruder was male?" he says.

"Excuse me?" I'm confused by his question.

"You called the shooter a guy, ma'am, so I was just curious if you got a good look at the person." He stares at me blankly, waiting for my response.

I hadn't realized that I had referred to the "shooter" as male. Most people tend to assume that it's typically a man. I'm not saying that women can't be shooters, but in nearly every crime show or movie I've watched, the intruder has always been portrayed as a man, so that influenced my assumption.

"I apologize; I wasn't paying attention when I made that statement. I just assumed…"

"Ma'am, in a case like this, I do not like assumptions. Assuming can land the wrong person behind bars, if you know what I'm saying. Assuming can also get someone hurt. So from here on out, we need solid facts, not assumptions. Let's refer to the intruder as the shooter and our friend…" he pauses and pulls out a small notepad from his suit pocket, "our friend Aaron here as the victim."

What a prick.

"I understand," I say.

"Did you get a good look at the shooter?" Detective Green asks again.

"No, I did not get a good look at the "shooter." The person wore a mask and was covered from head to toe in all black," I explain.

"Do you know who may have wanted to hurt you and your kids, ma'am?" he asks.

Well, I could tell him I hypnotized my mother, making her think she had dementia for the rest of her life. She would definitely want to kill me if she ever came out of her hypnosis. I could also say my brother, who helped our mother almost murder her two daughters and grandkids, could be a suspect, but I didn't say any of that.

"No, not at all; I have no idea who could have done this," I lie.

"I'd like to ask our friend here a few questions, but I see he is knocked out at the moment, and I don't want to wake him after having surgery. I can come back tomorrow and get a statement from him," he says.

"Thank you so much, detective," I say.

"Ma'am, can I just say..." he pauses before stepping out of the room. "Yes?"

"You got lucky. I've worked plenty of cases like this, and it's not always a happy ending. You got a good friend there. If I were you, I'd keep him close," he says and then steps out of the room, leaving me once again pondering what I would have done had Aaron not been with us last night.

CHAPTER 24

— · —

I step outside the hospital doors and look at the scene before me. I'm quickly reminded of how long we have been in this place. I'm reminded of how long it's been since I was awakened by Aaron telling me the last thing I wanted to hear: *someone is trying to break in.* The dark sky and streetlights reveal that we have been here for possibly over twenty-four hours now. The night breeze is exactly what I needed at a time like this.

I desperately craved fresh air to escape the stifling air filling the hospital room. I felt trapped, as if the walls were closing in on me, suffocating me with memories I dared not confront. My heart raced with an unsettling mix of fear and confusion stemming from the events that had unraveled my world.

The recent encounter with the mysterious woman, who claimed to be someone's Nana, kept replaying in my head. Her piercing gaze and mysterious words hinted at deep secrets that could shatter what little peace I had left. *Who is she? Why did her presence send an icy shiver down my spine?*

Then, there was the detective, whose voice seemed to echo in my head. He had calmly delivered a chilling message: *You got lucky.* Deep down, I understood exactly what he was saying. I got lucky because I'm still alive to testify to what I witnessed. Those words hung in the air like a loaded gun, and I couldn't help but replay the events leading up to that moment—the mysterious black sedan, the dream I had of James, and the ominous feeling of being watched.

Could James be back?

With each passing moment, paranoia began to creep in. Was there someone out there waiting to strike again? The sensation of invisible eyes on me intensified, causing me to stand outside the hospital doors, starting to go into a panic.

A weight settled heavily in my chest, tightening with every passing moment. My breath quickened, each inhale growing shallower and more frantic. The world around me began to shrink, and the people walking by blurred with each step they took, leaving me only able to make out their silhouettes. Although the person who threatened me and my family had not succeeded in their intentions, they had succeeded in instilling a deep, paralyzing fear within me, leaving me trembling at the very thought of their malice.

Is the shooter still out there? Is he or she still watching me? Could this person be watching me right now? All these thoughts ran through my head, and finally, my world stopped.

"What the..."

As I gaze up at the top of the hill, an eerie stillness surrounds me, as if time itself has frozen. The night breeze vanished, replaced by a suffocating silence that pressed against my skin. Despite the darkness surrounding everything, it felt like the streetlights had flickered out one by one, plunging me into an unsettling sense of unease. My eyes were drawn to the image ahead, an alarming sight that sent a chill racing down my spine.

As a child, this place was supposed to be my safe haven and source of comfort, but it was the opposite. It held dark memories, a place where our mother could inflict her torment on my sister and me. I can still recall the day she chased me through the house, my heart racing as fear consumed me. No one should ever feel that way about their mother—the one person who is meant to have that protective instinct. She should be the one to safeguard her children with every fiber of her being, but not Lily-Ann. Every time I look up toward the hill, the once-beautiful mansion at the top serves as a grim reminder of the hell she put us through.

The mansion at the top of the hill was no longer the reflection of the elegant portraits hung on the walls of the businesses throughout Shelly Grove. Instead, it was like a thorn on the hillside, a sad testament to the pain this woman had inflicted on our community. Even with Lily-Ann confined to the facility, the sight of her house evoked a chilling sensation, as if unseen eyes peered down from the dusty windows, silently scrutinizing each of us as we went about our routines.

It wasn't the sight of the mansion that caught my attention, though; it was the glow of light shining through the windows. I rarely look up at the hill because I already know what sits at the top. At this moment, my heart stops, and my world as I know it has come to a halt.

Who is in my mother's house?

CHAPTER 25

— • —

I f panic were a person, I would embody it completely. My heart raced as I sprinted through the hospital halls, urgency fueling each step. The air felt thick in my lungs, making them burn as I struggled to control my frantic breathing. All I could think about was reaching Sarah to tell her what I saw. *Was my nightmare becoming a horrifying reality? Is James really that crazy? Could he be the one lurking around in our mother's house?*

"Sarah... I... need... to... tell... you... something." I can't get the words out fast enough because, at this moment, I'm bending over with my hands on my knees, trying to catch my breath.

"Are you okay?" she asks, looking at me like I have gone crazy.

"Alice, what's going on?" Aaron says softly.

I burst into the room so fast that I failed to realize he was awake.

"Someone..." I pause and take a deep breath because my throat and chest are killing me at this moment from sprinting through the hospital.

"Someone, what?" Sarah asks.

I take a deep breath one more time before I blurt out the last thing Sarah would ever want to hear, "I think James is in Mom's house!"

Sarah looks at me with wide, startled eyes as if frozen in place like a deer caught in the glaring headlights of an approaching car. The air in the room has become heavy with silence, amplifying the sound of the many monitors plugged in to monitor Aaron. Her expression mirrors the fear I felt earlier when I glanced up at the hill and saw the warm glow of light shining from the windows, illuminating the darkness around it.

"Sarah, did you hear me?" I ask.

She is still looking at me, lost for words. I can only imagine what's running through her head at the moment. This was how I looked as I stared at Lily-Ann's house, watching the light shine through the many windows. I know the exact fear she is feeling at this moment.

Aaron slowly reaches out his hand, which has an IV attached to it, and touches Sarah, which causes her to jump. "Are you okay?"

"Are...are you sure?" she asks as she swallows what seems like a lump in her throat.

"Yes," I whisper as if I were to say it any louder, James himself could possibly hear me.

"Alice, did you see him?" Aaron asks.

For a moment, I pause and bring myself back to the moment I looked up at the hill. Technically, I didn't see James up there; in fact, I didn't see anyone at all—just the glow from the lights shining through the windows. There were no shadows or signs of movement. Perhaps I should have thought this through more carefully before assuming the worst, before taking my sister back to the very day when James held a gun to her head, threatening to pull the trigger.

"No...No, I didn't see him. I didn't see anyone, just the lights on," I explain.

Sarah let out a breath as if she was holding it the entire time. It reminded me of how a balloon quickly loses air when tightly held. It seemed like she had been waiting for the perfect moment to let go. Honestly, I don't think I saw her breathing at all.

"Alice, I know we have been through a lot, but what makes you think James is up there?" she asks. "He would be crazy to come here and not take you up on your offer."

Maybe Sarah was right. Perhaps I am overthinking this. James would be crazy to come here. I made a promise to him that I would kill him myself if I saw him again. He also saw what we did to Lily-Ann. He has to know I was serious about what I told him. If I ever see him again, I will kill him.

The thought of him pointing the gun at my sister's head and his willingness to pull the trigger stirs up a fire inside of me as I think about it. The thought of him smashing out the detective's car windows and dragging my children away into the darkness stirs up a rage inside of me waiting to be released. One thing that my mother and I do not have in common is that mothers love. I love my children with all my heart, and if anyone were to hurt them, I know that momma bear inside of me would kick in instantly.

At this point, I needed to see for myself. I hadn't willingly set foot inside that house since the night James took the kids from the car. To say I'm not nervous about going back would be a lie. I'm terrified to enter that place again, but there's only one way to find out why those lights were on—*we have to go back inside.*

CHAPTER 26

— • —

After Aaron was released from the hospital, we were all on edge. We felt it would be best if we stayed together at my house. There is a shooter on the loose, after all. I know having five people in my little three-bedroom, two-bathroom house will be hectic, but it is worth it. At least this way, there will always be someone here to help Aaron during his recovery.

Bang!

The door slams, and Aaron jumps as he lies on the couch.

"Sorry, Aaron," Kandice whispers as she shuffles through the house to get ready for school. "I can't find my jacket."

Though he tries to appear tough, I can see that the shooting has left him a little rattled. When we were leaving the hospital, someone accidentally dropped something that sounded like a gunshot, and Aaron jumped so fast I nearly had to catch him to keep him from stumbling. At least now, having several eyes on him, he might start feeling safer.

"What does it look like?" he asks.

"It's light purple, with rhinestones," she explains.

"I think your aunt moved it," he says. "She was cleaning and moved a few things from off the couch."

"Ugh! Really?" Kandice is starting to get frustrated with the number of people in our house.

"Mom, have you seen my blue and red controllers for my Nintendo Switch?" Adam yells.

"Sorry, buddy. I put it in the drawer in the kitchen," Sarah says quickly as she rushes down the stairs.

"What drawer, Aunty?" he asks.

"The one with all the stuff in it," she says quickly. "Bye, love, y'all got to go check on my horses and the donut shop."

Sarah rushes out the door, and Adam shoots an annoyed look at me as I descend the stairs.

"Ouch!" I stumble over a pair of size thirteen men's tennis shoes.

Did I really sign up for this? Maybe I should tell Aaron where we keep our shoes so I don't nearly break my neck again.

"Mom, really? You know I don't like people touching my controllers," Adam says, frustrated.

"Sorry, sweetie, it's only for a little while. We need to give the detectives time to figure out who hurt Aaron, and we also need to give his body time to recover. He doesn't have anyone else to help him." I explain.

"What about his parents? They're not around to take care of him? Couldn't Aunt Sarah stay with him at his house? I mean, you got enough on your plate as it is." Adam protests.

He does have a point.

I'd be lying if I said my child wasn't right. I do have enough on my plate, and my house isn't big at all, but what kind of person would I be not to offer him a place to stay while he recovers? He did get shot trying to protect us.

"First, I did not raise you to be selfish. Second, we owe it to him to let him stay here while he recovers. And finally, if it wasn't for him, it's possible that the person who broke into our home could have taken all your gaming stuff. So I think you need to change your attitude, mister," I say sternly, with my hands on my hips.

"Yes, ma'am," Adam says softly, lowering his gaze.

At this point, having all of us under one roof is starting to get the best of us, but in the back of my mind, I hadn't forgotten about Lily-Ann's house. In fact, it has been all I can think about. I wanted to go there badly, but Aaron insisted we wait until he was better so he could go with us. He told us he would never forgive himself if something happened to Sarah and me.

***

OUR MOTHER'S HOUSE STICKS OUT LIKE A SORE THUMB.

Weeks have gone by slowly, and each time I lift my eyes to the hill, a shiver runs down my spine, and I can feel my skin crawling from an inexplicable sense of dread. I wasn't expecting Aaron's recovery to take this long, and the sight of my mother's house was starting to get to me. No matter where you are in town, you can't help but see it. In the back of my mind, I think she did this on purpose. Perhaps, in her twisted way of thinking, she knew she wouldn't be around one day and wanted to ensure that this town would never forget the woman who had hypnotized an entire town.

"Alice, are you okay?" Aaron asks softly as he gently rises from the couch, clutching his stomach where he was shot.

"Yes, why do you ask?"

"You look like you got something on your mind," he says.

"Oh no...no, I'm fine. Just thinking about..." I don't know what to say. I don't want to worry him by telling him my mother's house has been on my mind. I also don't want to remind him of the night he got shot. I honestly believe it was James who did this, and my gut is telling me he's been hiding in our mother's house, watching us every day.

"Okay. Please give me more time to get better. I promise we are going to go up there. I just don't want you girls to go up there without me," he reminds me.

How did he know what I was thinking? I'm sure it's not hard to guess. I bet it's written on my face.

At this point, I'm starting to lose my patience as I listen to him plead with me to wait. He doesn't know how dangerous my brother is. The detectives haven't even found answers on who did this to him. Right now, I feel like a sitting duck. I should have killed my brother when I had the chance.

"Okay, I'll wait. I promise," I lie.

He still has a long way to go in his recovery process, but he is now able to get around on his own. Him and Adam have gotten closer, so close that they have become gaming buddies. I've had to cut both of them off from the game when it's gotten too late because they will stay up all night trying to beat each other.

Aaron had started to develop an appetite again because I'm constantly being asked to order pizza or pop some popcorn when they're nose-deep into a game. Even though he's able to do all these things, I can still tell the pain is still there.

Watching him, made me furious. Someone violated my home. They came in here trying to hurt me and my children. Not only did this person break into my house with the intention of harming my family, but they also hurt someone I care about, and for that, I urgently needed to get up that hill.

The detectives weren't moving fast enough for me. If it really was James who did this, I needed to get to him before anyone else did. If it was James who did this, I needed to make sure he wouldn't take the easy road out and spend the rest of his days in prison. He doesn't deserve to stay in a place that offers him three hot meals a day or a warm bed at night. Most people in this town are mentally struggling because of what they did to them, so I need to make sure this will never happen again. My brother belongs in a box six feet underground. I had already made up my mind what needed to be done; I just had to be patient.

CHAPTER 27

— • —

As the day slowly passed, I found myself transfixed by the clock, my eyes glued to its steady, relentless movement. I now fully understand the cinematic effects portrayed in movies, depicting time dragging on agonizingly as people waited in anticipation. The minute hand moved slowly, and its tick echoed throughout the entire house. *Could I be imagining that?*

"Hey sis! Do you have any more towels?" Sarah asks. "I wanted to shower while everyone is sleeping."

Ugh, it's finally past ten, and the kids are asleep, and I can hear Aaron snoring like a freight train. The only person still awake is my darling sister.

"Yes, I left a load in the dryer. I'll have the kids fold them in the morning," I say.

"No worries, I'll fold them when I get––"

"No!" I interrupt her before she can finish her sentence. At this point, all I want her to do is go to bed so I can do what I need to do.

"Um?" Sarah gazes at me with a puzzled expression.

"What I mean is, don't worry about folding the towels tonight. I can have the kids fold them in the morning." I lie.

"It's no problem, really, sis. That's the least I can do. We are invading your space right now," she explains.

"My kids are getting older, and it's time they learn to do some chores around here. What am I going to do when you go back to your house? It's best I teach them now," I lie again, hoping that she will believe me.

Sarah gives me a questioning look, as if she wants to say something. But then she says, "Okay. Well, I'm going to wash this horse smell off of me and hit the bed."

Bingo. That's exactly what I wanted to hear.

CHAPTER 28

— • —

The house is finally quiet; you can hear a pin drop. Everyone is out cold, and this is my chance to sneak out. I slowly get out of my bed and take off the robe I was wearing to hide my leggings and tank top. My bed squeaks a little as I lift my body from the mattress.

I approach my room door, and I place my ear against it to ensure I don't hear any movement. I was grateful because all I could hear was silence. Well, and Aaron's snoring.

As I open my room door and tiptoe into the hallway, I glance over to check on Aaron, who appears to be sound asleep. I head up the stairs and peek into Adam's room, where he's out like a light. I can't help but crack a smile as I look at him. He's such a tech guy! It's pretty funny. He's passed out with his game controllers in hand and his headphones still on. *Should I be concerned by the amount of video games this kid plays?*

Kandice agreed to let her aunt sleep in her room for the time being. Her room sits directly above the garage, and the floorboards leading to her room tend to creak when stepped on, so I don't take the risk. I decide to go with my gut feeling that they're both out cold.

I head downstairs in hopes of quickly getting out the door when I remember I need to grab something out of the kitchen.

"Shoot!"

Aaron's size thirteen tennis shoes are in the middle of the floor, and once again, I trip over them.

I pause like a deer momentarily, as they do when a car approaches with its headlights beaming. I'm startled at the sight of Aaron moving on the couch. He must have heard me trip. I stand there frozen as I watch him adjust the best he can on my couch.

Once he stops moving, I tiptoe into the kitchen. Squatting down, I open my cabinet and reach inside. I know it's there, but I can't feel it. "I could have sworn that I put it in this spot," I whisper to myself.

Panic starts creeping in as I'm unable to find what I'm looking for. I scramble to my feet and rush over to another set of cabinets. I do the same thing: reach inside and try to feel for what I'm looking for. *Where the hell did I put it?*

I make one last attempt and return to the first set of cabinets. This time, I sit on the floor so I can actually peek my head in. To my surprise, I was near it. My arms weren't long enough to reach it. I punch in the code, and a little chime sounds, ensuring it's open. I pull out the object and stare at it as I sit on the floor.

Did I really buy a gun? I stare at the black object in my hand, momentarily contemplating whether I'm really going to use it.

What has my family done to me? My reality is that I have to look over my shoulder every moment of the day. The night Aaron was shot, he asked me if I had a gun, and I didn't at that time. But after that night, I pushed aside my fears of owning one and bought one. It was an interesting experience. A guy named Randy helped me out and showed me everything from a Glock 19 to something called a Smith with Weston. *Wait, maybe it was a Smith & Wesson.* Who knows, I settled for a Glock 19. I wasn't playing this game with my family anymore—enough is enough. I knew what I needed to do, and this time, I'm prepared.

I close the cabinets and tiptoe back through the living room. I take one last look at Aaron: he's still out cold and snoring as loudly as a freight train. *How does he not wake himself with that snoring?*

At this moment, I feel like I'm in some James Bond movie. I reach out my hand and slowly turn the knob on the front door, but something quickly catches my eye; it's the little red blinking light on the alarm system.

"That was close," I say under my breath.

I pull out my phone and click the "Night Disarm" button. The person who invented that selection was a genius. This will allow me to disarm the alarm in my house without making any noise.

Looking at the alarm system, I patiently wait for the light to turn from red to green. If I open this door any sooner, I can give up trying to get out of the house tonight. The alarm will sound, not only waking up my house but everyone's house in our neighborhood.

I take another look at Aaron and notice him move again. *Come on, light, what's taking you so long?*

Finally, the light turns green, and I'm free to open the door. I slowly turn the knob and look over my shoulder one last time to ensure Aaron is still sleeping: he's out cold.

Sneaking out of my house, I felt like a teenage girl again. I remember sneaking out of Lily-Ann's house once. Sadly, it wasn't to go meet up with friends; my version of sneaking out was going outside and sitting on the grass to look up at the night sky. I loved looking at the stars. For some reason, I was able to imagine whatever I wanted when I looked up at the stars. They were peaceful, the total opposite of what we had to deal with.

Once I made it to my car in another desperate attempt to avoid getting caught, I put my car in neutral to let it roll out of the driveway. Call me crazy, but I couldn't let them hear me start the car. The only way I could get out of that driveway without waking any of them was to do what I did, and it worked.

Did this actually work? Was I in the clear? Was I getting ready to kill the only brother I had left? I start my car and immediately turn off the headlights. Once I'm no longer in front of my house, I give the car a little gas and head for the hill. *There's no* turning *back now.*

CHAPTER 29

—•—

A few days ago, I was watching the news, and they were discussing an ongoing trial. It was a big deal because of all the controversy over the rise in gun violence. Some men tried to steal this lady's sports car from her driveway while she and her family were sleeping. The husband heard a commotion outside and went to investigate. One thing led to another, and the robbers started shooting at the husband and killed him. What I found interesting about this case was that the wife went on the stand and told the robbers she forgave them and prays for them every night that the Lord will save their souls.

I grip the steering wheel as I drive through town, thinking about this case. The husband didn't deserve what happened to him, but it was the wife who had my mind all over the place. How could she forgive someone so easily who took the love of her life? How could she say she prays for them every night for the Lord above to save their souls? *Could I do the same?* I ponder the last question as I glance over at the black Glock 19 lying in the passenger seat. I made a promise to my brother: *if I ever see you again, I will shoot you in the head the same way you were willing to do to our sister.*

"Couldn't be me," I tell myself. I can't forgive James so easily. He took my babies, the loves of my life, and tried to murder them. He came into my house and wrestled with my daughter as she fought to get past him. I tighten my grip on the steering wheel as I recall her telling me he put a cloth over her mouth, drugging her. Suddenly, a realization dawns on me: *I can't forgive him, and I will kill him.*

Approaching the hill, I recall the panoramic view our mother used to have from living at the top of the hill. If someone is up there, it wouldn't be hard to spot me. I could be setting myself up. James could be inside, watching and waiting patiently for my arrival. It's clear to me that I can't risk him catching a glimpse of my car, so I decide to leave it hidden among the trees at the bottom. If he is in there, lurking, the last thing I want is for him to see me coming. I have to be careful... every second counts.

My heart is pounding, and I'm almost breathless as I climb the hill. *Ugh, I really should get a gym membership.* My crossbody purse feels heavier than usual, and I'm pretty sure it's because of the weight of my gun. Randy didn't tell me it would be this heavy to carry in my purse. *Should I have gotten something smaller?* As I reach the top, I'm quickly reminded of just how steep the hill is. My lungs ache from my heavy breathing, and my legs are trembling and refuse to move any further. James and Lily-Ann are the last thing on my mind. All I want now is a large glass of water.

Bending over with my hands on my knees, I lift my head, and that's when I see it. I straighten up, and everything around me, including myself, freezes in place. The front door to Lily-Ann's house stands directly in front of me, staring back as I observe it.

It's amusing how something so harmless as a door can unsettle the mind. As I stand frozen in front of the massive door, its once inviting appearance now looks like something from a nightmare. The front porch light flickers and dies, causing the area around me to fade into darkness. It takes my eyes a few seconds to adjust, but I'm sure I just saw a shadowy figure.

Oh, wait—it's just the vines. Thank goodness!

Looking at the vines makes my skin crawl. They resemble a tangle of snakes as they slither around the railing of the porch stairs. The sight is terrifying. Even the bushes give me the creeps. They are overgrown; you could once see through the windows, but now they are completely blocked by bushes. Our mother's house used to be a place for many parties, and even though we had some bad memories here, Lily-Ann always ensured that her home was well-maintained.

What would she do if she saw it now?

Crunch. Crunch.

The silence up here is terrifying. "Maybe I should have waited for Aaron to come with me. Is it too late to turn around?" I ask myself.

Crunch. Crunch.

Somewhere in the darkness, an animal moved through the underbrush, its steps crackling the fallen leaves. The sound sends chills through my entire body. *Do we have bears in Shelly Grove? Wolves?* The questions echo in my mind, giving me an unsettling feeling. I strain my ears, desperate for clarity, but all I feel is dread creeping into my bones.

Maybe I should leave... I could always come back another day. Maybe when it's daylight... that sounds like the better choice.

Crunch. Crunch.

Whatever creature lurks just beyond the shadows, my gun feels helpless. It was a toy against the immense threat of a bear or a wolf lurking in the dark.

Finally, I built up the courage. I decide it's time I go inside, even though, in the back of my mind, I had no idea what was waiting for me on the other side of that door. Reaching out my hand, I grab the knob and begin to turn it. To my surprise, it was unlocked. I push the door open, and the scene before me feels like I've just opened the door to a scene in a horror movie.

If I'm being honest with myself, this is a real-life horror movie. It's my real-life horror movie.

The door's eerie, creaking groan reverberates through the silent house, each squeal more sinister than the last. If James is inside, he must have heard it—every terrifying sound, every unnatural echo. Now, I realize with chilling certainty: if he's hiding in our mother's house, he must have figured it out by now—that someone's here and that he's not alone.

CHAPTER 30

— ⋅ —

It's pitch-black and eerily silent. The furniture and decorations remain exactly where she left them, covered in a thick layer of dust, as if abandoned for many years. A chilling stillness hangs in the air, intensifying the sense that I'm being watched.

"HELLO!" I shout, but there's no response. The house remains silent, and my scream echoes through the space. "IS ANYONE IN HERE?"

Each step I take uncovers a chill that seems born from a house haunted by terrifying memories. The squeaking floorboards remind me of the many times I ran away from our mother's attempt to beat me. Another step leads me below the sparkling chandelier she installed for the last party she held here. This was my party—my supposed welcome to a new town, where my children and I were new residents.

As I move forward, the floor continues to creak beneath me, echoing the day I entered this house and stumbled upon the chests and pictures with scratched-out faces. *How could my mother do this to me?* With another step, the floor creaks again, pulling me back to the moment I was tied to a chair and awakened by my sister. I'm reminded of how I had to watch helplessly as my children dangled above a pool of water.

In that moment, the thought alone made me sick. I close my eyes and try to shake off the horrifying memories.

I move forward, and the floor creaks again, sending a shiver down my spine. I slowly open my eyes and look at the walls. If they could speak, I'd fear the secrets they might reveal, the horrors this woman might have committed here. How many lives could have been lost in this place? It's clear that she can harm anyone; blood is definitely not thicker than water in her mind.

Turning on my cell phone's flashlight, I navigate through the house towards the upstairs bedrooms. I come up empty-handed, however, as I find no sign that anyone has been here. *I know these lights were on that night at the hospital.* I remind myself. If it had only been one light, I might think my mind was playing tricks on me, but it looked like someone was living here again since all the lights were on. *Was it a setup by my brother? A trick to lure me up here?* Suddenly, a noise downstairs startles me, causing me to jump.

I have to admit, I'm a little freaked out at this moment. If James were here, I feel I could handle him, but facing spirits coming back to haunt Lily-Ann is something I am not willing to confront.

Tiptoeing down the stairs, my hands begin to sweat as I grip my cell phone to use the flashlight. I try not to make a sound as I do my best to avoid any creaking floorboards. I need to make sure whoever or whatever is in here can't hear me coming down the stairs.

Once at the bottom, I stand in silence, hoping to hear which direction the noise came from. But there's nothing—not one sound. *Is it possible I could be hallucinating?* I wonder.

"Great, not only has my mother messed me up, let's go ahead and add hallucination to the list," I say to myself.

As I turn the corner, there it is, right in front of me—the door where it all happened—the room that led to Lily-Ann's secret basement. My body freezes. I want to move forward towards the door, but I can't. It's almost as if something is holding me back. *Is it the fear of what happened down there? Is it the fact that I found the evidence of my neighbor's murder in this very room?* I'm not sure what it is, but I need to see where that noise came from.

James is clever. What better place to hide than in the basement? Who in their right mind would want to go down there? *You'd have to be insane to go down there.* Then again, my brother is insane; it takes an insane person to kidnap their own niece and nephew, but it's clear to me that at this point, I need to be insane as well. My brother is here, hiding; I can feel it.

I grip my phone firmly and feel the outside of my crossbody purse to check that the gun is still in there. Mentally bracing for what might happen, I extend my shaky hand and carefully turn the knob.

"Alice, what are you doing?" I'm startled by a familiar voice. As I turn around, Sarah and Aaron are standing in the front doorway.

"What are you doing?" Sarah asks again.

I have what's called a light bulb moment; *maybe the noise I heard was the two of them trying to get into the house.*

"Seriously, sis, what the hell are you doing here?" she asks angrily. "What the hell are you doing here without us?"

"…" I have no words. How do I explain to the two of them that I needed to come here and that I got tired of waiting for Aaron to get better?

Sarah is pissed, and Aaron looks confused. I could only imagine the thoughts running through their head. At this point, I owe them an explanation.

"I know y'all are mad, but I needed to see for myself if James was here." I begin to explain. "I couldn't sit back and wait for the detectives to find answers."

My sister doesn't budge. She looks a lot like Lily-Ann with those eyes that could kill. At this point, I can tell she is ready to explode on me.

"You have some nerve—" she starts to say, then Aaron interrupts.

"I think what she was about to say is, 'We know you care about our safety, but we care about yours too, and we just wish you had shared your plan with us.' Isn't that right, Sarah?" he asks, holding her gaze.

He's right. What was I thinking trying to do all this on my own? I tell my kids not to make silly decisions, and here I am, breaking into my mother's house in an attempt to kill my brother. My very dangerous brother, by the way. This was a dumb decision, and my sister has every right to be angry with me.

Perhaps, in some strange way, I had hoped James was here so I could put an end to him for good. Maybe, in some way, I felt guilty for letting him go that day in the hospital. Whatever the case, I can't keep letting them continue to control me. Our mother is long gone mentally, and James is nowhere near here.

"Thank you guys," I say. "For coming up here to get me. To save me, really, from my own thoughts. To save me from opening a chapter in my life that I should keep shut."

"We care about you, sis, and your safety," Sarah says as she wraps her arms around me in a tight embrace.

"Yeah, I don't know what we would have done if something had happened to you up here while we were all at your house sleeping," Aaron says, also wrapping his arms around my sister and me, squeezing us in a masculine bear hug.

"Don't you ever scare me like that again," Sarah says, playfully slapping my shoulder. "Now, let's get out of here; this place gives me the creeps. Why haven't we knocked this place down yet?"

"You know, maybe we should talk to the mayor about finally demolishing this place. I mean, now that Lily-Ann can't do for herself, we have the right to do whatever we want to this place," I say as we begin to end this chapter of our lives for good.

Heading for the front door, Aaron walks out first, followed by Sarah. I grip the doorknob and take one last look at our mother's house. The feeling is something I can't put into words. I feel a mix of sadness and happiness simultaneously. I was finally about to leave this place once and for all.

CHAPTER 31

—·—

S tepping out of the house onto the front porch, I grip the door-knob to pull the door shut. Aaron and Sarah have reached the bottom of the stairs. Suddenly, I'm startled by a loud noise. At this point, I know I'm not the only one who heard it because Aaron and Sarah both stop talking and quickly shift their gaze to Lily-Ann's house.

"What the..." I begin to say something, but I'm at a loss for words.

"Did you hear that?" Sarah asks.

We all look at each other, unsure of what we should do next—frozen, as if we were waiting to see who would make the first move.

"I knew I wasn't going crazy!" I say excitedly. I'm honestly not sure why that excited me. Maybe it's because this entire time I've been feeling like my past has been haunting me. It's clear, though, I'm not crazy, and I know what I saw, and I know that we are not alone.

"Maybe we should call the cops?" Sarah suggests.

Bang!

We jump at the loud sound that comes from inside the house again.

"Forget this. I'm not waiting on the cops to get here," I say forcefully. "I'm going in," I say as I push the door all the way open and bolt inside.

The two of them follow behind me. At this point, we were eager to find out what the noise was. "I bet he's here hiding in the basement," I say, looking over my shoulder as I run for the basement door. We quickly make our way back to the room that sits at the end of the hall. I swing open the door and instantly feel a chill. "The door is open," I whisper.

"What door?" Aaron whispers.

"Our mother has a secret door disguised as a bookshelf," Sarah whispers. "It leads to the basement."

"What the..." Aaron is lost for words, forgetting that I've told him that our mother is a certified psycho.

"Now do you believe us that our mother is crazy?" I ask him.

I step onto the stairs that lead down to the basement, and I'm quickly reminded of how dark it is down here. I turn on my cell phone's flashlight. Reaching into my crossbody, I pull out my gun and remember what Randy told me: *flip the safety off and point at whatever you want to hit, little lady.*

"You have a gun?" Sarah's eyes widen at her sudden discovery. "Why do you have a gun? Do the kids know? What about Adam? All those video games he plays, he might think he can use that, sis, what are you thinking?"

She's clearly pissed, but it's this gun that's going to save us if it is James that's down here.

My hands are trembling at this point. I've never really used a gun to shoot anyone. I shot it once at the range with Randy's help to ensure I knew how to operate it, but am I really capable of pulling the trigger?

"Maybe I should take that," Aaron says. He must have noticed my hands trembling. He gently takes the gun out of my hand and instructs Sarah and me to get behind him.

"It's dark down here," I whisper. "Just keep straight."

We continue down the dark hallway until we reach a familiar spot. It's the spot in the hallway that is illuminated by a single dangling light bulb.

"This is some creepy mess," Aaron whispers.

"You think," I say sarcastically.

One thing I do remember about this particular spot is that if we turn left, it will take us to the area where the pool used to be, where they took my kids. If we keep straight, that is where they had me tied up. I quickly shuffle around Aaron.

"Wait, Alice!" Aaron yells as I take off, running down the dark, cold hallway.

Breathless, I keep running until I suddenly come to an abrupt stop. *Is this real?* I wonder. I blink multiple times, but nothing changes. I wipe my eyes with my hands, attempting to confirm I'm seeing clearly, yet nothing changes.

Sarah and Aaron finally catch up to me.

"What's wrong, Alice?" Sarah asks, unaware of who or what is standing before us.

I slowly lift my arm. I'm in shock and can't speak; I can only point in front of me.

"Oh God, this can't be real."

CHAPTER 32

— · —

The devil herself is standing before us. Her hair is tightly curled, and she is wearing a striking red dress that complements her curves. The glossy black heels she is wearing must cost a fortune. She has those iconic red-bottom heels. This woman undoubtedly commands attention wherever she appears. For someone just released from a mental facility, she certainly knows how to present herself. Lily-Ann is the type of woman who needs to be in a place far beyond a small town like Shelly Grove. In my opinion, she belongs in Beverly Hills.

Stuttering, I say, "How...how did you get out?"

She turns around slowly, and we're immediately taken aback. The woman in front of us resembles Lily-Ann, yet it's evident that she isn't her. *So, who is she?*

"Um, that's not your mom," Aaron says, confused—a feeling I know all too well.

"No...no, that isn't," I say softly, eyes fixed on the woman in front of me.

"But why does she look kind of like your mom?" he asks, a hint of panic in his voice.

"That's a good question," I say softly.

142

The shock is evident on our faces. There's a woman who looks almost exactly like our mother. She dresses like her and is in our mother's house. No, she's standing in our mother's secret basement.

"Who are you exactly?" Sarah asks, speaking up, asking what we are all thinking.

The woman chuckles. "I'm so sorry. How rude of me."

I offer her a curious smile.

"My name is Lily-Beth, but I usually go by Beth," she explains, as she reaches out her hand to shake mine.

Excuse me if I decide to be a little rude at this moment; I don't know this lady. I'm curious about the resemblance, but I've always told my kids to be mindful of strangers, and at this moment, there's a stranger in our house.

I tilt my head slightly, opting not to offer my hand for a shake.

"So Beth, why are you in our house exactly?" I ask. "A better question: why are you in our basement?"

Beth glances at me and then catches Sarah and Aaron's gaze from behind me. She's silent for a moment as if she's now the one lost for words.

"We're not trying to be rude, Ms. Beth, but we've been through a lot, and..." Sarah looks at me, "we don't have time for guessing games."

Beth continues to hold our gaze as if she is trying to figure out what she wants to say next.

"Alright, we don't have time for this. I'm calling the police," I say as I begin to dial 911 on my cell.

"Wait! Please don't," she quickly pleads. "I'll tell you who I am, but please don't call the police. This is a lot for me too."

"Maybe we should hear her out," Aaron says.

Beth takes a deep breath and exhales forcefully. "Your mother is my fraternal twin," she says. "Hence, the names Lily-Ann and Lily-Beth."

I give Sarah an uncertain look.

"What do you mean, fraternal twin?" I ask. "Our mother never had siblings."

Who am I really kidding? Our mother has kept a lot from us. She hypnotized an entire freaking town. How's that for keeping secrets?

"Your mother and I were close once upon a time, inseparable, to be exact," she starts to explain. "One day, we got into a nasty argument, and that tore us apart."

I nod, trying to understand all of this.

"After we graduated from high school, I left town and never looked back," she says.

"Over an argument?" I ask. "Sarah and I argue all the time, and we would never leave each other over an argument?" *We are talking about Lily-Ann, though.*

"..." Beth is speechless at this point.

"What about your parents? They didn't come looking for you?" Aaron asks.

"Well, you see, our parents always took Lily-Ann's side. "I honestly felt they loved her more and even wished I weren't there," she says. "So I gave them what they wanted, and I left."

Okay, note to self, I am officially a jerk. What she is telling us is terrible. I feel horrible for not welcoming her with open arms. Cameron was the golden child, and James was our mother's backup. Sarah and I meant nothing to her, so I can understand what Beth is saying. It's hurtful to hear that this happened to her, too.

Reflecting on Beth's words, everything begins to fall into place. Maybe Lily-Ann adopted this behavior from her parents. Perhaps witnessing how they treated Beth made her believe that was a distorted way of expressing love.

Beth's story is tragic, raising several questions: *Why is she here? Why return now?*

She gave us an earful as we sat around on the cold, hard basement floor, like a bunch of school-age kids listening to the teacher read a story. She told us she came back because she heard from one of their old classmates about Lily-Ann's condition. She had mentioned that even though they didn't get along, she still wanted to check on her. Apparently, she felt bad when their parents died. I guess she never thought about attending the funeral because of the way they treated her. She didn't want her sister to pass away without seeing her one last time.

I don't blame Beth for not attending her parents' funeral. *Will I do the same the day Lily-Ann passes? Could I live with myself if I didn't at least say goodbye? She is my mother after all.*

"Well, it's getting late, and we've been talking down here for a while now," I say. "It's also a little creepy down here."

For Beth, it probably wasn't so weird, but for us, there were too many memories in this basement.

"How about we pick up where we left off tomorrow?" Sarah asks. "I mean, we could maybe continue this conversation. It's kind of nice knowing we have an aunt."

"I agree, we have never met any other family members," I add.

"The donut shop is a pretty popular place around here," Aaron says quickly.

My eyes widen with excitement.

"I mean, if you girls would like to continue this conversation there," he adds.

Beth chuckles, "I love a good donut, especially if it's nice and warm."

"Great! How about we meet around noon? I can take a longer lunch from work," I say.

"It's a date!" Beth says excitedly.

CHAPTER 33

—·—

I t's eleven fifty-nine, and I haven't seen one car pull in front of the donut shop yet. Perhaps it's my nerves getting the best of me, or maybe it was just hard for me to trust anyone at this point—especially anyone outside of my little circle, which now included Sarah, Mr. Gerald, Sharon, and Aaron. I had never really known much about our mother's past. She always wanted things to be perfect. To finally get the truth from her sister, I know, it will be a lot to take in.

"Where is she?" Aaron asks.

"I'm not sure. Maybe she's lost," I wonder.

Aaron shoots me a look that tells me he's not buying it. "I really don't know about this. This is why I suggested you all meet here. A random lady pops up, claiming to be your aunt. That's a red flag if you ask me."

Aaron has been a supportive friend throughout this entire process. Even though he's technically supposed to be in recovery and resting, he has decided to be here with us to hear Beth out.

The bell above the donut shop door chimes, and there she is. Looking exactly like our mother, with her golden-brown skin and pin-tight curls. They are precisely the same. She is dressed to impress, just like

Lily-Ann. *What is it with these two dressing like they're heading down the red carpet every day?*

She is literally glistening with diamonds from head to toe. Today, she is wearing a navy blue one-piece pantsuit. She has a silver belt around her waist to complement her outfit and white heels. My goodness, her shoes even have diamonds on them.

Well, they could be fake, but they're very shiny, and I bet they're expensive.

This is crazy. I went to our mother's house, planning to kill James, but I ended up with a mystery aunt instead. Maybe therapy isn't such a bad idea after all. James left a bad impression about therapists after tricking me into thinking he was one, so I've been hesitant to see another shrink. However, after today's meeting, I wouldn't be surprised if I need to talk to someone immediately.

"Hi, dears. I'm so sorry I'm late. I put the address into my GPS, and on the way here, I got sidetracked looking at the town," Beth explains, giving each of us a kiss on the cheek like we were little kids. "It looks so different from the last time I was here."

"I bet. I'm sure a lot has changed since you left town," I say, shooting Sarah a look.

"Would you like a donut and maybe some coffee, Ma'am?" Aaron asks.

"Oh yes, that would be great! You three are so sweet and polite. I don't think anyone has ever called me ma'am," Beth says. "Honestly, do I look that old?"

I offer a questioning smile.

"Joking, sweetie. I'm in my sixties. I know I'm getting old," she says with a chuckle.

Aaron brings a warm glazed donut and a cup of coffee with cream and several sugars to our table. "I'll be over there if y'all need me."

"Well, I'm sure you two have plenty of questions," Beth says as she begins to pour cream and sugar into her coffee. "Let me just get something right. My sister had three kids: a boy and two girls, is that right?"

Sarah and I catch each other's gaze, both of us confused. "What do you mean, three kids?" I ask.

"Well, yesterday, the three of you were at your mother's house," she says, nodding toward Aaron. "I assumed you were all her kids. Is that correct?"

"Oh, Aaron, he's our best friend. He's just sticking around for moral support," I say with a chuckle. "But you can say he's like a brother to us."

Beth apologizes for her mistake. Apparently, his being here made her think he was our brother. It was an honest mistake. I'm sure it wouldn't be a good idea to tell her about our actual brothers. How do we explain that one of our brothers is dead because I killed him, and the other is somewhere in the world because I threatened him? She would probably catch the first flight out of here, leaving nothing but a trail of dust.

"So, what was our mother like growing up?" Sarah asks. "What were our grandparents like?"

Beth chuckles and raises her cup of coffee to her lips, lightly blowing on the steam. "Your grandparents, my dear..." She pauses and glances around, as if she were about to reveal a top secret and wants to make sure no one is around to hear it. "Your Grandparents... were crazy and very controlling," she says nonchalantly.

"That sounds familiar," I murmur.

"Your grandparents took punishment to a whole new level, ladies. We grew up in that house; the basement was their personal project. They used that basement as our torture chamber," she says.

Sarah and I exchange glances, understanding clearly now why our mother used the basement for the same reason.

Beth takes a deep breath. "They were the parents of the year if you ask me," she says, looking away as if trying to fight off tears. "You know they created that basement so no one would hear us scream when we were punished," she says, focusing her attention back on us and squeezing her lips together tightly.

"I'm so sorry y'all had to go through that," I say.

Beth lowers her gaze and fiddles with the coffee cup. "They would lock us down there for days with no food or drinks. I guess it was their own twisted way of teaching us a lesson."

By now, I understand what Beth was experiencing. Our mother was just as delusional. We never got locked in the basement as kids, but we sure have had our fair share of torture from her.

"It was hard once Lily-Ann and I got into our last fight; we weren't just sisters, we were best of friends. We always had each other's backs when we got in trouble. Often, we would be locked down there together because your mother wouldn't tell on me," Beth explains.

Tears slowly roll down my cheeks as I wonder how someone who gave birth to two beautiful twin girls could do this to them. At this moment, I begin to feel something for my mother that I hadn't felt before: sympathy.

CHAPTER 34

— · —

A s Beth continues telling us about their past and the crazy experiences they had in the house on the hill, she then says something that strikes a nerve for Sarah and me. She mentions constantly feeling like their parents were controlling them.

"What do you mean, controlling you?" I ask.

Sarah catches my gaze.

Beth chuckles. "You know what? Never mind, it was a crazy thought."

"If only you knew some of the things we have been through," I say, unaware that I spoke out loud. "What do you mean by controlling you?"

Beth leans forward to get a little closer to us. "There were these crazy accusations that our parents were hypnotizing people."

"Hypnotize? Really? Do you think they could do that?" I ask, eyes wide.

Beth takes another sip of her coffee and sits back in her chair. She holds our gaze and then begins to chuckle. "No, are you serious? There is no such thing."

Sarah and I exchange glances. Beth might not believe it, but we know firsthand that it exists. However, I'm unsure if I'm ready to explain that to our long-lost aunt. Besides, she seems nice—the complete opposite of our mother. I'm not prepared to mess this up. She is the first family member who appears somewhat normal.

The bell above the door to the donut shop chimes, and I jump at the sound. All this creepy talk about being locked in basements and hypnotizing people makes my skin crawl.

"Hey, baby girls!" Mr. Gerald says as he enters the donut shop.

I immediately jump to my feet and give him a tight hug. It's always a pleasure to see him. He's like the missing piece to our twisted puzzle. It's as if he's the dad we've never had.

"We weren't expecting to see you here today," I say.

"Yeah, I figured I'd come grab me a cup of coffee and one of those warm donuts before I get my day started," he says.

"Well, come on over. Pull up a chair. There's someone I'd like you to meet, by the way," I say cheerfully.

Mr. Gerald picks up the nearest chair and walks to our table. As he gets closer, Beth looks over her shoulder and instantly appears shocked. She observes Mr. Gerald. Studying his face as if she were trying to figure out something. She doesn't blink, not even once.

I look at Mr. Gerald, and his expression is identical to hers. He also looks shocked, and if I'm being honest, he almost looks like he isn't breathing. *Something strange is going on.*

"Are... you okay, Beth?" I ask hesitantly.

"Gerald! Is that you?" Beth says excitedly. "Man, give me a hug. It's been years since I last saw you. What on earth are you still doing here?"

I glance over at Sarah, noticing the wide-eyed disbelief etched across her features, before shifting my gaze toward Aaron, who is sitting at a table in the corner, observing the scene. He also has the same look on his face. The shock on our faces is palpable, an unspoken understanding passing between us as we process the unimaginable reality before us. *Do these two know each other?*

"Um! How do you two know each other?" I ask.

Beth looks at me and chuckles. "Sweetie, Gerald and I go way back. We went to school together."

Really? We have known Mr. Gerald all this time, and he never thought to tell us we had an aunt. It was time for him to start explaining.

I'm sure by now the look on my face says it all. "Why didn't you tell us we had an aunt?"

Mr. Gerald exhales deeply as though he has been holding his breath for a long time. "Maybe we should take a seat."

I plop down in my chair like a toddler upset with their dad for not letting them have candy at that moment. "Okay, we're sitting, and I need some answers."

"Everyone knew Lily-Ann and Lily-Beth's parents were different from most parents around town. When we graduated, everyone from our graduating class was devastated when Beth left town," he begins to explain.

"Okay?" Sarah says.

"So what happened?" Aaron asks from behind me as he pulls up a chair to hear what Mr. Gerald has to say, curiosity visible on his face.

"For some reason, I had forgotten all about her. It's weird. It was as if she had been wiped clean from my memory," he says, his face contorted with confusion.

Nothing in this town made sense. Over the years, after everyone emerged from their hypnosis, more truths were revealed to my sister and me. So what he told us, in some bizarre, hypnotic way, made perfect sense. Perhaps seeing her helped restore all his memories of her.

The only question I have now is, why now? Why did she come back now? Yes, she told us she came back because she discovered our mother's condition, but why did she wait so long? Their parents were already dead, so why not come back sooner to restore their relationship?

CHAPTER 35

— • —

After discovering that Beth and Mr. Gerald knew each other in the past, we had many questions. From what they told us, our mother was a sucker for Mr. Gerald. Apparently, she had a big crush on him since they were in elementary school. Beth described it as though she was crazy about him, but their parents couldn't stand him. No wonder she hypnotized him, of all people, to be her "husband."

"Honestly, dear..." Beth begins but pauses, looking at Mr. Gerald. "Everyone thought your mom and Gerald would be the ones to get married right after high school."

"What happened? Why didn't they?" Sarah asks.

"Well, she brought him home one day to meet our parents," she starts to explain. "You see, back in our day, the guy had to ask permission from the parents to take their daughter out. Our parents didn't know they had already been together; they just hid it. So she wanted them to finally meet him because they had talked about getting married after high school."

"Okay?" I scrunch my eyebrows, trying to figure out where this story is going.

Beth was sure that something went wrong the day Mr. Gerald met their parents. She told us that one day, Lily-Ann and Mr. Gerald were all over each other, but something changed after he met their parents. She mentioned that everyone at their high school believed they had a bad argument. She also pointed out that it didn't take him long to find another girlfriend.

"Your mother was always jealous whenever she saw them together. At one point, I swear she was going to blow a gasket," she says.

Interesting, I thought as I sat back in my chair, trying to piece together everything she had told us. Our mother is the devil in disguise, but maybe it wasn't just her parents who pushed her over the top. Perhaps Mr. Gerald had some part in that as well.

***

HOURS HAVE PASSED, and hearing some of Mr. Gerald and Beth's high school memories was great. Aside from our grandparents being psychopaths, it seemed like they had a pretty good time in high school up until the breakup between him and our mom.

We discovered things about our mom that are the complete opposite of the person she has become today. We found that she enjoyed attending high school parties, loved dancing, and occasionally indulged in a bit of teenage drinking. *Not saint Lily-Ann,* I thought.

Our mother seemed like a fun person to be around. I felt a twinge of sadness, wondering if she were still the Lily-Ann from high school, perhaps my sister and I would have had a better bond with her. I'd be lying if I said it didn't hurt knowing we will never see that side of her. I would kill to go back to the seventies to see her that way. *Is time travel a real thing?* Maybe that's what her parents should have invented instead of a freaking hypnosis tablet.

Getting to know our long-lost aunt has been an incredible experience. After a few hours of conversation with Beth, it felt like we had known her forever. We discovered her passions for nature and travel, along with a newfound love for glazed donuts, inspired by Sarah's donut shop. She was the complete opposite of Lily-Ann. *Why couldn't Beth have been our mother?*

You could sense her genuine heart; kindness flowed naturally from her. Yet, a troubling question nagged at me: *why did her parents treat her so poorly?*

"So where is she?" Beth asks.

"Who?" I ask.

"My other half," she says with a chuckle. "My sister. Your mother."

"Oh yes, sorry," I say. "She's in the facility for the mentally ill here in town because of her dementia."

Beth places her hand over her chest.

"I can only imagine it has to be hard for you girls to take on all that. Dementia is no joke. It's hard to care for those patients," she says.

"Yeah, it has been hard," I say. "That's why we decided to let the professionals care for her. She is in good hands, though."

"Yeah, Auntie... well, is that okay if I call you that?" Sarah asks cautiously.

Beth chuckles, "Of course you can, dear. It's not like it's a lie. I am your aunt. By blood."

"Well, like Alice was saying, she's in great hands. Our friend Aaron here works at the facility. He watches over her for the most part," Sarah explains.

Beth locks her gaze on Aaron and begins to observe him. She leans forward, taking his hands into hers, and gently squeezes them. "You seem like a really nice man, dear. Thank you for taking good care of my sister."

"It's my pleasure, ma'am," Aaron says, lowering his gaze as if he had a shy bone in his body.

"Do I know your parents? They did a fine job raising a beautiful black man like yourself," she says.

Aaron is now blushing and appears to be at a loss for words.

"No, Beth, he isn't from here. He's our newest resident in this town," I say.

"Oh, I see. Well, welcome to..." She pauses briefly. "What is it called now? Shelly Grove?"

I nod, "Yes, that's right."

"Well, welcome to Shelly Grove, dear. Please thank your parents on my behalf. We need more good black men in this world," she says. "And why haven't one of you ladies snagged him yet?"

I laugh so loud, it nearly startles her. "Beth, he is like a brother to us, and honestly, I don't look at him that way."

"No offense, bro," Sarah nudges Aaron jokingly.

"None taken," he says with a chuckle, nudging her back. "Honestly, Mrs. Beth..."

"Ms.," Beth interrupts. "I have never been married."

"Oh, sorry, got it," he says. "I was going to say, I'm just trying to make good friends here."

"So, does that mean you don't have any children, Beth?" I ask.

Beth looks at each of us and lowers her gaze. "Unfortunately, I never had that opportunity. My dad beat me so bad one time, turns out I was unable to have children after that."

I cover my mouth in disbelief. "Are you serious? I'm so sorry."

"I've learned to live with it, dear," she says with a smile, but it doesn't feel genuine. I guess it's a good thing we never got to meet our grandparents.

She claps her hands together. "So when can we see her?" she asks quickly, changing the subject.

"I actually need to get home. If I don't have dinner ready when the kids get out of school, I'll have two very hangry children on my hands," I say with a chuckle.

"Kids? You have two?" she asks.

"Yes, a boy and a girl. Adam and Kandice are their names," I say with a smile.

"How sweet," she says with a smile that doesn't seem genuine. Perhaps I shouldn't have mentioned that I have kids. She just told us she was beaten so badly she couldn't have children. "I'm so sorry I shouldn't have..."

Beth lifts her hand, silencing me. "Honey, I'm in my sixties; children are the last thing I'm thinking about. One thing I've found beneficial about not having kids is how much I get to travel."

We all laugh at her comment.

"How about tomorrow? At the same time, around noon. At least this way, she would have already eaten so that we won't disturb her lunchtime," Sarah suggests.

"It's a date," Beth says as one corner of her mouth rises to a partial smile.

"I'm going to run to the bathroom before I head back to work," I say.

Sarah nods.

I enter the bathroom and look at myself in the mirror. I place my hands over my mouth to keep from anyone hearing me. "What. The. Hell." I can't believe what Beth just told us. A tear appears in the corner of my eye. I'm saddened by what my mom and Beth had to go through in that house. I've always been the strong sibling. The one that's always been able to hold my composure. But this, this is nuts, and I can't help myself when a stream of tears starts pouring down my face.

Waving my hand in front of the paper towel dispenser, I pull off a few sheets. I turn the faucet on in the sink and wet the paper towels slightly. Dabbing my face to clear up any evidence of tears, I look at myself in the mirror and blow out a long sigh. "Alright, pull yourself together," I tell myself before tossing the damp paper towels in the trash can.

I walk out of the bathroom to say my goodbyes, and I notice Beth quickly placing something back inside her purse. Honestly, it could be nothing. She probably is trying to take her glazed donut with her.

Clapping my hands together, I say, "Well, are y'all ready to head out?"

Beth looks a little uneasy as she holds her purse close to her. Sarah is still focused on Beth, and Mr. Gerald is also staring at her. "Hey, are you two okay?" *Of course, they're not okay.* I mean, I had to take a minute for myself after that disturbing story she told us. The two of them are probably as shocked as I am.

"Maybe you all should get going. We can catch up tomorrow," Beth says, then grabs Sarah and Mr. Gerald's hands and gives them both a light squeeze. "I'm okay, really. This stuff happened years ago. I don't ever have to deal with this again." She lifts a corner of her mouth and smiles as Sarah and Mr. Gerald smile back at her, and also give her hand a light squeeze.

At this point, my mind is racing with a million thoughts, but I can't shake the nagging curiosity about what they were discussing while I was in the bathroom. Was it something they didn't want me to hear?

CHAPTER 36

— • —

U sually, the thought of seeing Lily-Ann makes me sick to my stomach, but today, I don't have that feeling. Surprisingly, I'm up bright-eyed and bushy-tailed, as the old folks used to say. I'm not the breakfast type, but I'm up early, making eggs, grits, bacon, and cheese toast. I've also invested in an excellent programmable coffee maker, ensuring my coffee will always be hot and ready in the mornings. If I'm going to be a coffee drinker, I might as well go all in and get the best coffee maker on the market.

I pull my cell out of my back pocket and call Mr. Gerald to inform him that I'll have breakfast on the table in about five minutes if he wants to swing by and grab a plate. He didn't plan to go with us to visit our mother because it's been hard for him to step foot in the facility. What she did to us is messed up, but making someone think they're married to you is a whole new low, if you ask me.

The phone rings a few times and then goes straight to voicemail. I peek out my kitchen window and notice his car is still in the driveway. *Maybe he is still sleeping?* He has a key to my house, so I'll leave him a plate in the microwave and let him know it's there so he can get it once he wakes up.

I open my text messages, scroll to the last text I sent him, and shoot him a quick message.

Me: Hey! Breakfast? It'll be in the microwave for you once you wake up. We probably won't be here when you wake up. Remember, we're going to see the crazy lady today lol. Just use your key to come in.

I wait a second to see if the three dots appear, indicating that he is typing something, but nothing appears. *Maybe he is still asleep.*

"Gotcha again, bro!" I'm startled by someone yelling from upstairs.

"Kandice! Adam!" I yell from the kitchen.

"Yes, Mom!" They both yell simultaneously.

"What are y'all doing?" I ask, curious who is screaming when they clearly need to be getting ready for school. "Y'all need to get going!"

"Sorry, Mom, coming!" Adam yells. "Aaron just beat me again in Mario Kart!"

Really, before school? These two have become best friends once Adam realized Aaron loves video games as much as he does. This is another reason I couldn't see Aaron as anything other than a friend. I find it hard to get used to a grown man sitting around gaming all day. Some women don't mind that, but it's not for me.

Adam rushes into the kitchen, opens the freezer, and grabs a toaster strudel. *So much for the breakfast I made.* He pops the toaster strudel in the toaster and plops down in a chair at the kitchen table. "So, Mom, how was your visit with... your aunt? Is that right?"

"Yes, sweetie," I say, still in disbelief that I have a living relative. A nice living relative at that.

"So how was it? When can we meet her?" he asks.

"Soon, sweetie. I want to make sure she isn't..." I jokingly twirl my finger around in a circle near my ear, gesturing that I want to make sure she isn't coo-coo like the rest of my family.

Adam chuckles.

"Kandice!" I yell. "Y'all need to get going so you can get your brother to school, so you're not late for first period."

"Sorry, Mom!" Kandice yells. "Aaron was helping me lace up my dunks! He said they weren't laced right!"

The doorbell rings as Adam's toaster strudel pops up. He quickly jumps out of his chair, grabs the pastry, and heads for the front door. "I'll get it!"

As I'm flipping another batch of bacon in the frying pan, Adam comes into the kitchen with a mouthful of his toaster strudel and says, "Uh, Mom, someone's here for you." She looks like—"

I quickly interrupt him before he can say another word, "Make sure my bacon doesn't burn," I say, putting the fork in his hand as I quickly rush past him.

There is a woman on my porch. Her back is facing me, and she is looking up at something. She has tightly curled hair and wears a sleek, all-black body suit that complements her Coca-Cola-shaped figure. A bright pink belt cinches her waist, matching her pink purse and heels. For a moment, I freeze, realizing how much she resembles Lily-Ann—especially from behind, but I snap out of it when I'm reminded it's Beth. *Wait, it's Beth at seven in the morning, standing on my porch with...*

"Donuts!" she offers as she turns around at the sound of me opening the front door.

"Beth? Good...morning," I say, curious why she's here and what she was looking at.

"Good morning, sweetie!" she says, her voice filled with excitement. "I figured I'd bring over some donuts and maybe enjoy a little breakfast before we go see your mom."

I love the kind gesture, but I'm not one for surprises. I'm also a little confused about how she got my address. I search my thoughts and go back to yesterday's visit. I don't recall giving her my address.

"Is it me, or does it look like your mother's house looks over the entire town?" she asks.

I step onto the porch as if I don't already know our mother clearly watched over the entire town from up there. I shrug my shoulders, "Hmm, I never noticed."

"That's a little creepy, don't you think?" she asks. "I could have sworn there were more trees up there when we grew up in that house."

"Maybe they cut them down," I say, quickly changing the subject, not giving her time to think about her next question. "Would you like to come in?"

"Yes! Thank you, sweetie. I'm so sorry for showing up unannounced. Your sister gave me the address yesterday before you all left. She thought it would be a good idea to meet here," she explains with a smile.

She can't see it, but I'm rolling my eyes on the inside. Beth is sweet, but something I've learned from my past is not to be so quick to let strangers around my kids, family or not.

"Who's at the door?" Kandice asks as she descends the stairs.

Well, I thought it might be a little too soon for this introduction, but here we go: "This is your great aunt, I suppose."

"..." Kandice is at a loss for words. I'm sure she doesn't even know what a great aunt is. Heck, she doesn't know any aunt but my sister.

"This is your grandmother's sister. Her name is Beth," I explain.

"Oh! Okay, I get it now," Kandice says as if she had a light bulb moment.

"You can call her Ms. Beth or Aunt Beth, whichever you prefer."

Adam walks towards the front door, clutching a few strips of bacon as if he had just discovered treasure. His cheeks are packed that he looks like a squirrel who's just come across the mother lode of acorns!

"Did you know we have an aunt?" Kandice whispers to Adam.

"Yeah, mom wanted to make sure she wasn't..." he mimics my gesture from earlier and twirls his finger in a circle around his ear, indicating that I wanted to make sure she wasn't coo-coo first.

Beth laughs because, at this point, neither of my children is being discreet, and I am officially embarrassed and at a loss for words.

"Well, it was nice to meet you, Ms. Beth. I wish we could stay longer, but we have to get to school," Kandice says as she and Adam head out the door.

"Y'all have a good day. Love you! And drive safe!" I yell as the kids get into the car.

Beth is here now, and there's not much I can do other than give her the grand tour and offer her some bacon, that is, if Adam left any for the rest of us.

"So is Gerald coming with us?" she asks.

I pause for a moment, my mind racing as I try to process the sudden, unexpected question. Caught off guard, I realize there's no way on this planet that I can tell her the truth: that Lily-Ann hypnotized him into believing he was married to her. My eyes widen in shock and disbelief, and with a trembling voice, I manage to say, "Not this time."

CHAPTER 37

— · —

I'm speechless because my sister didn't inform me that she shared my address with a stranger. Considering everything we've been through, she should understand, more than anyone, how I feel about involving unfamiliar people. Beth is sweet, I don't doubt that, but please understand if I need a little time before I fully welcome her into our lives.

Sarah walks into the kitchen, and at this moment, I'm feeling a bit annoyed. She seems surprised to see our special guest sitting at the table, enjoying one of her glazed donuts from the donut shop. "Oh, hey, Aunt Beth, I didn't know you were stopping by this early."

"Yes, dear. I figured we could have a little breakfast together before we head out to see your mom," she says. "You don't remember me telling you this yesterday?"

Sarah stares at her momentarily, as if searching her thoughts from yesterday. "Oh... yeah... right. I totally forgot."

That was weird. My sister is not the type who forgets an important detail like that. She owns a horse stable and a donut shop; she doesn't have time to forget details like inviting someone over for breakfast.

"Oh, hi, Ms. Beth! I didn't expect to see you so soon," Aaron says, walking into the kitchen and heading straight for the pan of bacon on the stove.

"Hey, dear. Yes, I brought some donuts from Sarah's shop. They were so good yesterday that I figured I'd bring some for breakfast before we head out to see my sister," she says.

"That's what's up, thank you," he says, grabbing a donut from the box. "Alice, you made bacon too?"

I find it challenging to discuss the small amount of bacon we have left with Aaron. Thanks to Adam for taking most of it. This morning's breakfast will likely be cheese toast and glazed donuts.

"Sarah, may I speak with you for a minute?" I ask, completely ignoring Aaron's questions.

"Yeah, sure, no problem," she says curiously.

"We will be right back. Aaron, can you help Beth if she needs anything, please?" I ask.

"Sure thing," he says, saluting as if he were addressing a high-ranking government official.

Sarah and I enter my room, and I express to her my feelings about inviting Beth over without telling me first. Sarah doesn't seem to understand my frustration, as she looks at me as if I'm speaking another language.

"Sarah?"

"Oh, sorry, sis," she says. "I honestly don't remember giving her your address. I was so excited to find out we had a long-lost aunt, but I can't remember writing your address down."

Now, I'm trying to understand why Beth lied. Why did she tell me Sarah had invited her over? The better question is, why did Sarah go along with it?

CHAPTER 38

— · —

O n our way to the facility, Beth asked if we could take the scenic route through town to see what had changed over the years. She mentioned that the old movie theater had been there since their teenage years, and our grandparents had funded the clock tower in Shelly Grove Park. Sarah and I exchanged a look upon hearing this discovery. While we knew the clock tower had been used to hypnotize people, we didn't realize our grandparents were responsible for installing it. Who am I kidding? Nothing about my family should come as a surprise to me.

As we get closer to the facility, I notice a black sedan following behind us. I don't want to alarm everyone, so I continue in the direction of the facility. I turn left, and the black sedan turns left. I turn right, and the black sedan turns right.

I must have missed my turn to the facility when I'm startled by Sarah, "Uh, sis, you missed the turn."

"What?"

"She said you missed your turn," Beth repeats.

"Oh, sorry," I say quickly.

"Are you okay?" Sarah asks.

"Yeah," I lie. I clear my throat and gather my thoughts. "You know how I get before going to see Mom."

"Oh, sweetie, I realize I can be selfish. I know this isn't easy for you," Beth says, holding her hands to her chest.

Easy? Please, little does she know I'm the one who put her in that place. I'm the reason she'll never walk the streets of this town again. I'm the reason she'll never be that woman of mystery.

I look behind me as I make a U-turn and notice the black sedan is no longer following us. *Get it together, Alice. Many people in this town drive Black cars.*

As we arrive at the facility, I park in my usual spot that offers a view of the front of the building. Beth appears excited to see her sister, as she immediately opens the car door and leaps out with impressive speed. I've never seen anyone in high heels move so fast. I can't criticize her, though; if I hadn't seen my sister for years and then learned she was unwell, I would react the same way.

"Oh goodness, that statue is very disturbing," Beth says. She seems disturbed by Big John's appearance, unaware that he and I now share an unspoken connection.

We enter the facility, and the lobby is quiet as usual. Today, Sharon is at the front desk, and I'm sure she can't wait until Aaron can get back to work.

"Hey, Sharon, how's it going?" I say. "This is my Aunt Beth. She hasn't seen our mother in quite some time, so we wanted to bring her here as a nice surprise for my mom."

"..." Sharon doesn't say anything. She fixes her gaze on Beth. She doesn't blink. I'm pretty sure she's stopped breathing. I'm no doctor, but from the looks of it, she appears to be losing some color in her face.

"Sharon! Sharon!" I say, but she doesn't say anything; she continues to focus on Beth. "Earth to Sharon."

At this point, I look at Beth and notice something odd about her as well. She, too, is looking at Sharon, and in my opinion, it would have seemed as though they had both just seen a ghost.

Did I miss something?

Something strange is going on between these two, and it's a little uncomfortable if you ask me. I can tell Sarah is thinking the same thing as I am. I shoot Aaron a look, and from the looks of it, I can tell he is also confused. Stepping directly in front of Sharon, I make eye contact with her, which causes her to snap out of whatever weirdness she's experiencing at this moment. "Are you okay?"

"Sorry," Sharon finally responds. "Your aunt just looks very familiar. I can't think of where I've seen her."

I glance over my shoulder and catch Beth's gaze, instantly understanding what Sharon means. I tell her that my mother has a fraternal twin, and we're just discovering this now. I also share that we felt the same shock when we saw her, as the resemblance is striking. Honestly, they could almost pass for identical twins, considering they dress alike, style their hair the same way, and, to our amazement, they both wear heels every day as if they were tennis shoes.

"Interesting," Sharon says.

For some reason, her response of 'interesting' doesn't resonate with me. If I mention that someone has a twin, the typical reaction is usually something like, 'Oh, that's cool' or 'I had no idea she had a twin.' However, Sharon doesn't respond that way. She seems to indicate that something is off, as if this new revelation does not convince her.

My gut has never failed me, and right now, my gut is telling me something isn't right with these two.

CHAPTER 39

— • —

When I say I'm tired of all the surprises, I really mean it. One day, I'm moving to another state, and the next I find out I was hypnotized and never left the East Coast. Let's not forget that the entire town was also hypnotized. We can't ignore the fact that my mother and brothers are all murderers. To make matters worse, now my mom has a twin who is acting very strange with the woman watching over our mother. Will my life ever be normal?

"Sharon, Beth would like to see Lily-Ann," I say. "Is that possible? Do you know if she is awake?"

"I think so. I just did my rounds and passed out meds. She was awake when I went in there," she explains.

"Great! Can we see her!" Beth eagerly interrupts.

"Yeah, no problem at all. Follow me," Sharon says as she reaches behind her and grabs the set of keys off the wall.

Walking down the hall is always the hardest for me. We have to pass many rooms, and it tears me apart to see all the sick people here. Our mother is here because she is truly unhinged and a danger to society. *I wonder what the rest of these people's cases are?*

We pause briefly in the hallway when Sharon accidentally drops her keys. I see an elderly Black man sitting on the edge of his bed, gazing at his feet. My heart aches for him as I wonder if his family comes to see him.

I peek in his room, and I don't notice a single picture. *Does he have a family that misses him or even cares about him?* Then I start to think about our mother. If this story were different and she truly had dementia, I would make sure our mother was loved and had many pictures hanging on her walls of her family. But does Bill have to spend his days in such an awful place, alone? *I'm not sure if his name is Bill; he looks like a Bill to me. So, for now, I'll call him that.*

My gaze is fixed on Bill when I'm instantly startled by the soft touch on my shoulder.

"Sorry, Alice, I didn't mean to startle you. We're heading to your mom's room," Aaron says. "Hey, I know you and Sarah have a lot going on right now, but I just wanted to check in and make sure you're okay."

"Yeah, I'm fine," I lie. "Why do you ask?"

"I know how hard it is for you to see your mom," he says.

I'd be lying if I said he wasn't right. Every time I see that woman, my mind goes back to the horrific scene of my kids chained up to be drowned. I can forgive my mother for all the beatings and the way she treated my sister and me, but to try to kill her grandkids is next-level. I will forever hate this woman. So he's right; it isn't easy for me to see her because every time I do, I instantly feel rage.

"Lily-Ann," Sharon says in a singsong voice as we enter her room. "There are some visitors here to see you.

In my opinion, she looks helpless. Today, she's sitting up in bed, gazing into outer space, dressed in a light pink gown adorned with embroidered sunflowers. She has three large cornrows in her hair, making her look less like a woman in a mental facility and more like someone who belongs in a prison yard. If she ever came out of her hypnosis, she'd be furious, not because we hypnotized her, but due to her current appearance.

"Maybe you should say something, Ms. Beth," Aaron suggests. "It will be a different voice, and maybe that will trigger a different response."

Currently, I struggle to face our mother after my last visit, when I tried to suffocate her. If it weren't for my sister showing up, I think I would have gone through with it.

"I think I'm going to stand out in the hallway," I say.

"Oh, sweetie, I understand," Beth says, clueless to the real reason why I can't be in this room. "I won't be long."

I stand in the hallway outside the room, leaning my back against the wall. I can hear Beth trying her hardest to get Lily-Ann to recognize her voice. I also hear my sister and Sharon whispering, "It's not working."

Yes, she is here for "dementia;" yes, she is also under hypnosis. But deep down, I feel rage. For some reason, I want answers. I want to know why she hasn't told us about our aunt our entire lives. I want to understand why she pushed her twin away. Sadly, deep down, I also want to know why she couldn't love us, not even a little bit. I want to know was it the fight between her and her sister that turned her into this terrible person?

At this point, nothing they are doing is working. I rush into the room with tears forming in my eyes and yell, "Mom!"

Dead silence falls over the room, and now all eyes are on me. Everyone wears the same shocked look on their faces. Before I can say another word, Lily-Ann fixes her gaze and stares back at us. But she doesn't look lost in her world of dementia. She has the same expression we had the night we found Beth in the basement. She appears to be staring into the eyes of a ghost.

CHAPTER 40

— • —

With her eyes fixed in our direction, she lifts her arm and points. I try to follow her arm, to see who she is pointing at, but I'm unsure. This is all new to us, and to be honest, my heart is pounding, and I'm a little freaked out at the moment. She doesn't blink, not even once; she just stares in our direction.

I'm feeling unsure about how hypnosis operates. I'm questioning if we made a mistake. I'm also concerned it might be fading. We lack detailed instructions for this process; we only followed what Mr. Gerald and Sarah observed her doing in the past, and we watched videos online.

"You! You!" Lily-Ann yells repeatedly.

We glance at one another to determine who Lily-Ann is indicating and addressing. It's still unclear to whom she is shouting "you."

Sarah rushes to her bedside, kneeling. "Yes, Mom, it's your sister. It's Beth. You know your sister Lily-Beth."

Lily-Ann doesn't budge. She doesn't acknowledge the fact that Sarah is kneeling right next to her. She continues to stare in our direction and point. *Something's not right about this visit.*

My heart pounds as if it's about to burst from my chest. *Could she be pointing at me because she knows I tried to suffocate her? Is she pointing at Beth because she recognizes her sister?* All these thoughts raced through my mind. Nothing makes sense at this moment.

"YOU! YOU!" I jump almost out of my skin as Lily-Ann shouts.

I look at Sharon and Aaron. They are the professionals, and I'm sure they encounter this daily. Mentally ill patients do things that don't seem to make any sense. However, as I observe them, I notice they both appear taken aback by the scene unfolding before them.

I fix my gaze back on Lily-Ann, startled by her next move. She leaps out of bed and charges toward us. Fortunately, Sarah reacts swiftly, grabbing our mother and holding on tightly. I have no idea what has come over Lily-Ann. She rushes at us like a wild animal in a zoo, ready to attack the onlookers. Her eyes have turned pitch black, and she no longer resembles that sad, lonely woman trapped in the facility. Instead, she appears like a lion poised to strike at anything in its path.

"Sharon!" Sarah yells. "Do something!"

Sharon, like all of us, is in shock at what is happening. I can tell she was not expecting this either. Snapping out of her shock, she rushes over to Lily-Ann. "Aaron, I need your help!"

Aaron quickly rushes over and assists Sarah in holding Lily-Ann steady. I find myself completely frozen, unable to move, as if my feet are glued to the ground from shock. I wasn't prepared for this. *Did something trigger her?*

Beth reaches out and squeezes my hand with one of hers while covering her mouth with the other. She appears surprised and didn't anticipate this reaction.

"I'm so sorry, dear," she says, continuing to squeeze my hand. "If I hadn't been here, she wouldn't have..."

"Don't..." I interrupt her before she can finish her sentence. "Don't blame yourself. She's really sick, Aunt Beth."

Beth snaps her head in my direction, surprised at the words that came out of my mouth: *Aunt Beth.* She smiles, and I smile back at her.

"What's that?" Beth asks as she quickly turns her head in the direction of Sharon, Sarah, and Aaron, who are holding Lily-Ann down.

Sharon has pulled a syringe out of the pocket of her scrubs. She lifts the needle to her lips and, with her teeth, pulls off the cap, spitting it onto the ground. She plunges the needle into Lily-Ann's thigh, holding the syringe down until every drop of the liquid inside has disappeared.

"It's a medication to calm her down," she says, out of breath. "It will relax her, and it may make her a little sleepy."

Aaron and Sarah lift Lily-Ann onto her bed as her body starts to go limp, and the fight has been drained entirely from her.

"Okay, can anyone explain what just happened?" Sarah asks.

"Maybe something triggered her reaction," Sharon says.

"Clearly, but what?" I ask.

Beth sinks into a small chair in the corner. Tears well up in her eyes, and her voice sounds slightly cracked. "Was it me?"

I place my hand on Beth's shoulder, "We don't know what caused her to react this way."

"I've never seen her this way," Sharon says softly.

The room is silent as each of us tries to process what we witnessed. I felt horrible on the inside. Poor Beth wanted to see her sister, and here she is seeing her in this condition. I couldn't imagine seeing Sarah in this state of mind. Part of me feels like this is my fault. I felt responsible for the way she reacted.

"Maybe y'all should try to come back another day," Sharon suggests as she brushes away a few strands of hair that are stuck to her now sweaty face.

"I was hoping for a different reaction, you know," Beth says, with tears now falling down her cheeks, causing her makeup to fall with each drop. "Some part of me had hoped she would have seen me and instantly jump out of bed to hug me."

"I can only imagine, Aunty," Sarah says softly.

"I just knew things would be different this time. I just knew we would fix our relationship," Beth says, tears streaming down her cheeks, falling into her lap.

Aaron grabs a few napkins from the counter and places them in Beth's hand. "Maybe we should take Sharon's advice, Ms. Beth. Maybe we should go. You don't need to be here right now. Not like this. Not seeing your sister like this."

He reaches his hand out to help Beth out of her chair.

"Maybe you're right," Beth says, dabbing her eyes with the napkins. "Maybe we can try again another day?"

"Of course, we can come back another day, that's your sister," Aaron says softly, wiping some of her tears from under her eyes.

"Thank you, baby," she says, sniffing.

At this point, I can tell Sarah and I are thinking the same thing. *What's going on between these two?*

"I'm so sorry, Beth," I quickly interrupt. "We will keep trying until she realizes who you are."

182

That's the least I can do. I thought to myself, considering this is probably all my fault. This poor lady is in here crying because I thought it was a great idea to hypnotize our mother into believing she has dementia. Now, our aunt is being comforted by our best friend, and it's making me uncomfortable.

CHAPTER 41

— • —

As we drove back home, a heavy silence settled over the car, and I found myself at a loss for words. I stared out the window, watching the scenery blur past as my mind kept replaying the events that had just unfolded in Lily-Ann's room. The memories were vivid and jarring, leaving a lingering sense of shock and disbelief. Sarah, noticing my distress, was kind enough to drive us back to my house.

Staring out the window, trying to piece everything together, I'm startled by a sudden vibration. I lift myself slightly to pull my phone from my back pocket. The screen is black, so I click the small button on the side to open my phone. I haven't heard from Mr. Gerald yet, and I wonder if he went to my house to get breakfast.

As soon as the screen lights up, I notice a new text message notification displayed on my lock screen. *It must be Mr. Gerald letting me know he got his food.* I enter my passcode to access my phone and see that the text message is from Aaron.

I pull down my visor and look in the mirror to see Aaron in the backseat. I glance over my shoulder and notice Beth is staring out her window in the backseat. She must still be shocked, as she doesn't see me looking at her.

I look down at my phone and open the new text message.

Aaron: Hey.

Me: Hey.

Aaron: Are you okay?

Me: Not really.

Aaron: I'm sorry this happened.

Me: Yeah, me too.

Aaron: I know it was hard for you.

Me: What?

Aaron: Going back to see your mom.

Me: Yeah, but I'll be okay.

Me: Can I ask you a question?

Aaron: What's up?

Me: Why were you comforting my aunt?

Aaron: She was really torn up from what happened.

Aaron: I mean, no one else was, and she came all this way.

Me: Yeah, I know, it just seemed a little odd.

Aaron: Odd? How?

Me: Because you don't know her.

Aaron: Alice, she came to see her sister, who just freaked out on all of us. Right then, she needed someone to comfort her.

Me: I didn't think about it that way.

Aaron: What other reason did you think I was comforting her?

Me: Well...

Aaron: Really? Goodness, Alice, the woman is half my age.

Me: I know. It was a stupid thought. Blame it on my mom.

Aaron: Do you really think I would try to get close to your aunt?

Me: I'm sorry, it's just been hard to open up to people, and trusting others isn't that easy right now. I'm sorry.

Aaron: You're my friend, almost like a sister to me. I would never hurt you and Sarah like that.

Me: I know. It was a stupid thought. Forgive me?

"Well, we're here," Sarah says.

I quickly lock my phone and return it to my pocket. I look back at Beth and apologize again for what happened at the facility. I let her know we will be in touch so we can get together another day. I also reassure her that we will try revisiting Lily-Ann, but it's probably best that we give her a few days.

Beth says her goodbyes, and at this point, all I want to do is lie in bed and sleep for the rest of the day. My head is pounding, and I don't want to think about anything else after the events that unfolded today. I just want to sleep.

"Kids, we're home!" I yell as we walk through the door.

"What's for dinner?" Adam asks.

"Tonight is fend for yourself. I need to lie down; I have a massive headache," I say. "There are some frozen pizzas in the freezer."

"I'll make sure they eat, sis. Just get some rest," Sarah reassures me.

"Adam!" Aaron yells.

Adam peeks his head around the corner at the top of the stairs.

"Put that Mario Kart on, bro. I'm ready to spank you again," Aaron says with a smile so wide you would think he was a kid walking into a candy shop.

"Bet," Adam says.

"Yeah, get some rest, Alice," Aaron reassures me as he walks past me, heading up the stairs, looking over his shoulder. "We got the kids. I'm going to spank Adam in this game real quick, and I'll help Sarah with dinner."

I walk to my room and shut the door. Leaning against it, I exhale deeply; it almost feels like I have been holding that breath for hours. I sit on the edge of my bed, placing my head in my hands, and reflect on everything that happened at the facility today.

I'm immediately reminded of the moment we arrived at the facility and the expression on Sharon's face when she saw Beth. That look felt familiar to me—it's nearly identical to the expression my neighbor used to wear whenever Lily-Ann visited. *Did Sharon truly seem surprised by how much Beth looked like our mom, or was there another reason behind her stunned expression?*

Something felt off about this visit. Heck, the moment we saw Beth in that basement, I knew something was wrong. I lift my head, and at this point, I understand what I need to do; I need to dig a little deeper and gather more information on Beth.

CHAPTER 42

— • —

I'm awakened by the sound of my programmable coffee maker's timer. I need to figure out how to adjust the time for each day. It's the weekend, and who wants to be up at eight in the morning on a Saturday?

I jump out of bed and notice I'm still wearing the clothes I had on yesterday. I rush into the bathroom, brush my teeth, sprinkle a little water in my hair to help bring out my curls, and, of course, change my pants. I can't go out there wearing the same clothes I had on yesterday.

I stumble into the kitchen on a caffeine mission, ready to pour myself a cup of coffee—because let's be honest, I've fallen hard for this magical bean juice. It's as if I've discovered the holy grail of adulthood! Seriously, I can't even think of starting my day without it. Now I get why they call it addicting—if coffee were a person, I'd be writing it love letters!

I set my phone on the counter and open the cabinet. My hand instinctively snatches the nearest coffee mug. The phrase on the mug makes me smile: "drunk off coffee." Sarah thought it would be a fun birthday gift, given my recent coffee obsession. I pour myself a steaming cup, then take one of Adam's toaster strudels from the fridge, and place it in the toaster. Today, I have a mission, and my breakfast choice is a quick, indulgent option, as usual.

I'm blowing the steam from my mug, and before my lips touch the cup's rim, my cell phone buzzes. "Who would be messaging me at eight in the morning on a Saturday?" I ask myself.

> **Mr. Gerald:** Hey, sweetie! Sorry, I didn't get back to you right away. I had to take a quick trip to Atlanta. I'll let you girls know when I'm headed back. Enjoy your aunt.

> **Me:** Oh, okay. Well, drive safe out there. You know that Atlanta traffic can be chaotic. We love you.

> **Mr. Gerald:** Love you girls, too.

I'm a little confused because Mr. Gerald hasn't left Shelly Grove since I've moved here. Heck, he's probably never left this town if I'm being honest with myself. My mind takes me back to the plate of breakfast I left in the microwave for him. *I wonder if he ever came over and got his food?* I open the microwave and I'm pleased to see the plate is gone. *At least he got a good meal before heading to Atlanta.*

"Good morning." I'm startled by Aaron as he greets me in the kitchen.

"Oh, hey. Did I wake you?" I ask.

"No... not at all," he says, pointing at my programmable coffee maker. "I think your coffee maker did. It smells good. I think I'll have a cup."

"Coming right up!" I say as I grab him a coffee mug out of the cabinet.

"So why are you up so early? Where are you headed this morning?" he asks.

"I was going..." I begin to tell him I want to speak with Sharon this morning, but for some reason, I can't bring myself to tell him the truth. After we visited the facility and realized something was off with Beth, I decided it was probably best to keep my thoughts to myself. I don't want to worry him or Sarah with my crazy accusations. It could be nothing at all. It could be me overthinking this entire thing. I just need to figure her out on my own.

If Beth is going to be spending time with my family, I need to make sure she checks out. I learned a hard lesson from my mother: You can't trust everyone, not even family. My sister can call me paranoid, but if you can't trust the one person who gave birth to you, then who can you trust?

I find it strange how Beth was standing in an empty basement the night we first met. It was late at night; shouldn't she have been sleeping? She also comes from a long line of crazies; it's very possible that she's putting on, as the older generation used to say, pretending to be a nice person.

I told myself I wouldn't step foot back into our mother's house, but maybe some of the answers I'm looking for are there. Beth says she came back because she heard her sister was ill, so why not start with checking the hospital? Why would she check an old, creepy basement?

"I want to visit the facility this morning and speak with Sharon about yesterday," I say. It's not a complete lie. I do need to speak with Sharon about yesterday, but not about my mom.

"Do you want some company?" he asks.

"No!" I say quickly.

Aaron holds my gaze, and now I can see the confusion on his face.

"What I mean is, no, I don't want to drag you down there with me. I felt horrible about yesterday and wanted to see what we could do to prevent that from happening next visit," I lie. "Beth needs to see her sister."

He furrows his brows and tilts his head slightly. Maintaining eye contact, he remains silent, staring at me. Meanwhile, I'm beginning to fiddle with my fingers, uncertain about what to say next.

"Is that right?" he finally asks.

Something about his question doesn't sit well with me. *Is he asking that because he doesn't believe me?*

I nod, "If you don't mind, could you please remind the kids to do their chores when they get up? I won't be gone long."

The room is now silent as I sip my coffee and ponder our conversation. *Why did that feel like I was being interrogated? Do I really have to tell my sister and Aaron where I'm going every time I want to walk out my own door, that I'm paying for?*

"Hey y'all!" Sarah says with a smile as she walks into the kitchen, breaking the tension. "No one invited me to the party."

"What are you doing up so early?" I ask, now surprised, why two adults aren't sleeping in. You can tell neither of them has kids because any other day, I would kill for extra hours of sleep.

"I couldn't sleep. Yesterday was a little crazy, don't you think?" she asks.

"Yeah, it was," Aaron says.

"And Mr. Beautiful Black Man over here was acting like Mr. Knight in Shining Armor!" Sarah chuckles.

I nearly spat out my coffee from laughing. "Sarah?" Leave it to my sister to lighten up the mood in a room.

"Yeah, yeah, laugh it up," Aaron says.

"You have to give it to her, Aaron," I say with a smile. "That was funny hearing Beth call you that."

Aaron throws a balled-up napkin at me. "Shut up!"

I smile, and for a moment, I've forgotten about his weird behavior just a few minutes ago.

"Where are you headed, sis?" Sarah asks.

Before I can say anything, Aaron interrupts, "The facility."

Sarah shoots me a questioning look. "Why?"

"I wanted to speak with Sharon about yesterday," I begin, telling her the same lie I had told Aaron. "I just want to see what we can do to prevent this from happening again."

"And you couldn't call her to ask her that?" she asks.

She isn't wrong, and for a moment, I'm speechless. How can I challenge that question? I could have picked up the phone and asked her; if that was all I wanted to know.

CHAPTER 43

— • —

After leaving the house, I had a single destination in mind: the facility. My curiosity was growing rapidly, overpowering my sense of calm, as I wondered what secrets Beth and Sharon shared with each other. The anxiety that had been building up inside me was now almost unbearable, making my hands tremble and my thoughts race. I desperately needed to understand what that strange look had meant to Beth—was it concern, suspicion, or something else entirely?

I pull into the facility's parking lot, my heart pounding with anticipation and a desperate need to speak with Sharon. As I hurriedly make my way toward the front entrance, I almost trip over my own feet, anxious to get inside. I stop suddenly, raising my hand to salute Big John, because somehow, we share an unspoken bond—an understanding forged in silence. I sense what he's reaching for—hope, perhaps, or help. His weathered face, scarred and broken, carries a weight far deeper than the physical; it tells a story of hardship and pain. To me, those scars symbolize the brokenness we both carry inside. I see myself in him—wounded, craving healing, desperate for a peace I've long yearned for but have yet to find. In that moment, I feel the ache of my own brokenness, and my soul reaches out for solace amidst the chaos I've been through.

I wipe away what I think are tears that have silently slipped down my cheeks, feeling their coolness on my skin. I take a slow, deliberate inhale, trying to steady my nerves and brace myself for whatever is getting ready to be revealed to me. I turn my head one last time to glance at Big John, and I nod subtly to signal that I finally understand him. A strange, nagging thought crosses my mind—*perhaps there's something wrong with me for shedding tears over a broken statue.* With a shaky breath, I gather myself, push open the door, and step inside. There, I see Sharon sitting comfortably in a chair, her eyes fixed intently on her phone, unaware of my presence.

"Sharon! Hey," I say

"Hey Alice! I wasn't expecting you so soon," Sharon says, quickly setting her phone down on the counter.

I'm probably the last person she expected to see today, especially after yesterday's events. But I'm not sure how to bring up my question without seeming abrupt. I don't want to jump right into it, since that might come across as rude. Lily-Ann always taught us to ask how someone is doing first before asking for anything. Sharon isn't stupid either. She has been working with us since we placed our mother in this facility. She knows I don't go to the facility just for fun, especially not to see my mother.

"What's up? You don't just come here to say hello," she says. "Heck, you don't even come here to see your mom like that," she says jokingly.

"You know me so well," I say, playfully swatting the air. "Since you're not the type to beat around the bush, I'll be upfront with you."

Sharon nods.

"Can you tell me what you know about Beth?" I ask.

"Beth? Your aunt?" she asks.

"Yesterday, when we came in, you looked like you saw a ghost when I introduced you to her," I explain.

Sharon holds my gaze and says nothing. It appears that she's trying to find the right words to say. My gut never lies to me, and this is proof that something isn't right about Beth.

"Sharon, if you know anything about this woman, please let me know," I plead with her. "She is coming around my family. I need to know who I'm dealing with."

Sharon holds up her hand to quiet me, "Look, I don't know much about Beth; when I first moved into this town, I was a little kid. All I remember is the creepy stories the kids at school told about the big house that sat on the hill. They talked about your mom and Beth's parents and how they used to trap people in the basement and sometimes even kill them."

"So you know about the basement?" I ask.

"I was younger when I came here, so honestly, I thought people were just saying stuff to scare me," she explains.

From what Beth told us about their parents, I wouldn't put it past them to do something like that. At least at this point, someone other than Beth confirmed that their parents were nuts.

"One day, I was playing with some kids from school, and they told me the only way I could keep playing with them was if I proved to them I wasn't a chicken. To do that, they said I had to sneak into the house on the hill, go into the basement, and sit down there for ten minutes," she explains.

Those kids were jerks.

"So, did you go?" I ask, eyes wide.

She assures me that the only way she could make friends was to go. Now that I think about it, I guess I can understand why she went. Kids are cruel and try to make other kids do stupid things to make themselves look big and bad.

"What happened when you went into the house?" I ask, curious, if she ever made it down to the basement or if she got caught.

"Heck yeah, I went. I wasn't going to be known as the town chicken!" she chuckles. "We waited until it got dark, like most silly kids do when it comes to a big, creepy house, and found a window on the side that opened up into an open area. Once my so-called friends helped me in, I noticed I was standing in a foyer with a door leading to the basement. I decided to go down there for ten minutes, like they told me to."

As Sharon explains that night, my mind takes me back to the night we escaped. *There was no foyer by the basement door.* Then it hits me like a load of bricks. The foyer she is referring to must have been upgraded over the years. Perhaps they closed it in and turned it into a room. My guess is that they did that to prevent people from entering the basement. They also built that big bookshelf in front of the basement entrance as a secret door.

"What happened once you got in? Did you make it down to the basement?" My curiosity starts to get the best of me.

"Yes. I stood in a dark hallway for what felt like an eternity. I was ready to leave the basement when I heard someone coming, so I ran into another area of the basement. At that point, I saw a young woman tied to a chair with tape wrapped around her head to cover her mouth."

"..." I'm at a loss for words. I knew my grandparents were crazy, but it seems official, hearing from someone outside of our family.

"I immediately ran over to her and tried to untie her, but I wasn't fast enough. So she nodded her head to instruct me to hide in this tool closet that was down there. I suppose she already knew who was coming, so she wanted me to hide."

"Who was coming? Who was the girl?" I'm full of questions at this point.

"I sat in the closet, waiting to see who was coming. That's when I saw a man and a woman approach her. They asked her if she was ready to comply, and she shook her head no. The woman slapped her so hard that it caused her nose to bleed. She had to remove the tape from around her head so she wouldn't choke on her blood from what I could see."

At this point, I can only imagine how this girl must have felt. Lily-Ann did the same thing to me and the receptionist. *These people are evil.*

Sharon continues, "Of course, being a kid, it scared me, and I squealed. I quickly put my hands over my mouth, hoping they didn't hear me. But the man, I think, heard something, so he began to walk toward the tool closet. I watched as he got closer. I just knew that was it for me."

"What happened? Did you get caught?" I ask eagerly.

"Thankfully no," she says. "Right before he approached the closet, the girl yelled for him to stop and told him she would comply. I wasn't sure what she was talking about, but he finally untied her. Then the woman put something in her mouth and gave her a glass of water to wash it down, and she told her she would never be better than her sister

198

(Lily-Ann). The young woman saw me looking through a crack and put her finger to her lips to signal me to stay quiet."

"What the..." I can't believe what I'm hearing, but I'm even more curious to know who the girl was.

Sharon chuckles, "Right, after she did that, she swallowed whatever was in her mouth. She had tears falling down her face. Whatever they had her swallow, she really didn't want to do it. But it took her about one minute until it looked like she went into a trance of some sort."

For a minute, I stand there in complete silence, unsure how to process what she just told me. "So, how did you get out of there?"

"Well, eventually, they all left the basement. I waited there for a while before I came out of the closet. I was terrified. I had no idea what I just witnessed. It was some pretty freaky stuff if you asked me. Once I noticed the coast was completely clear, I ran as fast as possible out of the basement and jumped out the window."

I place my hand over my mouth in shock.

"Of course, my so-called friends left me. I don't think they ever intended to stay there for the ten minutes waiting for me. But the next day at school, everyone had questions, and all I could think about was the girl's instructions for me to stay quiet."

"So you didn't even tell your parents?" I ask.

"After that day, I never told anyone what happened that night. When you and Sarah came to me about giving your mom this pill, it all seemed too familiar to me, but we were all still coming out of our hypnosis here in town, so I never thought about that night until I saw Beth." She explains.

"Wait! So, Beth is the girl you saw in the basement?" I ask.

Sharon nods yes, "The moment I saw Beth, something weird happened."

"What do you mean?" I ask.

"It was like a fast rewind through time. Apparently, everything came back to me about that night. About that house," she says.

Now it all makes sense. The reason she stared at Beth for so long. Beth did tell us their parents were crazy, but she never mentioned they hypnotized her or anyone else. She made it seem like it was just a silly thought to her. This is all too familiar for me. Our mother did the same thing to us. Sarah was right, this must go back farther than we thought. Our grandparents have been hypnotizing people for many years.

CHAPTER 44

— · —

After speaking with Sharon, she asked me to promise to keep our conversation confidential. I could barely wrap my mind around all that Sharon had disclosed to me. She wasn't sure if Beth remembered that night, and she didn't want to remind her of it either. Even though I don't know Beth that well, I wouldn't want to take her down memory lane and remind her of the terrible things her parents put her through.

Walking out of the building, I say my goodbyes to Big John and crank my car. I decide to sit in my car for a little while, trying to get the image of Beth tied to a chair out of my head. The more I try, the more images flash of Beth, myself, the receptionist, and sadly, the elderly lady next door, who, at the hands of our mother, has been tortured. I wasn't sure if I could trust Beth because she is my mother's sister, but now I feel bad for the lady. She is a victim in all of this, just like I am. In my opinion, she's fortunate that she escaped this place.

I wasn't going to share this information with anyone. But it did leave me with a question. *Why would Beth come back? Why would she want to see her sister after all of this? Why would she want to be down in the basement of all places?* Something isn't adding up.

My phone buzzes, and across the screen is a notification that I have a text message. I unlock the screen and click on the new text message alert. It's Kandice, and she's put together a group text that includes Adam, her, and me.

"What now?" I sigh.

Kandice: Mom?

Me: Yes.

Kandice: Aunt Sarah and Aaron told us to do our chores.

Me: That's right. What's wrong?

Kandice: Well, I'm doing my chores, but Adam is just playing his games.

Adam: Why you always gotta tell on me? Snitches get stitches, you know.

Me: Ugh, please, you two, can y'all work together for at least one day?

Kandice: Mom, I'm trying, but when I told him to wipe down the counters in the bathroom, he told me to get out of his room.

Adam: No, I didn't.

Kandice: So I'm lying? Do you want Aunt Sarah to vouch for me?

Adam: Man, whatever.

Me: STOP IT! I'm out trying to take care of something very important, and the two of you can't do a few chores?

Kandice: I can do my chores.

Me: How about this? I'm on my way home. If those chores aren't at least halfway done, Adam, the games are mine, and Kandice, the phone is mine.

Adam: See what you've done, Kandice. Thanks a lot. Yes, Mom, they'll be HALFWAY done.

Kandice: Yes, ma'am, got it.

I lock my phone screen, shaking my head. Taking a deep breath, I exhale slowly, trying to calm my nerves. I'm clearly not ready to deal with the sibling drama today.

"Why can't my kids just get along?" I ask myself as I lean my head against the headrest.

As I lean forward to start my car, something catches my eye. My heart skips a beat, and I can only imagine my melanin-rich complexion has become pale. I take a second look and rub my eyes to confirm what I see. The same mysterious black sedan has reappeared; this time, it's anything but discreet. It's evident that the driver wants to be noticed. I can feel their gaze piercing into me, taunting me. Whoever it is, they are now parked right beside me.

CHAPTER 45

— • —

In the back of my mind, a whirlwind of thoughts races as I weigh my options. The engine hums softly under me, and I know I could slam my foot on the gas pedal, feeling the adrenaline surge as I drive away from this tense situation. Alternatively, I could pick up my phone and dial the police, hoping that fate would smile upon me and they'd arrive in time to catch the car before it sped off again.

Another thought crosses my mind: perhaps rolling down my window could bridge the distance between us, opening a line of communication. If the driver recognizes I'm here, they may do the same and lower their window too. This will allow me to get a glimpse of who has been following me. It's clear that the person inside is no longer interested in taking off again and is ready to reveal themselves.

I roll down my window and wave for the driver to do the same, but the car just sits there, with its engine humming. The mystery is driving me crazy. I glance around, observing the area, and pray that someone steps outside to be a witness. Maybe an employee at the facility is getting ready to take their break, or someone has finished their shift. But no one does, and we are completely alone in the parking lot.

I brace myself as the driver-side door opens. A tall Black man steps out. He has a clean-cut appearance and wears a tight-fitting black shirt that showcases his muscular arms. As he turns to walk toward my car, he puts on a pair of black sunglasses, making it difficult to see his eyes. The sun obstructs my vision, and the only thought that comes to mind is that James is back. He is back and has been following me. He is back and was the one who shot Aaron. He is back and is going to try to kill me right here in the parking lot of the facility.

I can only envision my children visiting this spot daily throughout their lives. They will bring flowers, bears, and cards. This parking space will be where my spirit remains, as my brother has returned because he will surely kill me this time. I might consider resisting, but the odds are not in my favor. I don't even have my gun with me, nor do I have a bat. The only thing I have on my side now is my prayers and hope that the Lord above will send me some grace, just like Big John.

"Alice?" A deep voice calls out my name, finally stepping into the sun's path, allowing me to see clearly now.

This man is not James. *Who is he, and how does he know my name?*

"Yes?" I'm slightly confused and a little relieved that I'll live to see another day. "Who's asking?"

"My name is Detective Homes."

"Detective Homes," I repeat. *Why does that name sound so familiar? Why does this guy look familiar?*

"Do you have a minute to talk?" he asks.

Clearly, I have a minute to talk; I'm sitting in the parking lot of a mental facility. The better question is, why has he been following me if he's a detective? *Maybe he has some information about the shooter.*

"Yes, I have a minute, but who are you exactly? Haven't I seen your car around town?" I ask, trying to get answers from the man who has been scaring the living daylights out of me. "Are you a new detective here in Shelly Grove?"

"No, I'm not new here. I don't even work here. I'm looking for someone," he says.

"Oh, do you need me to show you where the police station is? I'd be glad to; follow me," I say quickly, preparing to shift my car in reverse.

"Please stop, just listen, please," he says, lifting his hand to ask me to stop what I'm doing and pay attention.

"Is something wrong?" I ask.

He removes his sunglasses and wipes his forehead with the back of his hand. "I'm looking for my brother. He's a detective as well."

I sit back in my chair, almost at a loss for words. *What makes this guy think I know anything about his brother?*

"He relocated here about two years ago. The last I heard from him, he told me something weird was going on in this town, and he was looking into it," he explains.

"What...what did you say your brother's name is again?" I ask cautiously.

"His name is David, but he usually introduces himself as Detective Homes," he says.

My heart races, and I can distinctly hear it beating. It's pounding so fiercely that it feels like it might explode from my chest. "David?"

"Yes, David," he repeats.

I swallow what feels like a lump in my throat.

"The last time I spoke with him, he mentioned that he was looking into a woman named Sally. He mentioned that the people in town were behaving strangely and mentioned something about a woman named Alice."

"I'm a woman named Alice," I whisper, barely able to get my words out.

"I spoke with a woman named—" he stops, pulls out a notepad, and looks at something he has written down. "Her name is Sharon. She pointed me in your direction."

My phone buzzes, and I glance at it, seeing Aaron's name flash across the screen. At this point, I'm not sure if I should answer because I can barely get my words out to the other Detective Homes.

"David..." I begin to say, but stop and look down at my hands, which are now shaking. "David isn't here."

"So he left? So he's okay?" he asks eagerly.

I shake my head and lower my gaze.

"No, he isn't here because..." I'm unsure how to tell him his brother is dead. "He isn't here because he is dead."

The other Detective Homes glances left, then right. I can see that his heart has become heavy by this revelation. He shuts his eyes tightly as if trying to block out the world and tilts his head toward the sky. When he finally lowers his head, he grips the bridge of his nose, fighting back tears that threaten to pour out of his eyes; the weight of his sorrow is almost too much to bear.

I slowly get out of my car and place my hand on his shoulder. "I'm so sorry."

This Detective Homes is much more muscular than his brother. He doesn't look like anything could make him cry. But losing a brother—heck, losing a sibling at all—must hurt. For normal families, that is, I couldn't care less about Cameron's death. He deserved that.

My phone buzzes again, and I glance at it and notice that Aaron is calling again. I press the button on the side to silence the call.

"What happened?" he asks. His facial expression has shifted from sorrowful to one that is dark and foreboding. "Why did this Sharon lady point me in your direction, and who is this Sally lady, anyway?"

I can tell at this point that he has quickly gone through some stages of grief. Now, he is in the stage of anger. "Do you need a minute?"

"No," he says softly, but in a way that lets me know this guy isn't playing. He is pissed, and his tone lets me know that if I don't tell him what he wants to know, he will blow a gasket. "No, I don't need a minute. I need to know what happened, how you are involved, and who this Sally person is."

"I honestly don't think you'll believe me, Detective..."

"Mike," he interrupts. "Call me Mike. I'm not on official business. Not yet, at least."

"Okay," I say softly, lifting my head towards the heavens the same way Big John is doing, hoping the Lord above will give me the strength to explain this story. "Okay, Mike, how about we take a seat in my car? I'll tell you everything."

CHAPTER 46

— · —

Mike's gaze pierces through me, filled with an intensity that unsettles me. At this moment, I'm at a loss for words—does he seem freaked out from what I told him, or does he believe I'm insane? For anyone unfamiliar with this town and its people, I can completely understand why they might dismiss my story as a mere fabrication of an overactive imagination. If I'm honest with myself, there are moments when I pinch my skin, wishing and hoping that I might jolt awake from this surreal nightmare that seems all too real.

Mike looks out the passenger-side window as if he is still trying to piece together my story. "So you're telling me one woman and her two sons hypnotized an entire town, including yourself and your sister?"

I nod, "Yes."

"And my brother did not get hypnotized, but he willingly stayed here to try to solve this mystery?" he asks.

I nod again. "That's correct?"

"And your dead brother, stabbed him, but you are not certain what happened to his body?" he also asks.

When he says it like that, I would also think something was off about my story. I'm not sure how I can convince him that his brother is dead. He didn't move when he hit the ground, and he lost a lot of blood. *There's no way he could have survived that, could he?*

"Look, that night, my kids' lives were in jeopardy, and your brother died..."

"You think he died." He quickly shifts his gaze and locks eyes with me.

"Right," I nod in agreement, even though I'm pretty sure he is dead. He has to be dead. "He did what he swore to do under oath."

"What's that supposed to mean? He didn't swear under oath just to get caught up in some hypnosis nonsense." He rubs his temples and looks back out the passenger-side window.

I attempt to put myself in his position right now. He arrived here to locate his brother and seek answers. Yet, a nagging thought lingers: *We never went back to check on David.* It fills me with dread. What type of person neglects to check on the person who saved their life? Mike will go home with a bunch of dead-end questions and a bizarre story about a woman who had hypnotized her town.

My phone buzzes again, and I glance at it and notice it's Aaron calling again. *What does he want?* I click the button on the side again to stop the vibration, and this time, I shoot him a text.

> **Me:** Hey, is everything okay?

> **Aaron:** Where are you?

> **Me:** I'll be home shortly.

> **Aaron:** Are you okay?

> **Me:** I'll be home shortly.

I put my phone in the cup holder and glance at Mike. He's continuing to stare out the window, and I can only imagine what's going through his head. I place my hand on Mike's shoulder, "I'm sorry I can't be of more help, but if it helps, I can take you where this all started."

He quickly shifts his focus back to me. "When?"

CHAPTER 47

— · —

We agreed to meet tonight on top of the hill at Lily-Ann's house. I told him we were near her house on a dirt road when his brother was stabbed. That will forever be a road that will haunt my dreams. I'll never get the image out of my head of Cameron plunging the knife deep into David's stomach. I'm not thrilled to be visiting that area again, but if it helps give his brother closure, I'm willing to take that trip one last time.

I pull into my driveway and notice Aaron sitting on the front porch swing. I get out of my car and slowly close the car door. He looks slightly upset, or at least like something is on his mind.

"What are you doing out here?" I ask, smiling at him.

"Where were you?" he asks, looking down at his fingers.

Okay?

"I had to take care of something. Is everything okay?" I ask cautiously as I slowly walk up the porch steps. I can tell something is bothering him. "You called me a couple of times."

He lifts his head, catches my gaze, and holds up three fingers.

"What does that mean?" I ask.

"I called you three times to be exact," he says.

"Right, three times," I repeat.

At this point, I'm confused about why he is acting like this. Yes, he called me three times, but I'm not his child. Heck, I'm not even his girlfriend. Why is he freaking out on me like this?

"I was trying to make sure you were okay," he explains.

What is that supposed to mean? I texted him back, so clearly, I was just fine. At this point, he is starting to freak me out.

"What do you mean?" I ask softly, slowly stepping towards him.

"Really, Alice?" He jumps to his feet, and now I have to look up at him. "There's a burglar still out there, and you're just running around like this person didn't target your house."

I'm at a loss for words. Who is this person, and what did he do with Aaron? "I'm... I'm sorry, I didn't know you felt this strongly about it."

"Really?" He points to the spot where he was shot. "What do you mean you didn't know I felt this strongly? I was freaking shot protecting you and the kids."

He's right. He was shot protecting us, but I can't live my life in fear. I'm grateful for him being here, but maybe he's been here too long; perhaps it's time I get my house back. Maybe it's time Aaron goes home.

I hold up my hands in surrender. "Look, I'm sorry for down-playing it. I feel like I can't..." I stop, realizing my error. "We can't live in fear. We would be giving this person exactly what they want."

"And what's that?" he asks.

"For us to be afraid," I say.

"Look, I'm sorry for freaking out like this. I just wanted to make sure you were okay. You, Sarah, and the kids are all I've got. Y'all are

214

the closest thing I have to family here," he explains. "This guy could be anyone. You have to be careful who you are talking to."

I gently place my hand on his arm, realizing I had no idea he felt this way. The truth is, I've never been shot before, and the thought of it is overwhelming, especially for someone else. I can see that my carelessness might be putting him on edge, and it breaks my heart. I can't help but feel like the worst friend right now, wishing I could ease the silent battle he is having within himself. "You're right, and I probably should stop keeping secrets from you and Sarah."

"Secrets?"

"Yes, I went to the facility today to talk to Sharon, and she told me something very disturbing," I explain. "She said..."

Aaron lifts a finger to silence me, "Hold up, let me get Sarah. She needs to hear this, too."

***

IT TOOK MORE THAN AN HOUR, to explain to the two of them what Sharon had told me about Beth. Both of them were just as stunned as I was. I think the fact that there were two people in this town years ago who could have been more dangerous than Lily-Ann is mind-blowing.

I also came clean about Mike and mentioned that I told him to meet me at the top of the hill tonight. Neither of them liked the idea, but they both knew that once my mind is made up about something, nothing can change it. They agreed to come with me so I wouldn't have to meet with some stranger alone at a big, creepy mansion at night.

"Mom, can I..." Kandice steps outside onto the porch, surprised to see the three of us out here. "Is everything okay? The three of you look like y'all just got the news that someone in the family died."

I scrunch my eyebrows.

Kandice quickly places her hand over her mouth, as if stunned by something. She then peeks into the house and screams for Adam to come here.

"What now? I've done all my chores, snitch," Adams says aggressively, quickly realizing his mistake when he steps outside and notices I'm back home and standing on the front porch.

"I told you he's always being rude to me, Mom," Kandice rolls her eyes and crosses her arms. "Anyway, I was calling you to come down because someone died, and I think it's Grandma."

"What?" I have no idea where she got that assumption.

"Grandma died?" Adam asks.

"N..." I try to reply, but I'm interrupted.

"I mean, grown-ups only look this way when someone dies, and the only other family we got that's near death is her," Kandice says.

"No, your grandmother is not..." I try to explain, but I'm interrupted again.

"I mean, people don't live forever. She is kind of old, and old people do die one day, right?" Adam is thinking too much into this.

"Oh yeah, wasn't she like in her seventies?" Kandice says.

"Sixties to be exact, but..." I still can't get a word in.

Adam snaps his fingers, "Maybe she died of old age, I heard that was a thing."

"Guys, please, your Grandmother is not dead!" I say quickly.

"Wait, I haven't seen Mr. Gerald in a while," Adam chimes in.

216

"N..." Before I can say anything, I'm interrupted again.

"Oh snap, Mom, is it Mr. Gerald? Please tell me it's not Mr. Gerald?" Kandice asks, placing her hand over her mouth. It actually looks like tears are getting ready to form in her eyes.

"Stop!" I shout. "No one is dead. We were talking about something very important. Now what did you need, Kandice?"

"Oh, why didn't you just say that from the beginning, Mom?" she says nonchalantly.

These kids are going to be the death of me.

I glance at Sarah and Aaron; they are eating this up. Both of them have the biggest grins on their faces. They think this is funny. I give the two of them the look I would give my kids when they know they are in big trouble.

"I'm sorry," Sarah mouths and draws an invisible line over her lips, indicating she is zipping her lips.

"What did you need, sweetie?" I ask Kandice.

"I wanted to see if I could go to the park with Jenny tonight? They're doing the movie in the park tonight."

This is actually perfect. I have to meet Mike tonight, and if Kandice is out with her friend, then I don't have to worry about dinner. They can grab something while they're out. I start to tell her yes when something else dawns on me: what about Adam?

"How about this, you can go, but you have to take your brother," I say.

"What?" she whines.

"I will give you some money so you guys can grab something to eat while y'all are at the park. Besides, he needs to get out of the house."

"What about you?" she asks.

217

"Well, not that it's any of your business, but that's what the three of us were talking about. We have to do something tonight, and I won't be home for a few hours," I explain.

Kandice sighs, "Fine. But can you add a babysitting tip since I'll have to watch him and keep him out of trouble all night?"

"That's how you do it, my niece, negotiate what you want, girl," Sarah says jokingly.

I roll my eyes, "Please, somebody shoot me and take me out of my misery."

"Don't say that too loud; there is still a burglar on the loose," Aaron reminds me, as if I needed a reminder that someone else has tried to harm my family. But he is right; maybe I shouldn't say that too loudly. My mother used to tell us that our words have power.

I suppose she forgot that we had no power; she had taken it away from us. We hardly spoke because if we said the wrong thing, she would twist it against us. She acted as both judge and jury. We were doomed regardless of what we did.

CHAPTER 48

— • —

We're sitting in the car, observing the scene around us. It's dark, and there is a full moon tonight. The trees look extremely intimidating, and even with the windows up, I can hear crunching sounds in the shadows of the night. It's definitely an animal, but this makes it out to be the perfect scene in a scary movie.

Three people are sitting in a car parked on top of a hill, waiting to enter an abandoned mansion, which I'm sure is full of dead bodies rotting away. The moon is also perfectly full, so the crazies are even crazier tonight. The killer would probably be lurking somewhere in the woods waiting for us to enter, just so that he can slit all of our throats one by one.

Bang! Bang!

I'm startled, and instantly my spirit must have jumped out of my body. I can see Mike standing at the car door, banging on the window, waving for us to come out. Maybe this is what death actually feels like. Maybe when I do die, my spirit will be looking back at me, wondering why the hell I took my black behind up there. My spirit will probably also be wondering what I was thinking by agreeing to meet a stranger I had just met at my mother's possibly haunted mansion.

"Alice?"

"Yes!" I jump from the feeling of someone touching my arm.

"Is...is that the guy you were talking to earlier?" Aaron asks, thankfully interrupting me from my intrusive thoughts. "Where did you say he is from again?"

"Sorry, yes, that's him," I say quickly. "Um, I think he said Atlanta. Why?" I ask as I swing the car door open, almost hitting Mike.

"Is everything okay?" Mike asks as he backs up to give me room to step out of the car.

"Yes, sorry, I was just daydreaming, I guess," I say, embarrassed to have been caught imagining myself in a horror movie.

Mike nods; he's probably asking himself the same questions I am. *Why did I agree to come up here?* I'm sure he thinks I'm just as deranged as my mother at this point, after telling him I was daydreaming.

"This is my sister and my friend. Sister and friend, this is Mike," I say.

"Nice to meet you two," he says, extending his hand to shake theirs, and Sarah is quick to offer hers, but Aaron isn't as generous. He places his hands in his pockets and gives a quick head nod. Aaron isn't very trusting of Mike, and I guess he has every right to be. I mean, it is a little odd that he wanted to come at night.

"So this is where our mother lives, well, lived, and this is pretty much the last place we all saw your brother," I say. "Well, this isn't the exact spot, but it's close."

"Can we go inside?" Mike asks.

"I don't think that's a good idea," Aaron says quickly. "I mean, it's dark. Do we really need to go in there? It's a little creepy out here."

I honestly can't believe what I'm seeing right now. Aaron has to be all of six feet tall. No, he doesn't have muscles as big as Mike's, but he's no scrawny guy. I'm sure with Sarah and me, if Mike did turn out to be a crazy person, it wouldn't be hard to take him.

"Can I talk to you for a second?" I ask Aaron.

Sarah and Mike scrunch their eyebrows. I can tell they're both confused about why I need to step away to talk to Aaron when we just got here.

"It'll just be a second, I promise, guys," I reassure them.

Aaron and I walk to the back of the car, and I'm a little frustrated now, "What. Is. Wrong."

"Alice, I'm all for helping people, but how much do you really know about this guy. You just agreed to meet him here at night, of all times. I mean, who does that? And now he wants to go inside an abandoned mansion. Really? The red flags aren't going up in your head?" Aaron protests.

I look over at Mike and Sarah and notice them chatting. From the body language, I'd say he was hitting on her if this were any other situation, but given the intense situation, I highly doubt that's what is going on.

"Look, his brother died from helping us. I owe it to this man to get closure for his brother. The least I could do is let him look around for a bit," I whisper. "It's not like he will find anything."

Aaron looks over his shoulder and notices Mike chatting with Sarah. He points to them and says, "I want you to look at what you're gambling with right now, Alice. Your sister's life could be on the line right now if that dude isn't who he says he is."

I hate that he is right. I'm not sure if Mike is really David's brother. All I have to go by is that they both have the same last name and resemble each other. Not to mention, he is a detective, but he could also be the psycho killer in my thoughts that was lurking in the woods, waiting for us to get out of the car. I peek over Aaron's shoulder, and my eyes are instantly widened by what I see on Mike's belt buckle.

"Holy crap, he has a gun," I whisper.

Aaron looks over his shoulder and notices the same thing. "See what I'm saying. What does he need to meet you up here for, and why does he have a gun?"

"Wait," I say as something has dawned on me, and I have a light bulb moment. "Aaron, he's a detective, of course he has a gun." Aaron's paranoia is starting to rub off on me. Had I been thinking straight, I would have said that when he mentioned the gun. "Look, if it makes you feel better, let's at least give the man ten minutes to look around. I already know his brother is dead; he just needs closure."

Aaron rubs his head and paces back and forth for a second.

"Okay, but if he shows even the slightest sign of being a nut job, I'm taking him down," he warns.

At this point, his confidence is intriguing. I'm sure he could probably take him down with his adrenaline pumping, but Mike is not normal. This guy looks like he was taken off the stage of one of those bodybuilder shows and placed right here in Shelly Grove. But Aaron is right. If he does turn out to be the psycho killer I was daydreaming about, there will only be three of us who will come down from this hill tonight.

CHAPTER 49

— · —

T he house looks the same as it did the night I came up here alone. The tree limbs look like snakes wrapped around the porch railing. The bushes are growing high, covering the windows, and the same light on the porch is still flickering on and off. *We must be crazy coming back to this place.*

When I open the door, dust instantly tickles my nose hair, causing me to sneeze. This place has not seen a living person in months... well, technically, a few days ago when Beth showed up. But who's counting?

"So, is there any particular place you'd like to look?" I ask Mike. "This is a huge house."

Mike glances at me briefly and then scans the house. "Does she have an office?"

I begin to deny the presence of an office in this house, because our mom spent all her time outside of this place, torturing other people. She was always in others' business; she definitely didn't have time to keep up with an office. But something hits me, and at this point, I can't help but think that Mike may be on to something. "She doesn't have an office..."

Mike scans the room once again, looking for another place to start.

"But her husband did," I say quickly before he can get lost in his thoughts. Trust me, I know how that is. I often get lost in my thoughts. "He used to stay in there all the time, working."

Perhaps he was never really working in there. Maybe he was in there for show. Whatever his purpose was behind those closed doors, it couldn't have been anything good. Our mother hypnotized him into thinking he was her husband, for God's sake. Who knows what kind of twisted stuff she made him do?

"Is this the office?" Mike asks as he slowly opens one of the doors to a room downstairs and flips the switch to turn on the light. "I mean, it surely looks like an office."

Inside, there is a cherry wood desk that seems sturdier than the house at the moment. A wardrobe closet sits tucked in the corner beside a large, dark brown leather La-Z-Boy recliner. The office is equipped with blackout curtains, which make the room look even darker at night. A bookshelf stretches all the way to the ceiling and is filled with hundreds of books. *Did Lily-Ann like to read?*

We scatter as we enter the office. I check out the bookshelf, curious to see if this is another trick door. Aaron heads toward the wardrobe closet. Mike examines the desk, and my darling sister, of course, decides she wants to see how comfy the La-Z-Boy is.

"Sis, why didn't we take this chair with us?" Sarah asks. "I would sleep like a baby in this chair. Maybe that's why Mr. Gerald stayed in this office so much. He'd rather sleep in here than with his devilish wife."

I chuckle.

"Alice, have you seen this?" Mike asks as he holds up a black book.

"What is that?" I ask.

"I'm not sure, but it has formulas and dates. It has articles that date back to the 1940s," he says.

"Formulas? Articles? Dates?" I'm confused and can't understand what this all means.

"Didn't you tell me that Mr. Gerald was doing his own research at one point?" Aaron speaks up. "Maybe that was his journal or his research."

"You could be right," Sarah says quickly. "And he was in here a lot. He knew something wasn't right, not just two years ago, but going all the way back to when our grandparents were around."

Mike continues shuffling through the desk and comes across several papers that sit inside a white folder. I notice the look of concern on his face, and I instantly feel horrible. This isn't good for any of us being back in this house, but for him, I know this has to be killing him, trying to find answers about his brother.

I place my hand on his shoulder, "I'm really sorry about David. Do you think we should look somewhere else?"

Mike doesn't respond; his eyes are fixed on the papers in the white folder.

"Mike..."

He still doesn't move, continuing to flip through the papers. His eyes have grown wider, and at this point, I'm starting to worry about him. This poor man is traumatized and has completely checked out.

"Mike!" I say again, a little louder this time. He doesn't move. He continues flipping through the papers.

Concern grows on my face, and Sarah and Aaron notice it. They are only here for me and couldn't care less about Mike. They know how much this means to me, helping this man get closure, but at the moment, he is starting to worry me. He is flipping through the pages like a madman, and honestly, what could he really find about his brother in a white folder that has probably been here since our grandparents were living?

"Mike!" Aaron yells, and with more bass in his voice than I have.

Mike lifts his head and catches Aaron's gaze, "Sorry, uh, what did you say your name was again?"

"It's Aaron," I say, interrupting.

"Got it, sorry, man, I just..." Mike pauses.

"It's okay, you were just flipping through the pages like a madman and completely zoned out," I say, interrupting him. "Is everything okay? Is this all too much? We can leave and come back another day."

"No!" he says quickly. " I mean, no, it's okay. I'm okay. I just found some paperwork about this house."

I scrunch my eyebrows.

"What about the house?" I ask.

"I'm not sure," he says, scanning the room, making eye contact with each of us. "I think I need to send this information off, though. If this is what I think it is, maybe I can have more answers for you girls about your mom and grandparents."

"Yes, please take what you need," I say. "I have concluded that we come from a jacked-up background, but it couldn't hurt to find out exactly how messed up our family really is."

Aaron gives me a look that indicates he disagrees with my decision. We still have many questions about our parents, and if Mike believes he can help, I support it. I match Aaron's energy and return the same look. He hasn't seen what we've endured; he only knows the watered-down story I shared. However, if he saw the determination

226

in our mother's eyes to kill us, he would understand why I'm willing to accept help.

Mike rolls up the folder the best he can and sticks it in his back pocket, and at this point, I feel it's time we move on to check out another area of the house. There's something about this room that gives me the creeps. Maybe it's the way Mike was flipping through the papers like the words possessed him. Perhaps it's knowing that Mr. Gerald was in here day and night researching our family. Whatever the reason, it's unsettling.

Aaron and Sarah are the first to leave the office, while Mike attempts to arrange the desk back to its original order as if Lily-Ann herself were going to come back in here to examine it. As I reach for the switch to turn off the lights, I observe that something seems to be troubling Mike. At this moment, I begin to think that he has more on his mind than just concerns about his brother.

"Mike?"

He catches my gaze, and this time, the fear is unmistakable. Mike's face shows pure dread, yet he stays completely still, as if frozen by the silence. His fear's heavy presence lingers in the air, suffocating, and I can't shake the uneasy feeling that something is terribly wrong.

"We need to talk," he says, leaving me questioning the real reason we are here.

CHAPTER 50

— · —

The basement will always be the place in this house that I dread the most. My children were almost killed down there. I was nearly killed down there. I was forced to give in to my mother's demands in the basement. I hate her for putting me in that predicament, and of all places, Aaron and Sarah have decided it would be best that we check the basement next.

"Sis, if it's too much for you, we don't have to go down there again. I just figured if Lily-Ann were going to store a dead body anywhere in this house, it wouldn't be Mr. Gerald's office," Sarah explains. "I think it would be the basement."

As much as I hate to say she's right, she does have a point. Checking the office was a little odd, but it was clear that Mike had found something. The last words he said to me before we left the office keep echoing through my mind: *We need to talk.* I'm curious what he wants to speak to me about, and what has him so frightened?

"Mike, are you okay with checking the basement?" I ask before taking another step towards the trick bookshelf doors.

"It's fine. At this point, I don't put anything past your mother," he protests.

Sounds like something I would say. Is he sure he doesn't know Lily-Ann?

Each of us turns on our cell phone flashlights, recalling that the only source of light in the basement hallway is a single dangling light bulb. We carefully descend the stairs, taking the steps one by one. I'm not sure what we will find down here. I've never really had the time to search the basement. I mean, who would want to?

We slowly make our way through the basement, approaching the area where the hallway splits. I recall that if we go left, it would be the area where my children were dangling over a pool of water. It is also the same area where James held a gun to Sarah's head.

"Should...should we go this way?" I ask hesitantly. I haven't seen this part of the basement since that day. I wouldn't put it past our mother, though, to store David in that same area. She would do anything to torture me. What better way to do so than to store the one person who almost got us out of here in the same area where she nearly killed her grandkids? She is still finding ways to torture my thoughts, and she isn't even walking the streets of Shelly Grove anymore.

Beep. Beep. Beep.

Before taking another step, I'm startled by the emergency alert siren going off on my phone. I don't get the chance to glance at the message because the alarm sounds again.

Beep. Beep. Beep.

I look around and notice the alert is also going off on their phones. *What's going on?* Nothing serious has ever happened in this town that warrants an emergency alert.

"Oh my God." Sarah is looking at her cell phone, and even though I can't see her face, the tone of her voice tells me something horrible just happened.

Breaking news flashes across my cellphone screen, and we rush for the exit in the basement. Once we are back inside the house, I click on the alert that says, "Two DOA, and two patients missing."

"They confirmed two people are dead?" Sarah whimpers. "What happened? Where is this at?"

I open the app on my phone that allows me to view the local news. As I flip through the channels, I notice this has made the top news. *This is a small town; what could make top news around here?* Every news station is reporting on this. I click on one of the news stations and widen the screen so we can all see what's going on.

A light-skinned lady with honey-blond hair and hazel eyes appears on screen. This is definitely live, because it's the middle of the night, and she's wearing a teal shirt and blue jeans. Most news anchors are always dressed to impress, and in her case, I can tell she just threw on something to report what's going on in town.

Flames and more flames. The flames are so high that it's almost unbelievable that only two people were killed. It's like a scene from one of those rescue shows. Ambulances, firetrucks, and police cars are everywhere. Firefighters are rushing to the hydrants to plug in their hoses, and people are being dragged away from the burning building.

"Where is this place?" Aaron asks. "This is horrible. You don't see stuff like this in small towns. You only see this in big cities."

Mike shoots him an annoyed glance.

"Are they saying where this is?" Sarah asks.

I can't make out the building because of all the flames, and the cameraman has it zoomed in so close I can't see what's around it.

"I can't tell," I say as my eyes frantically scan the scene displayed on my phone.

"Try another station?" Mike suggests.

I click the back button on my app and exit the news station, then scroll through the channels. This time, there is a white woman with brown hair who is also not dressed to impress at the moment. She is wearing what appears to be a pair of leggings and an oversized t-shirt. It seems that she is standing in a parking lot, and the camera has a much better view of the entire area.

My eyes widen, and my heart feels as if it has stopped altogether. Big John, with his wigs spread wide and his arms raised as if he is reaching for the heavens, sits in front of a building that is engulfed in flames. It's the facility—the very place where our mother dwells. A chilling wave crashes over me like a tidal wave of dread. The emergency alert that flashed across my screen haunts me: two people dead before the first responders even arrived, and two patients unaccounted for, vanished into the chaos. *Who are the two deceased? And who are the two missing patients?* My mind races, frantically piecing together the horror unfolding before me, as the grim reality sets in.

CHAPTER 51

—·—

"Two people who had been unidentified were confirmed dead when first responders arrived on the scene here at the Shelly Grove Psychiatric Facility. At the moment, all we know about these two victims is that one is a Jane Doe and the other is a John Doe," the news anchor says while holding her hand up to her earpiece.

"Thanks, Sherry. Have they identified the two patients who have been unaccounted for? Is it possible they were... you know, killed in the fire?" A black man asks as the screen switches to a news set for Channel Eleven News, where he and a female anchor sit around a desk as they interview the white woman reporting from the scene of the fire.

"Thanks, Dale. As of right now, they aren't saying anything because they are still trying to get staff members and patients out of the blast zone," the woman says, who is at the scene of the fire.

I'm gripping my phone tightly as my eyes follow every patient that is caught on camera. None of them are Lily-Ann. The fire is a tragedy, but knowing my mother may be one of those missing patients is a nightmare. If she were to get out, there is no denying her first stop would be—

Then it hits me, and my heart has stopped beating. I can't breathe, and at this point, I'm sure my melanin complexion has turned completely pale.

"Jesus, Alice, are you okay?" Mike asks.

My hands are trembling, and I can't get out a single word. Inside my mind, I'm screaming, yet no sound escapes. I'm paralyzed. I sense someone shaking me, but I'm in shock. I can't hear anything now. Everything is a total blur. The world has come to a standstill around me.

"Alice?"

My phone drops out of my hand, and I can feel my feet moving at this point. Tears are forming in my eyes, and my body is completely numb. It feels like I'm floating through the house as I make my way towards the front door.

"Alice?"

Out of nowhere, a burning sensation spreads across my face, and my vision returns. My sister stands before me, her expression frantic as she shakes my arms and calls my name.

"Alice, are you okay?" she asks.

"Sarah, you didn't have to slap her!" Aaron yells. "Jesus, Alice, are you alright?"

"Well, I didn't know what to do, so I slapped her. That's what they do in the movies," she explains. "It looks like it worked."

I slowly bring my hand up to my cheek and try to rub away the fiery feeling. "My..."

"I'm so sorry, sis. I know your face probably burns," Sarah says.

"No, My..." I'm breathing out of control, and I can't get my words out. I feel myself getting ready to have a panic attack because right now, I know there is nothing I can do. I'm at the top of the hill in this godawful place, and who knows how long she has been gone from the facility? It is weird that the building mysteriously goes up in flames, and all of a sudden, two patients are missing. I can almost guarantee that one of the two missing is Lily-Ann.

Sadly, our mother doesn't have a heart, and because of what I've done to her. She will not hold back this time. Instead of chaining my kids up, she would probably connect them to an anchor and drop them off the side of a boat somewhere. She would probably cut my eyelids off and force me to watch as my two babies sink to the bottom, and after several minutes, when we know for a fact that they are not going to make it, she would probably put a bullet in my skull. Then again, she also knows how much I despise her, so killing me would be an honor to get away from her. She would probably chain me up in the basement, forcing me to stay close to her.

Tears are streaming down my cheeks as the words finally escape my lips: "My kids! Oh God, my kids!"

CHAPTER 52

— · —

The fire at the Shelly Grove Psychiatric Facility has rocked the entire town. From what I've heard, firefighters from multiple districts responded to help. They worked all through the night trying to extinguish the blaze. I'm no firefighter, nor am I an arson expert, but that was a pretty large fire for an accident. The building, according to what I've heard, is a total loss. Surprisingly, Big John is still hanging in there; maybe whoever he is reaching out to really extend a helping hand.

After making it home last night, I found my kids doing what they always do when they have the house to themselves. Adam was locked in on a Roblox game, and Kandice was scrolling through TikTok, checking out her next greatest read from someone on something called BookTok. Not one hair on either of their heads was touched, and it didn't look like anyone had tried to get into the house. They were safe, and that was my biggest concern last night, but now that I know they are alive and well, it's still unclear who the two missing patients are.

You can tell something horrific has happened. There's an underlying heaviness in the air, reminding the residents of Shelly Grove that a tragedy has unfolded in our area. The sky is overcast, casting a gloomy gray hue over everything, and it has been raining steadily all day, creating a damp, dreary atmosphere. *Perhaps the firefighters would have appreciated the rain last night; it might have helped them better control the flames.*

I grab my robe hanging on the back of my bathroom door and head for the kitchen, knowing that to get through this day, I'll need a strong cup of coffee to ignite some energy and clear my mind. I've finally figured out how to turn the timer off on my coffee maker, for those days when I don't want it to start brewing automatically.

As I wait for my coffee to brew, my cellphone vibrates in the pocket of my robe, and I immediately stop at the breaking news alert flashing across my screen. I click on the alert, and the daily news report appears, highlighting the fire that occurred at the facility last night.

This is the aftermath of a tragic fire. The fire has shaken the people of Shelly Grove. "We haven't had a tragedy of this size in years," Martha Johnson stated. She is a native of Shelly Grove. The two deceased have yet to be identified. All we know is that one is a Jane Doe and the other is a John Doe. Authorities are asking if you have a loved one in this facility, whether they are an employee or a patient, to please reach out to the local police station to facilitate the identification process for everyone who may have been in the building during last night's fire. They are currently checking names off the list as people call in to give information about their loved ones, as we speak.

"I was outside walking my little JoeJoe, and next thing I know, there was a loud blast. I didn't know what that was, so I grabbed my little JoeJoe and went into the house. My momma always told me to run first and ask questions later." Mary Daniels, a local of Shelly Grove, Stated. As for the two missing, authorities are still unsure of who the two missing patients are. They are currently going through the camera footage. They are encouraging the community to review the images attached to this article. If you recognize either of them, please call your local police department. This facility houses not just sick patients, but sick patients who are labeled as very dangerous to themselves and to others.

As I scroll down to the bottom of the article, my eyes confirm what I suspected. There are two women dressed in white gowns. One woman appears to be in her eighties or possibly early nineties. Her face is very clear because she is looking back toward the facility. She looks familiar, but I can't figure out where I have seen her before. The area is well lit, but one thing stands out in this image: there is no fire.

The other lady in the image, whose face is not visible, has brown hair. She is holding the elderly woman's hand as if she is trying to guide her away from the facility. However, something about this feels completely wrong. Perhaps she isn't trying to guide the elderly woman at all. As I zoom in on the picture, I examine the elderly woman's expression more closely. Rather than appearing content to leave that dreadful place, the opposite seems true. What I see etched on her face is pure fear.

My coffee maker chimes, signaling that my coffee is ready. I reach for a mug and pour myself a cup, watching as the steam rises and drifts in the air. It takes my mind back to this specific day when my siblings and

I were younger. I will never forget this particular day. Mrs. Joan, who was our mother's supposed friend, came over to bring her little Toby. Apparently, she had a church retreat for the weekend, which was held in our town, so I couldn't wrap my mind around why Toby needed a sitter. She claimed she would be gone all day and asked our mother if my siblings and I could watch little Toby.

"Here is his bag, sweetie," Mrs. Joan said to me. "Make sure you feed him twice a day. He only likes to be fed out of his blue bowl with the puppies."

"Got it," I said.

"Can he sit in my bed?" Sarah's eyes widened with excitement.

Mrs. Joan chuckled, "Sweetie, he would love that. I let little Toby sit on my bed all the time. He is bathed and his teeth are brushed daily, so he is the cleanest dog you'll ever meet."

I believed her. Toby was a little white Yorkie Poo. His fur was white as snow. Mrs. Joan loved that dog. She treated it better than a child should be treated. Toby got the ultimate royal treatment every day, if you asked me. He had his own room, with pictures of himself plastered on every wall. She even had one right above his bed, which was made up every day with a fluffy pillow and a small blanket.

She bought him these small ice cream cups, which were specifically designed for dogs and sold at the grocery store. Rumor had it that she even had little Toby in her will to get all her money when she passed away. There was no denying that this lady loved Toby. Is it so bad that I used to wish that I were Toby and my mother loved me this way?

"Mrs. Joan!" James called out excitedly, his smile so big that we could see all his teeth, even the empty spots where he had lost his baby teeth. "Can I take Toby for a walk?"

She smiled at him, "Sure, sweetie, let me get you his stroller. Toby doesn't like getting his paws dirty."

Sarah, James, and I cherished spending time with Toby. He felt like a bright spot in our lives, almost like a gift that brought us closer. Although James was often treated better than Sarah and me, I could see it always bothered him. The first time he spoke up to our mother, she responded by balling her fist and punching him in the stomach, almost knocking the breath out of him. He was only five years old then, and his small body couldn't handle such a harsh blow. After that, he was terrified of our mother and would do whatever she said, even if it meant Sarah and I would suffer.

Cameron didn't care for animals, so he never helped us take care of Toby. But it killed him to see us laughing and playing with that little snowball. I honestly think he was a little jealous of the somewhat of a bond the three of us had when Toby was around. Maybe if he didn't want to be the only child so badly, he could have enjoyed his childhood with his only siblings. But no, he stayed by our mother's side as much as possible. He probably liked it when Toby came so that he could have Lily-Ann all to himself.

Once Mrs. Joan left, we took Toby to the living room and played with him with the ball she had left in the bag. He was so cute with his little paws and his little mouth trying to get his jaw around the ball. He always did this jumping movement as if he were a rabbit trying to dive after the ball.

Later that night, we put Toby in Sarah's bed, and, like a kid after a nice, hot bath, he was fast asleep. Before heading to bed, I did my nightly routine of using the bathroom several times to avoid having an accident in my bed. Yes, I was twelve at this time, but living with our mother caused me to have nightmares, and with nightmares come accidents.

I walked past Cameron's room and saw him talking to James through the crack in the door. He kept poking aggressively at his chest with his index finger and saying something to him. James didn't look like he was pleased with whatever he was telling him to do. But James also knew better. He knew deep down that if he didn't do what the golden child Cameron told him, he would be placed in the same category as Sarah and me.

I went back to my room and peeped at Toby and Sarah one last time before falling straight to sleep.

***

"ALICE! ALICE! WAKE UP," I was awakened by my teary-eyed sister shaking me out of my sleep.

Yawning, I said, "What's wrong, Sarah?"

"Toby, he's gone," she said frantically.

I quickly jumped up, "What do you mean he's gone? Where is he? Did you check the living room?"

"Yes, and he's not there. He's not anywhere, Alice," she whimpered.

"We can't tell Mom, let's see if he went into our secret room," I instructed her. I'm not sure how he would have gotten in there, because the room door is always shut.

As we quietly tiptoed through the house, something caught my attention outside the house as we walked past the window: flames.

"Is someone burning something outside?" I whispered to Sarah.

She shrugged her shoulders. "It's like midnight, who would be outside other than ghosts?"

I peered out the window, where I saw James and Cameron standing around the fire pit. James had what looked like tears in his eyes, and Cameron had an evil grin on his face. *What are the two of them doing?*

I rushed to the door, swung it open, and ran outside. "What are you two doing?"

"Alice," James whimpered. "I had no choice, I'm sorry."

I was confused and couldn't understand why he was apologizing. "Sorry? For what?"

I switched my gaze to Cameron, who still had the same evil grin on his face. He shrugged his shoulders and said, "I have no idea what this wussy is talking about."

James looked at the fire pit and back at me. He started crying even more and apologized once again.

"I'm so sorry. I'm sorry. I'm sorry. I had no choice. I'm sorry," James cried.

Sarah stepped closer to the fire pit and began to scream, "NO! NO! WHY WOULD YOU DO THAT? WHY?"

At this point, I put two and two together. I didn't have to look inside the fire pit. It was clear to me what I was going to find, and judging by the look on Cameron's face, he was loving every minute of it. He taught James how to start fires so he could be the one to do his dirty work. From that day forward, if anyone needed a fire started, James was the one to call.

Our mother grew to dislike Sarah and me even more after that night. Cameron convinced James to lie and say we started the fire. He claimed that he and James caught us. To make it convincing, Cameron

241

tried to appear emotional, pretending to have tears, but in reality, he had just peeled an onion to make himself cry.

Mrs. Joan was devastated. She loved that little snowball so much that she even held a funeral for him. She was so heartbroken that, a few months after Toby's funeral, she suffered from a heart attack and passed away. We were known from then on as the two crazy kids who started fires and killed old ladies. The people in town hated us, probably just as much as our mother did, and they praised our brothers.

CHAPTER 53

— • —

"Alice, did you see the news?" Sarah says as she enters the kitchen, taking me away from my deep thoughts. \

"Hmm?"

"Did you see the news?" she asks.

I clear my thoughts as I'm finally able to take in what my sister is asking me. "No, I didn't. I just saw the alert on my phone. It was saying what we already knew. Are there any updates?"

Hurrying to the living room, I grab the remote and turn the television to Channel Eleven News. The same Black male anchor and a different female anchor are sitting around the desk, giving a brief run-through of what they will be talking about this morning.

"A fire that strikes the entire town," the male anchor says. "Leaving two deceased and two missing."

"Authorities are looking for an intruder who is still on the run," the female anchor informs the viewers. She must be referring to the person who attempted to break into my house.

"Residents of Florida are bracing themselves for a possible Category four hurricane," the male anchor says.

I'm drawn to the television when Aaron comes downstairs. "Morning, Fam."

I give him a quick wave over my shoulder, still fixated on the television.

"Hey, um," Aaron hesitates. "There's a game Adam wanted to get; it was released this morning."

"Gotcha," I'm not really paying much attention to what he's saying.

"Hey, Mom!" Adam comes down the stairs and plants a kiss on my forehead. "So there's this game that just came out this morning. I really wanted to get it."

I glance at him for a moment, "Don't you have enough games?"

"There's no such thing as having enough games when you're a gamer, Mom," Adam says as if I'm supposed to know this already. "But my real question is, do you think you could buy the game for me today, and you won't have to give me my allowance for the next two months?"

I tilt my head and purse my lips.

"Please..." he begs.

"Fine, but I can't take you right now," I say.

"It's cool, it's cool," Aaron interrupts. "I was going to take him. That is, if it's okay with you."

"Okay," I huff. "Grab my card out of my wallet, use the black one."

"Alright, we'll be back later, hopefully he doesn't try to buy up the whole game store," Aaron chuckles.

Sarah hits my arm to get my attention and points dramatically at the television.

"Look," she says, her eyes wide.

I quickly wave Aaron and Adam off, "Drive safe."

The male anchor informs the viewers that they have just received some new information about Jane Doe and John Doe. He draws our attention to a photo of a heavy-set, older white man. He appears to be in his late fifties or early sixties. He has gray hair and a gray beard.

"Bill Sawyer was the janitor on duty the night of the fire," the male anchor says. "He worked for the facility for fifteen years. Locals say he was a kind man. He would give his shirt right off his back for anyone in need. He leaves behind his loving wife Thelma Sawyer, and his two kids, Jane White, and Bill Sawyer Jr."

"What a tragedy, Dale," the female anchor says, shaking her head with a look of remorse on her face.

The following image shows a black woman with bone-straight hair. Her smile is wide and bright, revealing all her white teeth. For a minute, it doesn't click as I continue to stare at the screen.

"Oh my God!" Sarah says, clasping her hand over her mouth.

The screen displays a picture of our friend Sharon's graduation photo. She smiles brightly with excitement, celebrating her achievement of finishing nursing school.

"Sharon Wright was the facility's main nurse. Locals describe her as also being kind, outgoing, and a hard worker. She leaves behind her parents, Brent and Mary Wright," the male anchor says.

"This is a sad day, Dale. Two lives lost at the hands of an arsonist," the female anchor says.

Arsonist?

My phone vibrates on the counter, and I'm instantly startled by the sound. I rush back to the kitchen and pick up my phone. I notice I have a new notification. I stare into the screen so the face recognition notices me, so that it can unlock my phone. I have a new text from Mike. He went home to Atlanta last night and told us he would be in touch once his team looked into some information about our family. *That was quick,* I thought.

> **Mike:** Hey, do you have a minute?

> **Me:** Sure, what's up?

> **Mike:** Can I call you?

> **Me:** Yeah, no problem at all.

> **Mike:** Are you alone and sitting down?

I glance up and remember that Sarah is standing in the room with me. Before I can respond, my phone starts to vibrate in my hand. I have an incoming call, and 'Shelly Grove PD' is displayed across the screen. *Oh God, what now?*

CHAPTER 54

— · —

I answer the phone and put the call on speaker. I wave my hand quickly to get my sister's attention, signaling for her to come over. We both sit at the table as I finally greet whoever is calling me from the police station.

"Hello," I say cautiously.

"Hey, Alice, this is Detective Hudson from Shelly Grove PD. You got a second to chat?" He has a strong southern accent with one of those voices that lets me know he could be a smoker.

I look up at Sarah, feeling slightly nervous about responding. I have no idea who this person is or why they are calling me, but if it has anything to do with the two who are missing, I'm all ears.

"Uh... hi, Detective," I say nervously. "What can I do for you?"

"Sorry, I'm sure this is a little awkward. We don't know each other," he says. "Yet that is."

I swallow hard.

"Anyway, I was brought in because I'm sure you've heard by now about the fire at the Shelly Grove Psychiatric Facility," he pauses, as if waiting for me to say something.

"Uh-huh," I'm not sure what to say in this situation.

He falls silent for a moment, as if expecting me to say more. Then he coughs forcefully, as if something is lodged in his chest, or more like a smoker's cough.

"Anyways, my team was brought in to help with the investigation of the fire. I've been getting calls all day from people checking on their loved ones. So far, we have everyone accounted for, but two people," he explains. "I also notice we don't have your name checked off as a person who has called in to check on your loved one."

I'm at a loss for words and unsure what he wants me to say. The person in that facility is incapable of being loved. A part of me wishes she were the Jane Doe so I could stop having to sleep with one eye open every night. A part of me wishes she had died in that fire because maybe all these bad memories will go up in flames with her. But the reality is she is still alive, and a part of me believes she is one of the two who got away.

I close my eyes and take a deep breath.

"You all move fast. The fire just happened last night," I say. "But I hadn't had the chance to call yet, because my main concern was my kids. I wanted to make sure they were okay. I wasn't home when I got the notification about the fire."

"I see," he says.

I receive a beep and notice it's an incoming call. It's Mike, and at this moment, I realize I didn't respond to him, but he will have to wait. I'm desperate to hear what the Detective has to say, so I click the button that sends Mike to my voicemail. *He will leave a message, I'm sure, if it's important.*

"I was planning to go to the police station today to talk to someone about the Jane Doe and find out if our mother, Lily-Ann, was okay," I say as I glance at Sarah. "She is a patient there. She was diagnosed with dementia. She's really sick."

Once again, there's silence, and neither of us is saying anything. The only thing you can hear is the sound of our breathing.

"Ma'am," he says sternly as if I just said something wrong. "I'm very good at my job; this is why they've called me in to help with this case. Can you guess why I didn't come to your house personally to talk to you?"

"Um... I'm not sure. Why?" I ask.

It sounds like he sits up in his seat and maybe gets a little closer to the phone.

"Because I pay attention to detail," he says.

What the hell is that supposed to mean? At this point, this Detective is starting to rub me the wrong way. He calls and addresses me as if he knows me, and now I could be overexaggerating, but something tells me he thinks I have something to do with the fire at the facility.

"Um... okay. That's good, I guess, but what does that mean, Detective?"

"You said you were going to come up here to check if your momma was okay..." he pauses.

"Okay, yes, isn't that what you all told us to do?" I ask, still very confused.

"Was is a past tense word, Alice. Most people would ask if their momma is okay," he explains.

I look at Sarah and realize my error. *Shoot.* I don't know if that really was our mother in that picture running away from the facility. My gut tells me it was her, though. Lily-Ann is a brilliant woman. This guy has no idea who he is dealing with. He has no idea what she is capable of.

249

I need to find her before anyone else does. I just need to confirm one more thing.

"Detective Hudson, I didn't realize you were calling me to give me a grammar lesson. Please excuse my error," I say with agitation in my voice. "But my family has been through a lot, and dealing with a loved one with dementia is not easy. So, can you please check your list to see if our mother "IS" okay? She is the only Lil-Ann in this entire town."

Silence fills the air once again, and I can hear him shuffling through some papers. He coughs heavily again, as if trying to dislodge something from his chest.

"Sorry about that," he says. "I've been trying to quit smoking for some time now. Them thangs are addicting."

I figured he was a smoker. I guess I pay attention to detail as well, Detective.

"To answer your question, her name and one other are the only two names that aren't checked off as being marked safe," he explains.

Bingo. I knew that it was her.

"Do you mind coming down to the station?" he asks. "I just have a few questions for you."

A new notification pops up on my screen, and I notice it's a text from Mike. He wants me to call him as soon as possible, but at this point, I'm beginning to get a headache knowing I'll be spending the rest of my Sunday answering Detective Hudson's million and one questions, so I don't respond.

I take a deep breath, "Sure, Detective, give me about thirty minutes and I'll be right there."

CHAPTER 55

— • —

S undays are supposed to be my rest days. I was planning to stay in the house all day and maybe binge-watch something on Netflix. Lucky me, after finding out our mother has not been accounted for, I get to sit in the police station with Detective Hudson, who looks exactly like I imagined—minus the Hollywood glamour. He's an older Black man with a receding hairline, which, if he shaved it and let it all go, might suit him better. His belly protrudes so much that it threatens to pop the buttons on his shirt, risking hitting someone unexpectedly in the eye. At this point, retirement may be an option for him, in my opinion.

He wants me to go over all the possible places Lily-Ann might want to go. The fact that she hasn't come to pay me a visit yet tells me one thing: she's out there, and I know she's watching me. How do I tell him there is only one place she will have in mind to go? People with dementia usually forget who they are and may even forget their family members. Given the situation, I need to play along with him. I need him to believe I am a worried daughter who has no idea where her mother might be. I need him to think she's out there, possibly alone if

251

she's ditched the elderly woman she was with—who, by the way, looks extremely familiar, but I can't quite place where I've seen her before.

"Do you have any other family in the area she may have in mind to go visit?" he asks.

Of course, I have someone in mind: me. She will strike when the time is right. It's too hot right now; she could be a possible suspect.

"Detective, I've told you this already. It's just my sister and me. Sharon, the woman who died in the fire, was the one watching over her at the facility," I explain.

He nods his head.

"We have no other family here. My sister and I have been going to the facility quite often to check on our mother," I lie, allowing a few tears to form in my eyes. "Please, you have to help us find her. She is really sick. We think she was in the last stage of dementia. She didn't even know who her sister was."

He sits forward and gives me a questioning look.

"I thought you said she didn't have no other family here?" he asks in his strong southern voice.

Shoot, I did say that. I forgot about Beth.

"Sorry, I… I forgot all about her sister. She just came back into the picture. She's been away for years," I explain. "You guys don't think a woman of her age and with this disease could possibly be the one to cause the fire, do you?"

He furrows his eyebrows.

"Alice, I'm not trying to find the person responsible for setting that fire. We already know who did that."

I stare at him for a moment, unsure of what to say next. *If he doesn't suspect Lily-Ann did this, then why have me come here?*

"I'm sorry, Detective, if you don't think my mother had anything to do with this, then why all the questions? Why am I here?"

He scrunches his eyebrows and looks a little taken aback.

"Well, it's protocol. Not only do we have a missing person, but we have a missing person with the possibility of being in the last stages of dementia, as you just mentioned," he says matter-of-factly. "I would think you'd be just as concerned as we are to find your momma."

I am officially lost for words. He's right. Why would they think she'd be the one to set the fire? If she has dementia, she probably doesn't even know what a lighter is.

"So if you don't suspect her, then who did it?" I ask. "If you can tell me that information, that is."

"Alice," he says, leaning forward to catch my gaze. "I didn't want to say anything, especially after what you just told me, but maybe you can help me figure this out now."

At this point, I'm slightly confused and have no idea where this is going.

"Sharon, the lady who died in the fire. The one you said has been keeping watch over your momma..." he pauses and notices my eyes have gotten wider as I continue to hear what he has to say. He pinches the bridge of his nose and takes a deep breath. "We have footage of her unlocking your momma and the elderly woman's room, who was with her in the picture. In the video, we see her with some headphones on, dancing as she sprinkles lighter fluid in several trash cans, and one by one, she lights each trash can."

I blink several times, trying to process the information he just gave me. There is no way Sharon would do something like this. She knows Lily-Ann. She knows everything about her and what she is capable of.

"So... so you're telling me Sharon did this?" I ask. "Detective, there is no way on this planet that she would do this."

My cell phone vibrates in my pocket, and I pull it out and notice another text from Mike asking me to call him as soon as possible. This time, he tells me it's urgent. Right now, nothing else can be more pressing than finding out that Sharon, of all people, started the fire.

"The footage doesn't lie, Alice. If I knew I wouldn't get fired, I'd show it to you myself, but I'm not ready to retire yet," he says with a slight chuckle.

Something isn't adding up. Sharon couldn't have done this willingly. She knew how dangerous our mother was. She knew what our mother did to the people in this town. She knew what she did to my family. Sharon wouldn't do this, I know that without a doubt. But if she didn't do this and they have her unlocking the doors, then who did? Who is really behind this?

CHAPTER 56

— · —

Walking out of the station, I'm reminded of how long I've been stuck here in an endless conversation with Detective Hudson. My Sunday is officially over now that the sun has set, and the moon and stars are lighting up the sky. The busy streets have fallen quiet, and the only sound I hear now is that of crickets.

I walk over to my car and click the unlock button. I decide to take a minute and sit in my car, trying to piece together everything Detective Hudson just told me. I lean my head against my headrest, and my mind is taken back to the day my father left. It was a day I could never forget. Nothing about it made sense.

It was right after Toby died, and everyone in the town hated Sarah and me for what happened. Our mother already hated us, but this just added fuel to the fire. Sarah and I were grounded for what felt like the rest of our lives.

Sarah stayed in our room all day, but I came out occasionally to get something to drink or eat. She always preferred to eat in our room because she was too scared of what our mother would say to us. I remember going down downstairs to get a drink of water because that's all we were allowed to drink. Our mother told us kids who kill little dogs, don't even deserve water, but because she needed us to get stuff done around the house, she had to keep us fed and hydrated.

I was standing at the counter drinking a cup of water when my dad walked through the door. He looked a little out of it as he peered ahead. He had what some might call a one-track mind. As he walked past me, I noticed something I've rarely seen my dad do: he looked like he had been crying.

"Dad?" he didn't look my way and he didn't say anything. It made me feel like he was upset with me as well, that is, until I overheard him and our mother's conversation.

"I'm leaving Lily-Ann," he said with no sound of remorse in his voice.

I could hear my mother laugh that same sinister laugh she always does when she thinks she's got the upper hand on someone.

"What do you mean you're leaving, Rick?" she asked him. "You can't leave me, you're nothing without me. Where are you going to go? You have no money. You were nothing when I met you, and you will be nothing when you leave me."

The room was quiet for a second, and then my father spoke. "I'm leaving Lily-Ann, you're too... you're too controlling, and I can't take it anymore."

She laughs again.

"Controlling? Me? Have you lost your mind?" she asked. "You made me this way. Did you forget? You wanted to keep those two girls. I told you from the beginning I didn't want girls. I only wanted sons who could carry my family's legacy. Why the hell do you think I didn't want to change my last name and gave the kids my last name, you idiot?"

My dad didn't respond. He didn't say anything at all.

"I didn't want to compete for your love with two little bratty girls. But no, you insisted we keep those two brats, and now you have the audacity to leave me? With them?" she asked him. "Why didn't you just let me put them up for adoption?"

Once again, silence filled the room until my dad spoke once more.

"I'm leaving Lily-Ann," he said as if it was embedded in his mind.

"STOP SAYING THAT YOU PIECE OF..." She stopped, and the room got quiet again. I could imagine her probably fixing her curls and adjusting her skirt like she always does, as if she is trying to compose herself from blowing a gasket. "Why are you leaving, Rick?" she asked softly.

"I'm leaving Lily-Ann, you're too... you're too controlling, and I can't take it anymore."

Our mother began to cry at that point.

"What am I going to tell people, Rick? How am I going to raise four kids all by myself? Why Rick? Why would you embarrass me like this? What is everyone going to think?" She was full of questions at that moment.

I stood there quietly as a mouse, waiting for our dad to say he was going to take us with him because she hated Sarah and me. I was praying inside that he would come back into the kitchen and tell me to get my sister and pack our bags. But what came out of his mouth next was the last words I heard my father say before he stormed out the door, and never looked back.

"I'm leaving Lily-Ann, you're too... you're too controlling, and I can't take it anymore."

The rest of my childhood, I grew up knowing two things about my dad. One, he left our mother because she was too controlling, and two, he didn't take my sister and me with him. I always felt like neither of us was worthy of either of our parents' love. Maybe that's another reason why I desperately needed to get out of this town. This town was a sad reminder of everything that was extremely messed up in my life.

As I continue sitting in my car with my head against my headrest, reminiscing about my past, that's when it hit me. The repetition, the dazed look, then I'm reminded of the last words I heard my father say: *I'm leaving Lily-Ann, you're too... you're too controlling, and I can't take it anymore.*

My father didn't leave our mother because she was too controlling—no, it's more complex than that. Part of me suspects he longed to, but I'm beginning to believe this was something else. Something that most people outside of this town would never think is true. I believe it was something that most could not wrap their minds around.

"He was hypnotized!" I quickly sit forward in my seat, as I come to this realization.

Our father was hypnotized, and from what Detective Hudson told me, I believe Sharon was too. I can't help but wonder: *what really happened last night at the facility?* Sharon has been walking around town wearing earbuds, singing and dancing in the streets when she should have been at work. She loved her job and knew our mother needed those pills more than anything. She knew how important it was to keep our mother under her hypnosis. She would have never let someone else take on the responsibility of caring for her patients, and I know for a fact that Sharon would not have set the building on fire. *She didn't do this, I know she didn't.*

But I'm left with one question now: who? Who did this?

My phone vibrates, and I jump, forgetting I left it in my pocket. I glance at the screen, and everything suddenly clicks into place.

Mike.

CHAPTER 57

— · —

I answer my phone, trying to steady my voice. I can't give it away that I know he's up to something. Mike is the only one new to this town. The answers were right in front of me, and I wasn't listening. Once again, I let myself open up to someone, a stranger to be exact, and once again, I've been burned. I told myself I wouldn't trust people again outside of Sarah and my kids, and look where it has gotten me: a burned-down mental institution and my mother running around town holding some old lady hostage. The poor lady is probably scared out of her mind, but if I know my mother, I know one thing to be true: she has something up her sleeve.

"Hello," I say, answering Mike's call.

"Alice!" Mike says quickly. "Is everything okay? I've been trying to reach you."

I can only imagine the real reason he's been trying to reach me. He probably wants to pick my brain some more to see how much I've figured out. God, I must be the dumbest person on this planet. Aaron tried to warn me that night at my mother's house. He said he didn't trust him. Now that everything is coming together for me, and I can see clearly what's going on, I've started to wonder why he wanted to check the office, of all places, in our mother's house. He didn't suggest checking one of the abandoned bedrooms, or even the freaking basement, to be exact. The first thought that came to his mind was to check the office.

"Alice? Are you there?" Mike asks.

"Sorry, yes, I'm here," I say quickly, shaking off my intrusive thoughts. "I'm in my car, leaving the police station."

I crank my car so Mike can hear what I'm saying is true. There is a brief moment of silence as my phone tries to connect to my car Bluetooth.

"I've been trying to reach you," he says. "I need to tell you something."

I put my car in reverse and pull out of the police station parking lot. I can't understand what it is that Mike is so eager to talk to me about. Is he ready to come clean and tell me he is the reason my mother is out of the facility? Is he ready to tell me he is the reason Sharon is dead?

Mike has been the one driving the mysterious black sedan that has been following me around town the entire time. He was also the person talking to Sharon that day in the park when we had Aaron's welcome cookout. He is the one behind all of this, but my mind leaves me with one question...

"Why?" I say unintentionally. Not realizing that I spoke out loud.

"Why, what?" Mike asks.

I'm lost for words as I didn't expect to say that. I come to a stoplight and only one thing comes to mind: "Why the hell did this car just run the red light?"

Mike chuckles, "You better be careful out there. There are a lot of dangerous people on the streets."

I grip the steering wheel tightly as I take in the words he just said. *What is that supposed to mean?* Is that a warning? A promise? Is he now toying with me? I swallow what feels like a lump in my throat. Mike knows everything. The whole story. Everything that has happened in this town, but I still can't piece together why. Why Lily-Ann? Why me? Why Sarah? Why do this to us, knowing what this woman is capable of? The question that I can't seem to wrap my head around the most is how? How is he doing all of this, and is he working with James?

"What...what is it that you need to tell me?" I say hesitantly.

Silence fills the air. The light turns green, and I sit there waiting to hear his response.

Beep!

I look up, and a black car is now sitting behind me, holding down on the car horn. The windows are pitch black, and I'm not able to see the face behind the glass. I glance at the screen on my dashboard, where Mike's name is displayed, then I look back at the car behind me in my rearview mirror. *No freaking way. Is he behind me?* I think to myself.

"M...Mike?" The phone is silent, and I swear he either has the phone muted or is covering the speaker.

"Yeah," he finally answers.

Right now, I am one hundred percent sure of one thing: Mike is the person behind me because as soon as he came back on the line, the horn from the car behind me stopped.

I hit the gas and speed through the intersection. I have no clear direction as to where I'm going. Going home is out of the question because I have no idea why Mike is after me. I can't lead him to my children, so I need to try to lose him in some way.

The car behind me also hits the gas, causing its tires to skid.

"WHAT DO YOU WANT?" I scream in panic as I make a quick right turn, trying to lose him.

"..."

He doesn't respond. All I hear through the phone is silence—nothing but dead air.

The car behind me stays close and also makes a right turn. It's clear I'm being followed now. The car speeds up and taps my bumper, not hard enough to knock me off the road, but just enough to let me know they're there, taunting me. This makes me squeal because I'm terrified at this point. Lily-Ann is heartless, and she has no problem getting rid of me for good. I bet my life she's sitting on the passenger side, calling the shots, while James is sitting in the back seat, rooting him on to bump my car even harder.

One thing about our town is that when all the businesses close, there's no one outside. It's a complete ghost town. So at this moment, no one is outside able to witness him chasing me.

"Alice..." he says my name in a singsong manner as if he is trying to taunt me.

I make a left turn, still not having any idea as to where I'm going. Heading back to the police station would be ideal, but how long would it take them to step outside before he murders me? How much time would I have to even run to the door before he catches up with me? At this point, leading him away from this town is my best bet.

I make a quick U-turn heading back towards the main road. This is the road we need to take to get to Atlanta. If I lead him away from here, that also stops whatever plan he and Lily-Ann have come up with.

Doing this causes my tires to skid. I'm sure they have left behind a dark tire mark. In the morning, someone will have to notice those marks and question what happened last night. I almost lose control of the car as it swerves from left to right. I grip the wheel, trying to regain control of my car.

The car behind me does the same, skidding its tires across the street.

"What do you want?" I ask again. "Why are you following me?"

Speeding through each light, I glance in my rearview mirrors. I say a silent prayer, hoping that in some way, shape, or form, I have lost him, but it's just my luck that he continues to tail me.

"Alice? Can you hear me? You keep going out? Is everything okay?" Mike asks, which takes me by surprise.

"No, I'm not okay, you psycho, what the hell do you want? Why are you following?" I ask as I grip the steering wheel with my eyes focused on the road in front of me.

" ... "

Once again, the phone remains silent, and I don't receive any response from him. So, I attempt a different approach: I try to provoke a reaction.

"I know what you did, Mike. I know you're the reason Lily-Ann escaped the facility. I know you're also the reason Sharon is dead," I say aggressively. "How much is she paying you? Is David even your brother?"

The phone is still silent, and he doesn't say a word. It's something about the silence that frightens me the most. At least if he's talking, I can see where his head is. I can hear what state of mind he is in. The silence, on the other hand, gives me nothing. It leaves me in the dark, with no clue as to what his next move is.

"The police know you had something to do with the fire and with Sharon's death," I lie.

"What?" he says as if he is surprised.

The car behind me slams on the brakes, and the call drops.

Bingo. I got him.

I continue driving, unsure if he will speed back up to catch me. Looking in my rearview mirrors, all I can see are the headlights from the car, and they are drifting in the night as my car gets further and further away.

"What the heck was that?" I say to myself.

CHAPTER 58

— · —

Before leaving town, there is a small corner gas station that used to be run by an older lady, but I assume she has retired. I pull over at that gas station, which is now a Quick Mart. The sign is not lit up, which lets me know they are closed for the night. I decide it's time I get the police involved. I begin to dial 911 when my phone dings, indicating that I have a text message.

Mike: Alice, are you okay?

Mike: You kept going in and out.

Mike: I heard bits and pieces—something about my brother.

Mike: Something about me and the fire.

Me: Please leave me alone.

Mike: Alice, I really needed to talk to you.

Mike: It's important. I found out something.

Mike: You remember that paper I took?

Mike: You know from your mom's house.

Mike: I don't think y'all are safe.

Me: I know we aren't safe, you made that clear tonight.

Mike: What are you talking about? I'm in Atlanta.

Me: You know what I'm talking about.

Mike: I've been trying to reach you for hours.

Mike: I'm about to call you, pick up. Please.

My phone rings and I stare at the screen as I see Mike's name flash across. I shouldn't pick up his call after what happened, but I'm getting that gut feeling that I need to. He says there's something he needs to tell me. This doesn't make any sense at all. He also said he's in Atlanta. How is that possible when he clearly just chased me through town? Something isn't right here, and the majority of the time, my gut is right.

"What is it, Mike?" I say softly, answering his call. I'm agitated because I have no idea what's going on.

"Alice, you need to get out of town. Now," he says quickly. "You remember when we went into your mother's house and I put that folder in my pocket."

I nod my head as if he can see me on the other end. "Yes."

"Well, I had my guy look into what I found, and Alice let me tell you something, really weird is going on in that town," he tells me, but he is still not saying anything that makes sense.

"Mike, what are you talking about?" I ask.

"Alice!" he shouts. "You need to get your family out of there! You are not safe!"

"Mike, what the hell is going on. You were just behind me, trying to run me off the road. If I'm not safe, it's because of you," I say.

The phone goes silent, and all I can hear is his heavy breathing.

"What do you mean? Someone just tried to run you off the road?" he asks. "Alice, it wasn't me, I'm still in Atlanta. I'm at the station as we speak."

My heart feels like it has stopped beating, and I can't breathe. I'm gripping the phone tightly because, clearly, someone just tried to run me off the road, and I could have sworn it was him.

"Hey Mike! We're about to head downtown to the bar to have a few drinks. It's been a long day, bro. You coming?" I hear someone say in the background, which lets me know he is definitely not in Shelly Grove. This town doesn't have bars.

"Na, go ahead. Y'all take it easy. Chief will be pissed if he has to clear y'all's names from another bar fight," Mike says playfully to whoever was talking to him.

Then it hits me, "Oh God, oh God, oh God, oh God, Oh God. Mike, what the hell if it wasn't you, then who the hell is following me?" I begin to panic.

"That's what I've been trying to tell you. You're not safe. Go get the kids and get the hell out of there," he warns me.

"Wait, what did the paper say?" I ask as I begin to put my car back in drive to head back to my house. "It is James? Is he back?"

"Alice, it's not James. It's..." The call drops again, and I'm left feeling uneasy.

I try to call him back, but the screen keeps displaying 'Call Failed'. *Ugh! I hate living in a small town.* I look up and I see nothing but darkness all around me. I look back down, trying to get him back on the phone, but the call keeps dropping. Luckily, with iPhones, you can text as long as you have Wi-Fi. I go to the setting, hoping the new owner of the Quick Mart offers free Wi-Fi for his customers.

As the phone searches for nearby available Wi-Fi, I look up again, and the only thing around me is darkness. There's something about being anxious and scared when it's dark outside. Your mind starts to play tricks on you. The stick in the road looks like it could be a snake. The trees on both sides of the road make me think someone is standing there watching me. The shadow down the road makes me think it could be an animal. A very big animal if you ask me.

I look back down at my phone and lift my head to the heavens, thanking God when I see "Quick Mart guest" pop up for free Wi-Fi. I click on it and wait for the Wi-Fi to kick in and load my browser.

My phone dings multiple times, alerting me to several text messages. I check my messages and see that I have numerous texts from Mike.

Mike: Alice, it's not James, it's—

Bright lights blind me as a car speeds up towards the Quick Mart. The car is moving extremely fast and coming from the direction where I saw that huge animal. Now that I think about it, maybe it wasn't an animal. Perhaps it was a car all along. My eyes couldn't make out the image because it was dark, and the car had its headlights off.

My body feels frozen as I stare at the blinding lights, helpless like a deer. A chilling silence grips me until I allow my eyes to glance down, staring at the message from Mike, revealing who's behind the wheel. It's not James.

I scream one last time.

Bam!

CHAPTER 59

— . —

D rip! Drip!

I hear water dripping on the floor, and my vision flickers. The last thing I recall is a black car crashing into me at full speed, with screeching tires and a bright flash of headlights. After that, everything went dark. I regain consciousness, noticing my car rolling over multiple times—metal twisting, glass shattering, airbags deploying. I can hear the metal impact as the car hits the ground, breaking apart with each hit. The sound of crunching metal and breaking glass echoes around me. Eventually, all I hear is ringing in my ears. I remember hitting a tree—the collision felt like an explosion, shaking my body. At least, I think I hit a tree.

Once I felt the car come to a stop, there was an overwhelming silence around me. Almost immediately, I felt an intense heat spreading rapidly, and within moments, the car erupted into flames. I could see the world around me upside down. I was overcome with a sensation of paralysis; my body refused to respond or move. Despite that, I could sense a desperate scream building within me—though no sound came out. Instead, I was screaming silently in my mind, feeling an unbearable pain that seemed to radiate through every part of my body, adding to the overwhelming sense of helplessness.

The black sedan was parked further away. I recall seeing the silhouette of a person rushing towards the car. I can't make out who they are, but what I can remember is the boots. The person who pulled me out of the vehicle was wearing black boots. They weren't just any black boots, though; they were black Timberland boots with the gold Timberland symbol on the side.

Drip! Drip!

Where is that water dripping from? I try to lift my head as my vision continues to go in and out. My wrists are in pain, but I'm sure everything is in pain at this point. I try to open my eyes a bit more and glance at my wrists.

They are tied down to the arms of a chair. *What the...*

My head hurts so bad I can't bring myself to lift it. I keep hearing a dripping sound that seems to echo, which is causing my head to throb even more. My head feels heavy, but lifting it to see where I'm at seems almost impossible. Everything is blurry, but it looks like I'm sitting at a table. A huge table, to be exact. I drop my head again because at this point, it's way too heavy to hold up on my own. My eyes close again because I feel drained. I want to go to sleep.

Drip! Drip!

I'm startled by whatever is dripping, as it sounds like it's been amplified and echoes, causing my head to hurt even more. I open my eyes and see a crimson colored puddle on the floor below me. *Am I bleeding?*

Looking down at the puddle, I can hear someone say my name. The person's voice sounds muffled. I can't make out who is talking to me.

"Help," I say softly because my voice can't seem to get any louder. Even when I try to move my lips, the pain is unbearable. "Help."

My eyes close again because I feel incredibly tired. I might have a concussion, which I've read affects many football players due to severe impacts. Alternatively, I could be dying. Honestly, death doesn't seem so bad right now; it's peaceful, and all my worries would disappear. My kids would lose their mother, but I trust my sister and Mr. Gerald to care for them. I'm just so exhausted, and my eyelids feel heavy.

When I open my eyes again, fear takes over me. I can't move and I can barely talk, but something catches my attention, letting me know that the person in the room with me isn't here to help.

"Boots. Boots," I say softly before everything goes black.

***

MY MIND TAKES ME BACK TO MY CHILDHOOD. I was around ten years old, and Sarah, James, and I were playing hide and seek. Sarah was probably around five or six because she had just started kindergarten. That day I hid in our pantry because no one would ever think to look there. We all knew our mother would kill us playing around the food. This particular day, she wasn't supposed to be home.

I sat there quietly waiting to see if Sarah or James would run by searching every corner for me. Then I heard what sounded like the door opening. I was scared because our mom wasn't supposed to be home for hours. She told us she was going shopping and instructed Cameron and me to keep an eye on our younger siblings, because we were the oldest. If I had been caught in the pantry, that would have been another reason for a beating.

"So, how was it?" a woman's voice asked, which sounded like our mother's.

I looked through the small opening in the pantry door and saw our mother in the kitchen with an older man. He looked familiar, but I couldn't put my finger on where I'd seen him before.

"Are the kids around?" he asked.

"They're playing upstairs, they don't even know you're here, and if they did, they wouldn't know you are their Grandfather," Mom said.

Grandfather? We never got the chance to meet our grandparents because our dad didn't think they were good for us. But I do recall seeing a picture of him.

Our dad was in the military, so he was deployed overseas around this time. I remember our mother saying something like, 'His job was a part of some reserves,' or maybe she said, 'He was in the reserves,' which is why we didn't have to live directly by a military base. Dad always said stuff like he wanted to go full-time, whatever that meant, but our mom wouldn't let him.

"It was as expected. They're living a life of luxury," The older man, I'm assuming, is our Grandfather, said.

Who are they? I remember thinking to myself.

"She still doesn't have a clue?" my mother asked.

Our Grandfather put his hands on our mother's shoulders, giving them a light squeeze, "Don't worry about it, sweetie, you're my girl. I will do what I do best. No one will know anything."

"But, Dad, how? Don't you think one day—" she's quickly interrupted before she can finish her sentence.

"Shh," he held up a finger to his lips. I remember seeing our Grandfather pull something small out of his pocket that looked like maybe a piece of gum, or a piece of candy, or perhaps a pill, and show Mom. Whatever it was, it put a smile on her face. "I'll do what I do best, dear."

"And there's no way she'll know, right?" she asked.

"Not at all, we convinced her this was all her doing. She thinks she shamed the family. She'll never bother this family again," he said with a sinister smile on his face.

"You're the best," Mom said, and wrapped her arms around him, giving him a tight squeeze.

"You just go do your shopping and stop worrying your pretty little head about this. Worst case scenario, I'll do it again," he explained.

Do what again? I wondered.

"Great!" she said, excited, and then she walked back out the door. Leaving me confused about whatever code they were talking in.

CHAPTER 60

— · —

I jump, startling myself from my sleep. I don't go very far because I realize my wrists are tied down to the arms of a chair, and my ankles are also tied to the legs of the chair. I begin to panic trying to lift my arms, but they can't move due to being restrained. I try to speak, but I can't because something is in my mouth keeping me from saying anything. I look around the room and notice the puddle of blood on the floor. I'm sitting at a table that's large enough to feed a family of twelve or more.

I look up and notice the chandelier hanging above me. It feels so familiar. *Have I been here before?* I glance over at what could be a window because there are black curtains covering something. My assumption is that it must be a window because you can see a small streak of sunlight spilling out from the sides.

I quickly scan the room in panic, realizing I'm back in my mother's house. I'm in my mother's house, restrained to a chair. I'm in my mother's house, restrained to a damn chair in her dining room. I'm in my mother's house, restrained to a damn chair in her dining room, and I'm... not... alone.

I blink my eyes several times at the sight before me. I'm sitting at one end of the table tied to a chair, while my sister is sitting to my left. Tears streak down her face, terror and helplessness flashing in her eyes as she watches me. I lean over and notice her wrists and legs are also restrained. She's unable to speak because she also has a white cloth in her mouth that is tied behind the back of her head.

My anger boils over instantly. I've always been there to protect her, and seeing her like this breaks my heart. I snap, ready to lash out, but I'm held back. For a moment, I forget I'm restrained, and I try to speak, but all that comes out is a choked sound. I lock eyes with her, hoping she knows what I'm thinking: *I'll get us out of here. I promise.*

As I glance to my right, I'm hit with the sight of Lily-Ann sitting beside me. She locks eyes with me, and for a moment, all I can think of is how badly I want to rip her apart for what she's done to us yet again. But then reality sets in, and I realize she's not in control of the situation. My mother sits to my right, also restrained and with her mouth covered. I shift my gaze back and forth between her and my sister, wondering why they don't look half as beat up as I feel. I mean, I was hit by a freaking car. Now I'm curious—how did they get here?

I'm caught off guard by the elderly woman who escaped the facility with our mother, now sitting next to her. Her eyes are fixed on me, as if I'm the main attraction. She's also restrained with her mouth covered. I tilt my head to one side, and as I stare at her, I'm hit with a sudden realization: *I've seen her before.* She was the creepy old lady who called herself "Nana" the day Aaron was brought to the hospital when he got shot. My mind starts racing, and I'm left wondering: what brought her to this point?

What hurts just as bad as seeing Sarah tied to the chair is when I look in front of me and notice the person sitting at the other end of the table. It's Mr. Gerald, and he definitely looks as bad as I feel. Someone has beaten him to the point where one of his eyes is swollen shut. His lips are puffed up, giving him a look that suggests a Botox visit gone wrong. From where I'm sitting, I can only imagine his wrists and legs must also be retrained because he isn't moving at all, and his mouth is also covered.

What... the... heck... is... going... on?

CHAPTER 61

— · —

When I was in high school, I remember my mom tying me to a chair once because she caught me kissing a boy. His name was Charles, and he was the pastor's son. She told me I'd sinned by kissing. If I recall correctly, that was the first time she called me a whore. Over time, it became a nickname because she called me that so often. Even now, as an adult, the echoes of it still play in my head: *Come here whore. Wash the dishes whore. Watch your brother and sister, whore.*

If I didn't know any better, I would have believed I was a whore for an innocent peck on the lips. But I knew better, I knew I wasn't a whore, and I knew I wasn't going to hell for kissing nerdy Charles once on the lips. If anyone deserved to go to hell, it was her for how she abused her children. Maybe she was right several years ago when she asked my dad to let someone adopt my sister and me. I'm curious how our lives would have turned out. Would we be tied to a chair right now, possibly having to fight for our lives?

As I look down at my wrists and see the knots, my mind goes back to what Sharon told me she saw in this house when she was a kid: Beth tied to a chair.

My eyes go wide as I realize something. Did Beth do this to us? She appeared out of thin air. The first day she arrived, she was eager to see our mother. Then I recall our visit. Something startled Lily-Ann that day, when she kept screaming, "You." At the time, I thought she was talking about me, because honestly, I did try to suffocate her. But I don't think that's what she meant. It's Beth. She's the one who did this. But why? Why Lily-Ann? Why Mr. Gerald? Why her nieces?

My thoughts are interrupted by the screeching sound of the front door opening. All of us begin to look around, trying to figure out who is coming into the house. I try moving around in the chair to make noise, just in case someone is here to save us. The person who took us didn't think this through all the way. My kids and Mike know I would never abandon my children. Between the three of them, they have already alerted the authorities that I'm missing. *At least I hope they did.*

"Well, isn't this a nice surprise. The whole family is finally here," Beth says as she turns the corner, entering the dining room.

Beth and Lily-Ann are very much alike; they can never dress normal. I mean, if she has plans to kill us, I would think she would at least want to put on some jeans or sweatpants. This lady is wearing a black pencil shirt, with a ruffled white top and a pair of platform heels. I have to hand it to her, though; she does have the body to pull off that outfit. Her hair is nicely curled, and her nails are perfectly manicured. Perhaps she is crazy. You have to be if you plan on killing someone in that outfit.

"It's like we are having our own little family gathering," she says with a sinister smile on her face while clasping her hands together.

"Mmm. Mmm," I try to speak but can't.

"What's that, dear?" She asks as she walks over to Lily-Ann and runs her fingers through her hair. "Oh, sis, you look like you've been to hell and back."

"Mmm. Mmm," I try to speak again, but I can't with my mouth covered.

Beth rolls her eyes and hurries over to me. She pulls down the cloth that's tied around my head, "Are you trying to say something, sweetie?"

"Why...why Beth?" I ask, struggling to get the words out. "We...we welcomed you. With...with open arms."

She's towering over me, looking down at me with a smile on her face, "Why? Why me? Why are you doing this? What are you going to do to us? Those are all the questions people like to ask when they are in your situation. But you will find out the why very soon, dear. You just have to be patient," she says in a singsong voice, touching my nose with her index finger.

She'd better be lucky I'm tied down because right about now I'd like to take that finger and snap it in half.

"What...what about my kids? Please...please don't hurt them," I beg.

She places the cloth back in my mouth and secures it tightly behind my head. I'm left trying to figure out what she is talking about. Confusion clouds my mind, and I struggle to identify this version of Beth. She is definitely not the lady we first met. She's also shown me another truth about my family: they are all psychotic.

***

BETH HAS BEEN GONE FOR HOURS.

She left us all unsure of what she has planned. If she's anything like her sister, I can only imagine what's going through her head.

When you're stuck in a room unable to move or talk, there's only one thing you can do, and that's think. As I sit here, glancing back and forth between all of them, my mind takes me back to the first day I thought I was leaving this hellish town. After finding out that I never left, I ask myself now, why didn't I go after finding out the truth? There is nothing left here for me or my family. *Why, Alice, why didn't you leave and never look back?*

The door slowly screeches open, and I can hear footsteps approaching.

Thud. Thud.

They sound thunderous, like someone heavy-footed has walked into the house.

Thud. Thud.

Each step is slow, but powerful, as if whoever is walking into the house wants us to know they're here.

My eyes widen, and I can't help but try my hardest to get out of this chair when I see who appears in the doorway.

"Mmm. Mmm," I try to speak, but I'm hoping that he understands what I'm trying to say, hoping that he can read my mind when I'm trying to tell him to get us the hell out of this place.

"Oh my gosh, Alice, are you okay?" he asks, rushing over to me.

I always wanted to keep my family in the past, but I can't help but thank God for giving me the crazy idea to tell him about my past. About the things our mother has done to us. He knew I would never leave my kids alone.

"Mmm. Mmm," I point my head towards everyone else sitting around the table with me. Then I point my head to my wrists, hoping he understands he needs to act quickly and untie me so we can help the others.

He removes the cloth from my mouth, and I take a deep breath, "She will be back soon, you need to hurry."

He nods his head and rushes over to Sarah, removing the cloth from her mouth. "I need to find something to cut the rope from around y'all's wrists."

Bam!

The door slams, and at this moment, my heart is pounding so intensely that I believe it's about to leap out of my chest.

"She's back," I whisper, fearful of what's going to happen next. Afraid that our only help is also going to be her next victim. Terrified that there may be someone crazier in our family than Lily-Ann.

"You need to hide," I whisper, but by then, I realize it's too late because Beth has already returned and is standing in the doorway with a look I recognize. Lily-Ann always wore the same sinister smile—a look that told us we were caught and she was about to tear us apart.

"Well, isn't this a nice surprise?" Beth says as she slowly enters the dining room. She stands next to Lily-Ann and begins to twirl her hair through her fingers. "Were y'all expecting guests?"

She continues to wear the same smile on her face. At least with Lily-Ann, we knew what she was thinking when she had that look on her face. What scares me about Beth is that I don't know her, and I have no idea what she is thinking at this point. Heck, I have no idea why we are even here.

"Beth, please. Just let us go?" I beg. "I have kids, you know, your niece and nephew. I don't even know you. Why are we here?"

She shifts her gaze and stares in his direction. At this point, I recognize that look. Our mother always wore that look on her face when she was ready to hurt someone.

"Please, Beth, leave him alone. Focus on me. Talk to me," I plead. "He was just here to help. He won't tell anyone about this. None of us will."

I look around the table and notice that everyone is desperately nodding their head. Well, everyone but our mother and the elderly lady next to her.

"Tell her, Lily-Ann, tell her you won't say anything. Tell her we will put this behind us, and no one will ever know about this," I say.

Beth pulls the cloth out of Lily-Ann's mouth and the elderly lady next to her. "Did you have something to say, sis? Your daughter here seems to think you do."

Lily-Ann doesn't say anything; she continues to stare into outer space. However, as I follow her gaze, I notice something is off. I shift my gaze and see that the elderly woman is staring in the same direction.

Lily-Ann looks over at me, and for once, I notice something on her face other than her usual devilish look: fear.

"Aaron, sweetie, maybe it's time we tell them what's really going on," Beth says as she makes her way over to him.

"Aaron?" I'm confused because my friend is here to help us. He's here to save us and get us away from this crazy lady. Something tells me my assumption is wrong, though, because now he has his arm around Beth. My head is now spinning, and I'm struggling to make sense of all this.

"Alice..." he says as he catches my gaze.

Tears have begun to flow from my eyes down my cheeks. An icy dread grips me inside, warning that whatever he is about to say will haunt my nightmares. I sense that his words will shatter our lives beyond repair, perhaps making me sick to my stomach with fear. The silence before his revelation feels like the calm before a storm I can't escape.

"I'd like you to meet Beth, your aunt and my mother," he says, but this time wearing the same sinister smile on his face as Beth: his mother.

CHAPTER 62

— · —

When Sarah and I were kids, we used to play in this abandoned room in our mother's house. It had two beds, covered with white, dusty sheets. That was our secret hideout, a place we went when we wanted to escape or hide. We always thought our mother avoided that room for a reason. Sometimes, it felt like someone might have died in there, considering how neglected it was. That room held secrets we never fully understood, until today.

I walked into the same room again when I thought I was searching "Mrs. Sally's" house for clues, but I was confused by all the blue baby clothes and blankets. It never dawned on me why those things were in her house until this moment: *Beth had a baby.* What I can't understand is why we are here. Why didn't Aaron just come out and tell us he was our long-lost cousin? Sarah and I would have welcomed him with open arms. Just because his mom is crazy doesn't mean he has to be. *Does it?*

"Mom?" I turn to Lily-Ann, searching for answers. "Why didn't you tell us about our aunt? Why didn't you mention a cousin? WHY ARE WE HERE?" I shout, losing my composure. I'm strapped to a chair and was hit by a car. Mr. Gerald looks worse than I feel, and everyone seems to exchange secretive glances, as if there's something much bigger going on.

"…" She doesn't speak; she just continues to stare at Aaron and Beth.

My eyes are burning because I'm trying to hold back a pool of tears. The one person I tore my wall down for has been lying to me this entire time. I let him into my home and around my children.

"Why, Aaron? Why didn't you tell us? We would have excepted you. I've always wanted to know about my family," I say as a tear rolls down my cheeks.

Aaron walks over to me and wipes the tear off my cheek with his thumb.

"Shh! Don't get yourself worked up, lil sis."

My eyes widen as if I'm a deer staring into an eighteen-wheeler's headlights. I look over at my mom, who is still staring at him as if she is seeing a ghost. The old lady next to her is also staring at him as if she has seen a ghost. I can't bring myself to think of anything else at this moment, except one thing. "Who is this lady?" I say with agitation in my voice.

Beth chuckles and crosses her arms in front of her chest. "Well, this is going to be interesting."

CHAPTER 63

— · —

My head is spinning, and I'm trying to make sense of every-thing. The kids are probably scared because they have no idea where I am. The last thing I can remember is being hit by a black car and someone wearing black Timberland boots with the gold logo. I'm taken back to the last thing Aaron said to me before walking out of the house: *We'll be back later, hopefully he doesn't try to buy up the whole game store.*

I'm questioning what has happened to my kids and struggling to understand why I chose to stay. I've always believed I am a good person, so it's hard to accept that bad things happen to good people. I've never harmed anyone, so why am I suffering? It feels like my bad luck is a result of being born into this family. If I could, I would go back to where I came from and ask to be born through another woman's womb—definitely not Lily-Anne's.

"Alice?" Beth calls my name, pulling me from my thoughts. "Aaron is not your cousin, dear."

I nod my head, letting her know I'm following her.

"Your mother and grandmother," she says, gesturing her arm to-ward Lily-Ann and the lady next to her. "Well, also your grandfather, rest his pathetic soul. The three of them decided it would be a good idea to hypnotize me into thinking I had a sweet baby boy," she says as she gently rubs the back of Aaron's head, as if he were a toddler.

My eyes widen at this revelation, and I quickly glance over at my mother and my supposed grandmother. I shift my gaze and notice tears streaming down Sarah's face.

"Sarah?" I say softly. "Did you know?"

She nods her head no.

"Oh no, sweetie, she didn't know anything. As a matter of fact..." Beth says, walking towards Mr. Gerald, pulling the cloth out of his mouth. She places one hand on his shoulder. "The two of them have been most helpful. I've been able to get quite a bit of information out of these two."

I scrunch my eyebrows, which tells her she's lost me.

"Oh, I'm sorry, sweetie. Let me slow it down a bit for you. You see, the day I met you at the donut shop and you needed to go to the bathroom, well, let's just say these two gave me the information I needed about you, dear, and my sister," she says.

"I don't understand," I'm genuinely confused.

"God, you are an idiot," she rolls her eyes and then rushes over to me and squeezes my cheeks in the same manner our mother has done in the past. "I. Hypnotized. The. Two. Of. Them."

Beth smiles, but her gaze pierces me with an unsettling intensity. I have no clue why she is doing this or what she is thinking. I have no idea as to why we're here. If Aaron is my so-called brother, then why hold Sarah, Mr. Gerald, and me hostage? We didn't do anything to her.

"How do you think I knew where you lived. I needed her to tell me because I couldn't risk my baby boy telling me, and you starting to suspect him. Now could I?"

"I'm still not following," I mumble because Beth is still squeezing my cheeks.

"How about we start from the beginning," she says.

***

I HATE MY MOTHER WITH EVERY FIBER IN MY BODY. After what Beth revealed to us, I despise her even more. I hate my newly discovered grandmother and my deceased grandfather, whom I never got the chance to meet in person, other than seeing him through the crack in the pantry door when I was younger. Now I see why my father didn't want us to meet our grandparents. They're monsters.

Beth's story now makes complete sense. Sharon shared that when she was younger, she saw Beth's parents beating her in the basement, trying to force her to do or take something. It wasn't until Beth thought her father might have overheard Sharon that she decided to go along with what they demanded.

Her parents looked at Lily-Ann as the golden child. The prettier one. The one with a leveled head on her shoulder, or should I say the one who would do whatever they wanted her to do—the one who was more like them. It's pretty ironic because this is precisely how Lily-Ann treated Cameron and James.

The three of them decided to take Beth's agencies and hypnotized her into thinking she had Aaron. They couldn't stop there, though; they made her leave town and told her never to return. They told her she wasn't wanted or welcomed in this town anymore because she had a child out of wedlock, when really, it wasn't Beth who had the child, it was Lily-Ann. However, one thing I still struggle to understand is that our mother was married. Why not keep her own child? No one would have looked down on her because he wouldn't have been a child out of wedlock.

"Why didn't you keep him?" I ask Lily-Ann. "You were married; no one would have looked down on you for having a child out of wedlock."

Lily-Ann glances at Mr. Gerald, then Beth, and finally back at me. An instinct warns me that this story is about to become even more intense.

"Should I tell her Lily-Ann or would you like to do the honors?" Beth asks.

Even in the worst situations, our mother will never give in to anyone. She looks away from her sister, rolling her eyes.

"Guess I'll tell it," Beth says.

I swallow hard, bracing myself for what she is about to reveal to us.

"You see, your mom and Gerald dated in high school. They were oh so in love," she says sarcastically. "Our daddy dearest did not like the two of them being together, but he didn't want to make his precious daughter upset, so he tolerated it. But, get this, here comes the plot twist, your mom and Gerald committed the ultimate sin."

Right now, she's speaking in riddles, and I'm not following. "I'm sorry, what?"

"The two of them slept together, sweetie! It was after graduation, to be exact, and I guess they didn't use protection, so whoops, mommy here got knocked up," she says with a pretend sad face. "She had to run

291

to daddy for help, and well, they decided I was the key. They couldn't let their prized possession look bad to the townspeople. She had a reputation to protect."

"Okay?" I'm not sure what to say at this point.

My gaze quickly shifts to Mr. Gerald because at this point, I'm starting to put two and two together.

"So Aaron is..." I can't bring myself to finish my sentence.

"That's right. My sweet boy is your half-brother, dear," Beth's voice lowers. "And he's not happy being tossed aside like he's garbage."

CHAPTER 64

_– · –_

AARON

All my life, I knew something wasn't right about my relationship with my mother. Don't get me wrong, she raised me, and I will always love her for that. She didn't throw me away like I was trash. She was a single mother, and she did her best raising me in a big city, but we never lacked for anything. There were things about her, though, that didn't seem right. We didn't look alike. Her eyes were dark brown, and mine were hazel. I always felt a disconnect between the two of us. She struggled to exhibit the nurturing aspect of motherhood that you often hear about on television and that I've observed in the medical field.

When I was younger, I remember falling while trying to ride my bike. My leg was broken, and she rushed me to the emergency room. She seemed like she was scared to touch me, as if her motherly instincts didn't kick in to tell her to hug me or try to keep me calm. She did her best trying to show me that she cared, but still, something was missing.

I lived a life that some would have killed for. We lived in the Buckhead area of Atlanta. We had the privilege of living in a four-bedroom luxury townhome nestled in a prestigious country club community. I had the luxury of wearing some of the most expensive brands. I had a freaking Louis Vuitton bookbag in middle school. I attended some of the best schools, where chess and lacrosse were the highlights of our school experience. I attended Morehouse, where I earned my degree in nursing, paid in full somehow. You would think I would never have questions, but when I have a mother who never spoke of my father and never lifted a finger for anything, of course, I would have questions.

I never really had a good example of what love is supposed to look like because I didn't have a father around. My mother was never successful in the dating world, so I guess I have to thank her for my many failed relationship attempts. It was always just my mom and me. We were all each other had, which is why, as a grown man, I was still living with her. To be honest, she was well-off, and I didn't have to pay for anything, so why would I put myself in debt by trying to get my own place?

She always walked around with this smile on her face as if she was forced to be happy. No one walks around all day this happy.

Over the years, I have enjoyed nursing, but I grew especially passionate about it when I started working in the emergency department. There was something fulfilling about treating a patient, sending them home, and advising them to follow up with their primary provider. Job, well, until the next patient arrived, that is.

One night, a child was brought in because his parents had decided to throw a Fourth of July block party, and everyone was outside enjoying their beers and fireworks. The kid decided he wanted to take a stroll on his bike and somehow hit a light pole, causing him to be thrown off the bike. He came in with a broken arm and a missing tooth. As always, we patched him up, sent him home, and told his mother to follow up with the kids' primary provider. She kissed her son and apologized for not being there to tell him the light pole was in the way.

At that moment, everything I've tried to shake off from the time I was little all came back to me. Something didn't feel right about my mom.

If you've never seen a black man cry, I can tell you I was bawling my eyes out heading home after my shift was over. I'll never forget this day because it was now a little after midnight, and I was checking a voice message from my mom. She was singing Happy Birthday to me because I had just turned forty-two. I was wiping the tears from my eyes, thinking about how that kid's mom embraced her son after being thrown from his bike.

I clicked the button on the side of my phone to make the screen go dark and placed it in my cup holder. When I looked up, all I remember was headlights, and I was waking up in a hospital room patched up, but I wasn't able to go home. Apparently, I had lost a lot of blood. It would have been easier for them to get my blood type from my mother, the person who should know this information about me, but she didn't know. Call me crazy, but this was a major red flag for me. Perhaps it was because I worked in the medical field and felt that this should be something parents should know about their kids.

After several days in the hospital, I was finally given the usual instructions to follow up with my primary care provider. I went home just like the kid—arm in a cast and a bandage around my head.

Six months after my accident, I was cleared to go back to work full-time. I remember this day as if it were yesterday. I had just woken up because I was scheduled to work my first twelve-hour overnight shift. It was eleven in the morning, and I had just put a few pieces of

French toast sticks in the air fryer. I checked the fridge because my mom always leaves a note on it for me, as if I were still her little boy. I think she also forgot that technology makes it easy for us just to send a quick text message. I took a seat at the kitchen table while I waited for my food to cook. Deciding to waste a few minutes of my brain cells, I checked out TikTok, where I came across a video of several kids from around the world entering haunted mansions.

The air fryer dinged, indicating it was time to flip my food. I stepped away from my phone to turn the sticks over. I went back to the table, where I saw a group of kids playing around in this older mansion in the unspoken town that had been the highlight on the news stations lately.

Apparently, no one knew about this town out in the country, and some crazy stuff had been going on there. While looking at the video, I heard the door slam shut, and my mom came inside. She looked at me, and her face was wet, and her eyes were red as if she had been crying. I began to get up to see if she was okay, but she just waved me off. She didn't say a word. She went straight to her room.

I gave her a minute before going to check on her. I wasn't sure what to expect. Perhaps her doctor had given her some bad news about something. My mom has always been pretty healthy, so I couldn't believe it was anything too bad.

Standing in front of her room door, I overheard her crying hysterically. She was throwing things, and it sounded like she broke a few items in her room.

"I WANT THEM DEAD! I WANT THEM ALL DEAD!" she shouted.

I slowly opened her door, unsure of what I was getting ready to walk into.

"Um... Ma? Are... you okay?" I asked hesitantly.

She looked at me, black eyeliner smeared under her eyes and on her cheeks, "No, Aaron. No, I'm not okay."

"What's going on? What did the doctor say?" I asked. "Is it something major?"

She stared at me for a moment as if she had to think about my questions. I braced myself for what she would say next. Silently praying that they didn't tell her she had some form of cancer.

"Come here son. Sit down, we need to have a long talk."

CHAPTER 65

— • —

AARON

My whole life had been a lie. My mother went to the doctor with pelvic pains, and her doctor decided to do an exam. She was asked how many pregnancies she's had, and she told them she had only had one child. To her surprise, the exam revealed that she had never given birth, which left her confused. She didn't want to seem crazy or even raise any red flags, making the doctor think she had kidnapped a child, so she told them she misunderstood their question, and she told them I was adopted.

"I remember everything, son," she said to me. "I remember what they did to me."

"Ma, what are you talking about?" I asked her. "Who did what to you?"

That's when my entire world came crashing down. She told me everything. She told me how her parents treated her like the redheaded stepchild. She told me how they tied her to a chair like a dog and beat her until she took some pill that would keep her under their hypnosis. I didn't even know hypnosis was real. I mean, you see it in movies and stuff, but who would have thought it was a real thing?

She told me one day she woke up, and it was like a fast rewind through time. She said it was all unfolding as if it were a movie of her life over the past forty-two years. Her stomach was hurting, and she felt she needed to get checked out to make sure something serious wasn't wrong with her or that she wasn't going crazy. This was the reason she went to see her doctor.

"But how? How ma? If this is true, how did you come out of it?" I asked her. "Doesn't someone have to like snap their fingers to bring you out of it?"

Shaking her head, "I'm really not sure, sweetie. Something had to have happened, though."

She told me how her twin sister got pregnant right after they graduated by a dude she was dating. I was furious, and at this point, all I could see was red. These people tortured the only woman that has ever loved me, but what made my blood boil and took me to the darkest of places I had never been able to come back from was when she told me she was forced to take me and raise me as her own child to keep her sister from looking bad.

"Ma," I whimpered. "I...I'm so sorry they did this to you. We can't let them get away with this."

What kind of people do this? What type of parents send their child to raise an innocent baby that actually belongs to her sister, to preserve their other daughter's reputation? They couldn't accept that their golden child had made a mistake and might bring shame to the family, so they chose to hide it. They decided to hide me.

"What can we do son? They've already gotten away with it," she said as tears poured down her cheeks.

"Don't worry, ma, they will get theirs. I promise you that," I said as she leaned her head on my shoulder, and I rubbed the back of her hair.

After conducting my research, I discovered that the mysterious town that has been all over TikTok is where my so-called mother lives, and she has four other children that she raised and loved. *What made them any different from me? Why did they have the privilege of staying and growing up with a father and a mother?*

Months went by, and I researched hypnosis, Shelly Grove, and my family. I learned that I had two sisters, both now living good lives, owning their own businesses and working side by side with the Mayor. It must be nice. I don't even know the mayor's name here in Atlanta.

I learned that my sister Alice has two kids who have probably had the luxury of growing up knowing their grandparents. The more I researched, the more I wanted to kill them. I missed out on the life they all had the privilege of having. My mother or father never lifted a finger to find me. I was now the new redheaded stepchild in the family, and I was out for blood.

CHAPTER 66

— • —

He told us everything—he watched us obsessively, day and night. Studying our behaviors, obsessing over our schedules, knowing every detail about what my kids liked and which schools they attended. He was here the entire time, lurking in the shadows, even while the mayor had Sarah and me address the town. I always feared James coming back, but I'm not sure who to fear more: the brother who is mad because I kicked him out of town, or the brother who is furious because he's lived a lie his entire life.

When we finally met Beth, it wasn't her first visit; she's been here helping Aaron set everything up. It seems she has been at our mother's house the entire time, watching us all, just like her sister used to do. From the top of the hill, she observed the whole town—or more accurately, she watched us from up there. She uncovered the family inheritance and discovered where Lily-Ann had hidden the pills and the instructions to produce more. It turns out, the basement contained more than just dark hallways and pools of water for drowning their victims.

They told us how they got Sharon involved by hypnotizing her. This broke my heart more than anything because she was just an innocent bystander caught in the crossfire. This is how Aaron was able to get the job at the facility because they made her think she needed the extra help, when in reality, Sharon had been holding that place down with little help, ensuring Lily-Ann never escaped.

I asked them why they had to murder Sharon. She didn't do anything to them. If she were hypnotized, she had no way of knowing what she was doing, but Beth told us she had to die because she knew too much. Sharon was there from the beginning of it all. She knew what our grandparents did to Beth. At least Beth thought she knew. Little did she know; Sharon didn't know all the details of what happened that night while she was in the basement. She only knew our grandparents beat her and put something in her mouth. They killed her for nothing. She was clueless.

We found ourselves back in this nightmare, but now we're in a completely different game with all-new players. It made my skin crawl because Aaron managed to deceive us all. Living among us, playing us, and the frightening truth is, he didn't even need to hypnotize us to do it.

"Please, we had no idea you even existed," Sarah cries. "If we had known, we would have tried to find you. Aaron, we love you. I promise we didn't know."

I nod my head quickly in agreement with my sister. "Aaron, all Sarah and I have ever wanted is to be loved by our brothers. Our mother took that from us, so to know we had another brother out there who we possibly could've had a better relationship with, we definitely would have come searching for you."

At this point, the person we once knew was gone, replaced by a figure driven by pure vengeance. His face was set in a cold, merciless expression, disregarding everything we said. His eyes, now pitch black, gleamed with a relentless fury, and I could feel it—there was only one thing on his mind now.

"ALICE!" Aaron snaps at me. "Did you hear me?"

"I'm sorry, I didn't hear what you said," I mutter.

"I said, now that you mention brothers, it's unfortunate that James can't be here for this little family gathering," he tilts his head with a disturbing smile.

"What are you planning to do, Aaron?" I ask.

"Oh, lil sis!" he says excitedly, clapping his hands together. "I forgot to thank you."

"Thank me?" I ask. "For what?"

"Well..." he says, smiling. "You helped a brotha out if you know what I'm saying."

I scrunch my eyebrows, confused at what he is talking about.

"You took out one of my siblings already for me, so that's one less person I have to..." he takes his index finger and slides it across his neck as if it's a pretend knife.

Grabbing a chair, he sits it next to Mr. Gerald. He looks at him as if he were observing his features.

"Well, I'll be damned! We do look a little alike, pops," he says with a chuckle, slapping Mr. Gerald on the back. "Who would have thought I had a father this whole time?"

Mr. Gerald looks at him, "Son, I didn't know."

Aaron's face instantly changes from smiling to pure darkness.

"Son! Don't call me your damn son!" he says through gritted teeth and then punches Mr. Gerald in the face. He grabs his face, squeezing his cheeks together in the same familiar way Lily-Ann used to do to us, "You knew she was pregnant! You had to know! You're a man; you knew you messed up the moment you didn't wear a condom!"

I'm startled by the loud thunderous rumble coming out of his voice. I had no idea he could get that loud. I had no idea he could get this upset. Aaron never showed us this side of him other than that moment on the porch when he got upset about me being gone. This is all new to me. It's hard to process the man I'm currently seeing.

"Aaron, please, this isn't you," I say softly, but before I can say another word, I'm caught off guard by a blow to the face.

"Don't you dare say this isn't him. You don't even know him," Beth retorts.

I look over at my mother because all of this is because of her. We are in this situation because she threw her child away. After all, she is the real psycho here. *Well, if I'm being honest with myself, they're all a little psychotic.* She can't even look at me because, for once, she's not in control of the situation. For once, she is the one being victimized.

"So what's the plan here? We're all here now. We all know the truth," I say, spitting blood out of my mouth after Beth hit me in the face. "What's the plan huh?"

"Well, you all like having parties. What should we call this one?" Aaron asks, cupping his hand under his chin. "How about the welcome home for the lost son?" he says sarcastically, holding his hands in the air as if he is displaying an invisible banner.

Beth chuckles.

"My sister is so pathetic. Who names her gatherings? I bet you had nice little invitations made for them, didn't you, sister?"

"This will be the last gathering any of you will ever have," Aaron says with a sinister look on his face. "Let's play a game.

304

CHAPTER 67

— • —

A aron and Beth have left the room, and we are left staring at each other, trying to figure out what they have in store for us. The last thing he said to us keeps playing on repeat through my mind: *Let's play a game.* This isn't a freaking game show, and we aren't his contestant, or are we? Somewhere in the back of my mind, I'm praying and hoping that this is Aaron and Beth's sick way of a joke. I'm praying that any minute now one of them will say, "Gotcha!"

I keep opening and closing my eyes, hoping that the next time I open them, I'll be waking up in my bed with Kandice and Adam standing over me, waking me from a bad dream. But nothing changes. Nothing Freaking changes! I'm scared, and I have no clue what's going on.

"Don't let them see that your scared child," Lily-Ann finally says something.

"What?" I'm a little confused and shocked that she is actually speaking.

"Don't. Let. Them. See. That. Your. Scared. Child," she says as if she is annoyed. "Trust me, I know. When you show them you're scared, they're able to mess with your head."

"How about you do what you do best and shut the hell up!" I'm pissed. The first words that come out of her mouth are to tell me what to do. She's done that all my life, and if I'm going to die here, I will not die letting her control me. "We wouldn't be in this situation had you kept your legs shut. Who's the whore now, mom, hmm, who's the whore now?"

Mr. Gerald looks at me. I can tell he is caught by surprise at my tone. At this point, I really don't care what he thinks. I thought he was better than that. I thought he had more dignity than to sleep with my mother. How could he? I don't know him at all.

"Baby girl, just calm down," he says. "I know you're scared, but yelling and using all your energy will not help you get out of here. Trust me."

For a minute, I want to tell him to leave me alone because I'm furious at the fact that he slept with our mother, but then I'm reminded that he's been gone for quite some time now. The last we heard from him, he had texted me telling me he was heading to Atlanta.

"Oh my gosh, how long have you been here? We had no idea. We thought you were in Atlanta," I explain.

"I stopped counting the days," he says as he looks away.

"Gerald, I had no..." Lily-Ann starts to say something.

"Please save it," I say, rolling my eyes.

"Gerald, I really had no idea. She was supposed to be long gone. Our parents set her up to be well taken care of," Lily-Ann explains. "I'm not sure how this happened, how she came out of it. This wasn't even supposed to touch our family. No one was supposed to know."

"How could you keep something like this from me, Lily-Ann? How could you hide this from the kids?" Mr. Gerald says softly, almost in a whisper. "These kids deserved to know they had another sibling. I deserved to know I have a son. I knew you weren't right in the head, but this is a new low."

"Well, hold on, dear, she didn't really have a choice," the elderly lady speaks up.

"Hold on; we don't even know you or your name. You don't have the right to speak right now. We're stuck in this mess because of you and your crazy husband," I say angrily.

"I'm your grandma, sweetie, and your mom had no choice. She was looked up to by many. She had a reputation to protect. She had no choice. We couldn't let our baby girl face the backlash and people turning their noses up to her. Do you know what people said about you back then when you got pregnant out of wedlock? It won't nothing good. We couldn't let her go through that," Grandma says.

God, my entire family is crazy. This lady has to be in her eighties. You would think she would be wise beyond her years. At least that's what most people say. It's clear to me that I have no chance at a normal life. How is that I'm not crazy? How is it that Sarah hasn't lost her mind? What was the universe thinking when it chose this family for us to be a part of?

My head is killing me from the crash, and I have so many questions running through my mind. *How will we get out of here? Where are my kids? What do they have planned for us? How fast can I get my things and get the hell out of this town once this is all over?*

Bam!

The door slams, and Aaron appears in the doorway of the dining room. He's not the guy I thought he was. I can see nothing but pure hate in his eyes. As I observe him, I can tell what his true intentions are.

He's wearing all black: black pants, black hoodie, and those freaking black Timberland boots with the gold logo. No one wears all black unless they mean business.

Aaron pulls up a chair next to our grandmother. "So Grammy, question for you, why did my mother come out of her hypnosis. I'm just curious, you and Gramps are the master mind behind it all. What caused her to come out of it?"

"Child, I have no idea," Grandma says.

"Aaron, our grandfather, is dead," I say softly.

"Obviously," he says, rolling his eyes.

I try to win him over by helping him figure this out. Maybe if I give him what he's looking for, perhaps he'll let us go. If I show him we're on his side, maybe we can all walk away from this.

"When we made our mother think she had dementia, everyone came out of their hypnosis because she couldn't control them anymore," I explain. "It's possible the same thing could have happened in Beth's case. Maybe she came out of it when her father died, and her mother clearly isn't all the way there because she was also in a mental institution."

He doesn't say anything, he just stares at me as if he's trying to comprehend what I just said to him.

I try to sit forward so that he will only look at me. "Aaron, we love you. We would have really loved to have another sibling. It kills me knowing you were out there this entire time."

Tears begin to form in his eyes, and for a moment, I can see what I'm saying is working.

"Aaron, can't you imagine us going back to my house and us telling the kids you're their uncle. Adam will be thrilled," I smile. "Kandice

308

will brag about how she has the coolest uncle on the planet. The kids love you so much. We love you so much."

He tilts his head and offers a gentle smile. Maybe what I'm saying is getting through. Maybe all he needed was to feel welcomed in our family. Perhaps this will be...

My thoughts are quickly interrupted. He goes into the pocket of his hoodie and places something on the table. Perhaps it's the accident that's preventing my mind from registering what's in front of me at the moment.

He slowly leans forward, resting his arm on the table with an intense gaze fixed on me as he cautiously extends his arm. My eyes drop to a glint of gold—a chain with a cross gently swinging from his neck. I spot the Timberland logo on his hoodie, and for a moment, I wonder: *What is it with him and Timberlands?* My focus then moves to the dirt under his nails, rough and unclean. Suddenly, my eyes widen in shock as I see the shiny barrel of a small silver gun aimed directly at me.

CHAPTER 68

—•—

I swallow hard, feeling the uncomfortable lump in my throat as I struggle to keep my voice steady. I realize that what I just said wasn't effective and may have even been ignored. His unwavering gaze fixes on me, emotionless, as he calmly holds the gun steady, its barrel aimed directly at my chest. The silence stretches between us, thick with tension and unspoken threats.

"Are you done?" he asks without emotion.

"Yes," I say softly, fear visible in my eyes.

"Alright then," he claps his hands together. "Here's how this is gonna go: I ask the questions, and if the answer is right..." he pauses and chuckles. "Well, right to me that is, then I won't shoot you, and you get to live another day."

I look at Sarah and notice the tears flowing down her cheeks. Mr. Gerald's one eye that isn't swollen shut looks like he is worried. Lily-Ann still looks like nothing is bothering her; she's probably plotting in her own head how she's going to get out of here, and her mother, well, her mother may have just dozed off. She probably forgot that we're all here, possibly getting ready to die.

God, we are all dead.

310

"How many questions are asked in this game?" I ask, unsure if I should speak right now. He is still pointing the gun in my direction.

"Until you're all dead, that's when the game is over, lil sis," he says with a smile that sends chills down my spine.

What do I say to that? No one knows we're up here, and it's clear to me that the only way out of here is in a body bag. Aaron has one goal here, and that's to kill us all.

"Grammy!" he sneers bitterly. "So, what the hell made you and your spineless bastard of a husband beat your innocent daughter bloody until she finally gave in?"

Our grandmother lifts her head and looks at Aaron. She lifts one side of her mouth into a devious smile. One that I'm all too familiar with. Now I know where Lily-Ann gets it.

"She wasn't listening. The brat deserved it," she says and then spits on his shoes. "You know what? We were right to get rid of you. You're just like her—ungrateful. Your grandfather and I made sure you two were well off. Y'all had more than enough. We saw that big house you had in that expensive neighborhood."

My eyes widen because, at this moment, I know Aaron is thinking the same thing I am. *How did she know where they lived?* How did she know anything about the neighborhood unless they'd been there before? They probably watched them on numerous occasions.

"What. Did. You. Say," his expression has changed and his eyes have gotten wider. He's leaning in closer as if he were having trouble hearing her.

"You heard me, you little punk. You don't scare me. You should be afraid of—"

For a moment, my mind struggles to process what just happened. It feels like time has slowed, and everything around me moves in a blur. Sarah's mouth is open in shock, and she seems to be bouncing slightly in her chair. Mr. Gerald's only unswollen eye widens, and his mouth stays agape. He's saying something, but I can't hear anything. Lily-Ann's face is bloody, and she remains completely still. Her eyes are wide open as she stares blankly ahead, frozen in place.

"OH MY GOD! OH MY GOD! OH MY GOD!" My mind finally registers what's going on around the table. Sarah is screaming hysterically.

"NO SON! NO SON! NO!" Mr. Gerald is yelling with his one eye open as wide as it can go.

"I'm going to kill you," Lily-Ann mutters as she sits still, looking forward, not making eye contact with Aaron or looking over at her mother, who is now face down in a puddle of blood on the table.

"DO Y'ALL THINK I'M PLAYING!" Aaron yells. "YOU'RE ALL GONNA DIE. EVERY, LAST, ONE, OF YOU!" His face now appears unrecognizable, with his hazel eyes now turning jet black. An overwhelming darkness has overtaken him, and the Aaron I once knew seems to have completely checked out. It's like he's possessed—his body physically present, but his soul gone. The man who risked a bullet for me and the kids is gone. The guy who spent hours playing Mario Kart with Adam has disappeared. Now, I see only someone screaming and banging the back of his gun against our now lifeless grandmother's head.

CHAPTER 69

—·—

A aron left the room, and we were left looking at a dead body, leaning over, face down on the table. None of us is saying anything. I can't speak for the others, but I know what I'm feeling right now: *I had no idea he had it in him.* I have tears flowing down my cheeks, not necessarily because our grandmother is dead, because if I'm being honest, she might have deserved that. What our grandparents did was awful—their monsters.

Our mother is no better. She allowed this to happen. She begged her dad to make this go away, and he did. Well, for a little while that is. She never once considered what discovering this dark secret could do to a person.

"Why?" I ask in a low tone.

Everyone shifts their gaze at me, but my gaze is fixed in one direction.

I look at Lily-Ann and ask again. "Why?"

"Why, what child?" she responds.

"Why did you do this?" I whimper. "Why couldn't you have been a good mother? Why couldn't you have kept the damn baby? Why did you hypnotize your freaking sister? Why!" I yell.

"Why do people do any of the things they do, child?" she responds with no remorse.

"Do you have one kind bone in your body? Do you even have a heart?" I ask her.

"You don't know what I went through, child. I loved one man, and my parents took him away from me and made me marry a man I didn't even love. Made me have children by a man I didn't care for. The only thing I had left was my legacy, and when I had boys, I knew they could at least carry on my legacy," she says. "What good were you two girls anyway. Only thing I saw in you two was..."

She pauses and, for the first time, gazes down at her mother's lifeless body, seemingly unaffected by the fact that her mother was brutally murdered right beside her.

"What did you see huh?" I ask aggressively. "What did you see?"

"The only thing I saw in you girls was myself. I saw me, okay!" she yells, snapping her head toward me and holding my gaze. "I saw myself in you two—my mother forcing me to do what she wanted. I saw my inability to live the life I desired. I saw falling in love only to have it taken away. I was jealous because I knew you two would grow up and enjoy things I could never."

I swallow because for the first time, I actually believe what's coming out of her mouth. Her parents really screwed her up. They didn't cherish her because she was the golden child; they controlled her just as she had controlled us. Beth was the child they couldn't control, and that's the real reason they didn't want her around.

"My parents controlled everything about me, child. They didn't care what I wanted. Gerald was the love of my life. We were together through high school. I made one little mistake and asked my parents for help. I didn't know they were going to hypnotize him and make him break up with me," she explains.

This is so wrong. How could they do this to her? These people were heartless.

Taking a deep breath, Lily-Ann says, "Gerald didn't know about the pregnancy. I was too scared to tell him. I went to my parents for advice, and they must have thought it was a good idea for him to end things with me. They hypnotized him into telling me he was in love with another girl. I was left feeling stupid and helpless, getting ready to raise a kid, and I was barely out of high school. I needed my parents to help this go away, so they did what they do best: they convinced Beth that Aaron was her child."

"..." I'm lost for words.

Lily-Ann chuckles, "You know, I didn't even know at first what they did to Gerald until your Grandfather came clean about your dad."

"Wait, what do you mean?" Sarah asks.

Lily-Ann takes a deep breath, "Your grandparents also hypnotized your dad when he decided they couldn't be a part of our kids' lives. They made him leave me as well. They couldn't stand the fact that someone else was in control, so they did what they did best."

I knew something was off about our dad the day he left. He loved our mother, but he loved us more, and there's no way he would have left us with this woman. There's no way he wouldn't have taken us with him.

"Where did he go?" Sarah asks.

"He's dead," she blows out a long breath. "They killed him."

"How? Why? How do you know that?" I ask.

"Many years later, your grandfather was sick, and I went to visit him in the hospital. Your grandmother was already starting to show signs of Alzheimer's, so she couldn't really tell me how he was doing. He came clean on his deathbed and told me where I could find your father's body," she explains. Then her expression darkens. "Don't get me wrong, I cared about your father, but what sent me over the edge was when he apologized to me for hypnotizing Gerald years ago. At that point, I knew what I had to do. I took the pillow and held it over his face until the monitors started beeping, and then finally he was gone."

"Wait, so you killed your father?" Sarah asks.

"I was going to kill my mother, too, but she was already losing her mind, so I didn't bother," Lily-Ann says.

Well, I'll be Damned.

CHAPTER 70

— • —

I guess killing our grandmother was enough for one night for Aaron. He didn't come back the rest of the night. There is no clock in the room, so I'm unsure what time it is, but the sun had already risen. I only knew that because of the little sunlight that peeked in from behind the black curtain earlier. Now it seems like it's getting ready to go down again, leaving me feeling a glimpse of sadness knowing I'll be in this place another night without my babies.

I can't stop thinking about the kids and wondering how they are doing right now. *Are they in school? Did they eat today? Are they scared? Are they even alive?* I have no idea what Aaron has up his sleeves, but if he were so heartless as to shoot an old lady in the head without even blinking, I can only imagine what he would do to two teenagers.

Bam!

The door slams, and this time, both Aaron and Beth have returned.

My eyes widen because I'm hopeful one of them will tell me how the kids are doing.

"Please, are my kids alive?" I ask before either of them can say a word.

Aaron chuckles.

317

"Alive? Lil sis, what kind of person do you think I am?" he smiles, placing his hand over his heart as if he's shocked that I asked him that. "I would never kill innocent kids."

"Relax," Beth rolls her eyes. "We told the little rugrats you and your sister had to go check on Gerald in Atlanta."

Joy is all I feel in this moment. I'm not happy that these two are looking after them, but I am glad to hear that they're alive and they don't have any intentions of hurting them.

Beth walks over to her mother and kneels down as if she needs a closer look. She stares at her lifeless body and then looks back at Aaron. For a moment, it seems like she is sorrowful. *Perhaps she is starting to feel bad about what he did. Is it possible she didn't intend for things to go this far?* My thoughts are quickly interrupted when...

"You did well, son," she stands to her feet and brushes out her skirt. Even in the messiest of situations, this woman will not dress for the part. She is wearing yellow stiletto heels, a green pencil skirt, and a yellow button-up top, and she's carrying another purse that must have cost her thousands of dollars.

"My kids know I wouldn't just run off without telling them myself," I say.

"Lil sis, don't you know me and Adam are besties now. All he keeps asking about is when we're going to play Mario Kart again," Aaron says puckering out his bottom lip, making a sad face.

He walks over to me and kneels so that we are eye to eye. I try to swallow, but nothing goes down because my throat is starting to dry out from lack of water.

"He can careless where you are," he smiles as he holds my gaze.

He slowly stands to his feet and peers down at me, still smiling. The same familiar smile my mom used to give us. The exact same devilish smile, letting us know she has the upper hand.

"Anyway, sweetie, I need to head out," Beth says. "I just wanted to see how things were coming along."

"What's the problem? Can't you do this yourself, Beth?" Lily-Ann asks, shifting her gaze to her sister. "Are you too much of a coward to get your hands dirty?

Beth's expression darkens, and I can see nothing but rage in her eyes. Before I can blink, she's made her way over to Lily-Ann. Staring at her, she slowly removes a small, shiny silver gun from her very expensive purse. I'm surprised it's not covered in Louis Vuitton symbols as bougie as she is! She gently places her purse on the table, making sure it doesn't touch any of the blood that has spilled from her mother's head.

"Say it again," Beth says softly, almost a whisper.

Lily-Ann looks her in the eyes, fearless of what her sister has in store for her with the gun in her hand. "Coward."

Without hesitation, Beth starts beating Lily-Ann across the face with the gun, and her face swings from left to right with each strike. I jolt in my chair, but I'm not sure why. We've been in this situation before because of our mother, so why does it feel like I should help her even though it is clear that I can't?

"Beth!" I yell. "Stop! Please!"

Aaron places his hand on Beth's shoulder, which causes her to stop. It was almost as if she was just brought back from another universe she had let her mind drift off to. He places his hand over hers and slowly lowers the gun. "Ma, I got this. Don't stress yourself. You've been through enough."

Beth shakes her curls and straightens out her shirt. She puts her arm through the straps of her purse, lifting it off the table.

"That was generous of me, sis," she says, peering down at Lily-Ann, with a cold expression. She doesn't have one remorseful bone in her body. She's here for revenge. She wants to see her sister suffer the same way she did the day her parents beat her. She's out for blood.

My gaze drifts back to Lily-Ann, who is smiling after a horrific beating. Her face is bloody, and yet she still seems unmoved. She almost looks possessed, if you ask me. She leans her head back, her eyes lifting as blood drips from a gash over her eyebrow and spills from her mouth. Her teeth are stained crimson, but she keeps smiling, her focus entirely on Beth. "Is that all you got?"

"You deserve much worse," she says harshly, then spits in Lily-Ann's face. "I want to see you bleed out. I want to see you suffer. I want to hear you beg for us to stop. This isn't over, sis, until I'm done, and I'm just getting started."

Beth walks out of the house, and I'm left gazing at my mother's now beaten, bloody face, shocked from what just took place.

That's when it dawns on me: *We're screwed.*

320

CHAPTER 71

— : —

A aron is pacing back and forth, nibbling on his thumbnail. He looks as if he has something pressing on his mind. I'd like to imagine he is second-guessing his current choices, but from the way he shot our grandmother and the way Beth beat Lily-Ann, it is clear to me that these two have one agenda and one agenda only: they're not going to stop until we're all dead.

"Aaron?" I can barely get his name out of my mouth because my throat is dry.

He stops pacing and catches my gaze.

"Can we please have some water? It seems like we're going to be here for a little while?" I ask.

He chuckles.

"Aaron?" Sarah clears her throat. "My horses need to be fed. Do you think you could go by the stable and feed them?"

Aaron glances at Mr. Gerald, who is looking down. I can only imagine how he feels. His only child is a psychopath.

"Do you have any requests?" Aaron asks, gesturing at Mr. Gerald.

Mr. Gerald shakes his head no and returns to looking down.

Aaron chuckles, "This isn't Burger King. You can't have it your way. What do I look like, a freaking server? Did I say I was taking orders?"

"If you don't mind me asking," I say hesitantly. "What are you going to do next?"

Frankly, I'm not sure if I should bring this up. I'm clearly looking at a monster now, and I have no idea what he will do if I push him too far.

"Eeny, meeny, miny, moe," he says, his smile sending a shiver down my spine. "Cut a liar in its throat."

I swallow what now feels like sandpaper in my throat. I'm familiar with the nursery rhyme, but I clearly don't remember anyone getting their throats slashed when picked.

Aaron circles the dining table, touching each of us on the shoulder. "Eeny, meeny, miny, moe."

He stops behind Sarah, and she jolts in her chair, fearful as she feels his hand on her shoulder. He retrieves a pocket knife from the front pocket of his hoodie, pressing the button to flip the blade open. Carefully, he slides the blade along Sarah's shoulder, moving towards her neck, then lightly presses it against her skin. It's obvious he's taunting us now, and if I'm being honest, it's working.

Tears begin to fall down her cheeks, and it's obvious she's scared. We've seen this man kill without hesitation. Who's to say he wouldn't do the same to her?

"Focus on me," I mouth to her.

She nods carefully, trying to avoid the blade.

"If you hurt her, I'll kill you," I say through my teeth.

Aaron smiles at me, "Promise?"

He continues to walk around the dining table, touching each of our shoulders. In my mind, I can hear him singing the nursery rhyme as he touches each of us. *Eeny, meeny, miny, moe.*

I always imagined my last days would be peaceful. I would be on my deathbed, possibly in my late nineties, dying of nothing but old age. I'd have my kids and grandkids sitting at my bedside, singing beautiful songs that would remind me of nothing but the good old days. My kids would be reminiscing about the good times we had together, and their kids would be laughing at the silly mistakes their parents made as teenagers.

My thought is quickly interrupted when I hear "moe," and I see Aaron is standing over Mr. Gerald, peering down at him with the knife barely touching his shoulder.

"Ding. Ding. Ding," Aaron's smiling as if he just picked the winning lottery numbers. "Pops, you're up!"

My eyes burn as I try to hold back the tears that are building up. Glancing around the room, I search for a way out. It's obvious what will happen to each of us, but maybe there's some way out of here. My heart aches at the realization that I can't get us out of here. I've always been the one my sister looked to for help, and this time, my hands are tied; literally tied. I'm conflicted because Aaron is ruthless, and I know he won't hold back.

"Please, Aaron?" I cry.

"Pops, why didn't you ever check on Lily-Ann after sleeping with her and knowing you didn't..." Aaron sways his hands back and forth as if he's trying to figure out how he wants to ask his question. "Strap it up."

Mr. Gerald lifts his head, and with his one visible eye, he catches me and Sarah's gaze and mouths, "I love you."

"Son, I really didn't know. God knows I've always wanted kids. Better yet, I've always wanted a son. Lily-Ann took that ability away from me the day she sent you off with your aunt. Had I known, I swear I would have taken you and left this town so I could raise you myself and give you all the love you deserve," Mr. Gerald explains as tears begin to flow down his cheeks. "You're my son, and I even through this, I love you."

Aaron remains still, his eyes fixed on Mr. Gerald. Maybe what he said struck a chord. Perhaps all he needed to hear was that one of his parents would have loved him if given the opportunity. If Aaron would give his dad a chance, he would—

"NO! GOD NO! NO! WHY! YOU PIECE OF SHIT! WHY!" I scream, eyes wide open, as I watch Mr. Gerald fall face forward on the table.

For a second, I thought what he said to Aaron had meant something. Aaron smiled, and I was sure this night was over, until we watched him glide the knife across Mr. Gerald's neck with such ease, as if he were a chef slicing meat.

Sarah has looked away, but I can't take my eyes off the scene in front of me. Blood is pouring out of his neck onto the table, and his body is jerking as if it is now in shock. He was the closest thing I had to a father, and Aaron just took him away without a care in the world. He bore his soul to his son, and Aaron didn't even blink before slitting his throat.

Lily-Ann, with her bloody face, is surprisingly saying something, but I can't hear anything but my own screams.

"WHY!" I shout as tears pour down my face. "YOU BASTARD! WHY! I'LL KILL YOU!"

Aaron takes the knife and wipes it off on Mr. Gerald's shoulder as if he were just a mannequin lying face down on the table.

"I told you, lil sis, this is the last gathering you'll ever have," he says, his voice cold, as he walks out of the house.

CHAPTER 72

— · —

I t's been days since I last slept. Aaron's been gone for three whole days, and I've lost track of time. The sun has set and risen three times, at least from what I can see of the little bit of sunlight that's peeking in from the side of the curtains. I'm not sure what's keeping him away for so long. Maybe murdering his father got to him more than he thought it would.

My wrists and ankles are tightly bound, immobilizing me, and all I can do is sit here, trembling with a desperate urge to run over and shake Mr. Gerald's body, begging him to wake up. I haven't stopped looking in his direction at his lifeless body. He's just lying there face down in his own blood. I can't help but feel the bile trying to come up as I imagine the way he felt as the blade slid across his neck. He was the missing piece of my chaotic life—his being gone will now feel like an unfilled void, a heartbreak that cuts so deep. We've lost him, and it's as if everything has crumbled into darkness.

"I'm so…" Lily-Ann begins to say, but then gets choked up. "I'm so sorry."

This is all her fault. Lily-Ann had one job, and that was to be a loving mother, but she failed. She had a kid and couldn't stand anyone looking down on her because they weren't married. Who the hell cares? No one is perfect. She should have kept her son and moved out of this town if people gave her a hard time about it. But she took the coward's way out.

"I hate you," I say softly, never taking my eyes off of Mr. Gerald's lifeless body.

"That should have been you," Sarah cries. "Because of you, we're all going to die because someone is more psychotic than you are."

"I..." Lily-Ann hesitates. "I messed up."

"You messed up?" I'm angry and I can't hold back any longer. If my wrist weren't bound, I would jump out of this chair and wrap my hands around her throat, as I look in her eyes, watching her slowly drift away. "You messed up is an understatement. You mess up when cooking, you mess up when writing something, and you mess up by picking the wrong color shoes to go with an outfit. You don't freaking mess up by keeping a whole kid from the supposed love of your life!"

Lily-Ann swallows what I can imagine feels like a lump in her throat.

"I'm going to kill him and I'm going to kill you," I say as I slowly turn my head, making eye contact with Lily-Ann. I want her to see how serious I am. At this point, nice Alice is gone. Right now, all I feel is rage. "Sarah was right that it should have been you. Not him. There's a place in hell for people like you."

My gaze returns to Mr. Gerald's lifeless body, and all I can do is stare.

***

"WE'RE BACK!" a familiar voice announces. At this point, I'm too numb to think. "Ew, y'all stink. Don't you three know how to wash?"

We've been here for days, and I think we have gotten used to the smell of death and piss because Aaron has succeeded by scaring the piss out of us. This situation we are currently in is inhuman if you ask me. They haven't even removed our grandmother or Mr. Gerald's body. Aaron must have left them here as a reminder of what he has in store for us.

"Aww, sweetie, are you okay?"

I shift my gaze towards the doorway and notice it's Beth standing in there with a grin on her face. As I hold her gaze, I imagine myself slitting her throat the same way Aaron did to Mr. Gerald.

"Ma, she's probably still upset with me for," Aaron lifts his index finger and slides it across his neck. "She'll be fine, though. We got some work to do, let's head down to the basement."

"You're not going to get away with this, you know that, right, Aaron?" Sarah says. I'm almost caught off guard because Sarah is usually the one to smooth things over in the family. She's never really been the type to speak up in challenging situations.

Aaron pauses in his tracks and holds her gaze as if he's contemplating something in his head. He rushes over to her side and dares her to say another word. I remember this scene all too well from what happened between Beth and Lily-Ann.

My head is spinning, and I'm too shaken to speak—my throat is parched, and I'm still reeling from what we've witnessed. Aaron is towering over Sarah, daring her to repeat what she said. Sarah glances over at me, as if seeking my silent approval, but at this point, I'm exhausted, so all I can do is hold her gaze.

"I said, you're not going to get away with this," Sarah says softly.

Aaron tilts his head, "Oh, baby sis, you should have just kept your mouth shut."

Aaron takes out his knife, the same one he slit Mr. Gerald's throat with, and begins to taunt her. He slowly slides the knife from her wrist up her arm. He goes over her shoulder blade and around her neck to the next arm. He grabs her head forcefully, pulling it back, and slides the knife across her neck, barely touching the skin.

Sarah is shaking at this point because, in her head, I can tell she knows he's about to do her the same way he did his own father. I swallow what feels like nothing because my throat is dry. Lily-Ann, with her face swollen from the beating Beth gave her, has sat forward as if she's worried about what he's getting ready to do to Sarah. I honestly believe at this point we can't put anything past the two of them.

"Baby sis, do you know why a teacher tells a student to stay quiet in class?" Aaron asks as he slides the knife around in a circle, outlining her face, just barely touching the skin.

Sarah barely shakes her head, trying to avoid any contact with the blade of his knife.

"Because the teacher wants the other students to learn. If the student keeps blurting out in class, how are the students going to learn?" he explains.

"I...I understand," she says softly.

"This is my learning environment, baby sis," he says, grabbing her face, squeezing it.

"I...I understand," she says again.

"Do you, though?" he asks, looking into her eyes.

She nods her head yes.

"WELL SHUT THE HELL UP!" he shouts, his voice booming, and then he raises his arm and stabs the knife into her thigh.

Sarah opens her mouth and begins to scream, but Aaron covers it with his hand.

"Scream and I'll slit your throat just like pops over here," he yanks the knife out of her thigh, taking some of her flesh with it.

Sarah bites down hard on her bottom lip to keep from screaming, causing her lip to bleed. Tears are flowing down her cheeks as she shifts her gaze to me. It's almost as if she's looking at me for help. I'm her big sister, the strong one—the one who promised her years ago that I would get her out of this town.

I've failed her. I've failed my kids. We're all going to die in this place.

CHAPTER 73

— · —

A aron and Beth are down in the basement, like every psychotic person, they always have to reveal their big plan before killing everyone. They informed us of their plan to finally burn down this house now that they had the stash of pills and the instructions to keep producing more. Beth didn't feel like she needed to hold on to the house because of all the awful memories.

For once, I can agree with her on this. If I ever make it out of here alive, the first thing I'm going to do is sign the paperwork to get this place demolished.

Aaron told us that they plan to hypnotize the entire town again, so Beth can have what's rightfully hers. I'm assuming they are referring to the town since their parents practically owned everything in it. Also, they don't want anyone asking questions about our whereabouts, so he figured they'd have everyone, including my kids, forget we even existed.

Aaron was nice enough to wrap Sarah's leg before they headed to the basement. He told her it wasn't her time to die yet, so he wanted to make sure she didn't bleed out from the stab wound. Freaking crazy if you ask me. He doesn't want her to die yet, so his bright idea was to patch her up to save her temporarily.

"Are you okay?" Lily-Ann asks in a low tone.

"Yes, Mom, I'm just fabulous," Sarah says with a bright, overly cheerful smile, meeting our mother's gaze. "I was just 'kindly' stabbed in the leg—just a little pinch, really. It hurts like crazy, but at least I'm still alive," she adds, with exaggerated cheer.

I can tell Lily-Ann is regretting asking her that question, so she looks away, trying to hide her shame.

My body is exhausted, and I'm starting to feel drained. I try to rest my head against the chair's back, but it feels like it weighs a ton of bricks. Instead, I lean sideways and let my head fall onto my shoulder, wishing I were anywhere but here. My mind flashes back to the day I gave birth to Adam. I'd tried to be a hero and push him out without an epidural, but the doctor gently reminded me that this medicine was created so women like me didn't have to suffer through the pain if we didn't have to. The kids' dad had already left, but at that moment, nothing else mattered—I was holding my precious little bundle of joy, who weighed seven pounds and ten ounces.

The nurse handed him to me, wrapped in a hospital blanket. His eyes were wide as he stared at me. I softly kissed his forehead and reassured him that I would always be there for him and his sister. I promised him I would never abandon them, unlike their dad. He was too weak to be around my mom, so he walked out on his family. I assured my son that he could always depend on me.

Sarah was there for moral support, and I remember her smiling at me, telling me how I did a good job pushing Adam out. She was so excited to be an aunt again. She felt bad that the kid's dad had left, but she admired my strength to keep pushing forward, even with a new baby on the way.

Looking up at her as I lay on the hospital bed, she towered over me, smiling. She gently brushed the wet strands of hair from my forehead, wiping away the sweat that had built up during delivery.

"Alice, you're so strong, sis. I love you," she said as she planted a kiss on my forehead.

"Alice?" I hear my name. I keep seeing my sister's face staring down at me.

"Alice?" Someone whispers, and I imagine my sister planting a soft kiss on my forehead.

"Alice?" I blink, and the image of that day begins to fade away slowly.

"Alice?" I blink again, and at this point, I know I'm dying from lack of food and water, and maybe from blood loss from the accident, because I can see a man kneeling beside me, trying to untie the rope from around my wrist.

"It's okay, Alice, I'm gonna get you out of here. Help is on the way," the man says, his face a blur, so I can't make out who he is.

"Am I dead?" I ask because most people say your mind is taken to a happy place before you die, and my last memory was of the day Adam was born.

"It's okay, Alice, I've got you. Hang in there, don't close your eyes," the man says. "Oh God, there's blood everywhere."

"Are you an Angel?" I ask, still unsure who this person is.

"It's Mike. I need you to hang in there. If not for me, for Kandice and Adam. They need you," he reassures me.

"Mike?" My eyes widen at the mention of his name. "Mike, is it really you?"

A single tear starts to roll down my cheek as my head is leaning over, too heavy to hold up.

Mike pulls out a pocket knife, and my instant reaction is panic at the sight of the knife. I honestly don't think I want to see another knife again. If I survive this, I'll never cut a piece of chicken or slice a loaf of bread with a knife ever again—I'll just become a professional fork user.

"Knife," I say as another tear falls down my face. "Oh God, the knife," I cry.

"It's okay, I got you. I'm here," he says.

With the knife, he lowers it to my wrist, and I believe my mind is now playing tricks on me. I don't think this is Mike at all coming to save us. I believe it's Aaron getting ready to cut my wrist so I can bleed out a very slow, torturous death. Realization hits me when I no longer feel the tight restraint around my wrist. I'm able to move my arm, and the first thing I do is lift my hands at eye level so I can see for myself that I'm free.

"Oh God, Mike. It's really you," I cry. He wraps his arms around me and holds me tightly as I cry on his shoulder. In that moment, I'm thankful that someone is here to save us.

"Come on, we don't have much time before they come back," he reminds me.

He cuts the rest of the rope from my other wrist and my ankles and makes his way over to Sarah and frees her as well. He looks at me for approval to free Lily-Ann, because let's be honest, we are in this situation because of her. In this town, because of her. In my mind, I feel we should leave her here to die next to her mother, but something happened between the three of us while knocking on death's door. She opened up and let herself become vulnerable, something I've never seen our mother do before.

"Help her to," I nod my head in Lily-Ann's direction, hoping that I'm not making the biggest mistake of my life.

Mike rushes over to Lily-Ann and cuts the rope from around her wrists and ankles. She rubs her wrists, and I notice the marks around them from the rope. Her gaze falls on Mr. Gerald's lifeless body, and I notice the tears forming in her eyes. *Maybe she really did care for him, in her own twisted way.*

"Well, well, well," Beth says as she appears in the doorway of the dining room, startling us. "Look what we have here."

CHAPTER 74

—·—

Mike reaches behind him and grabs his gun, which he must have had tucked in his pants. He steps in front of us and tells us to stay behind him. Pointing the gun at Beth, he informs her that he's going to take us out of here and for her to stay where she is. He tells her that backup is already on the way, so she doesn't have anywhere else to go.

Beth smiles that same sinister smile as if she's already won this battle. She walks all the way into the dining room with her hands raised. She sits in the same chair I was bound to for days. Probably forgetting I pissed in that chair. *Oh well, I'm not going to tell her what she's sitting in.*

"Do you know how fast a house can go up in flames, dear?" she asks, getting more comfortable in the chair and crossing her legs.

"That's not going to work with me, ma'am," Mike says, still pointing the gun at her.

Beth smiles.

"Did you know that most older homes used gas for both heating and cooking?" she asks, cupping her hand under her chin.

"What's your angle here, Beth?" Mike asks, intensely focused on her.

Beth chuckles.

"Well, dear, if you shoot me with that gun, I promise you just signed your own death certificate because we're all going to die from the explosion," she says, leaning forward, holding Mike's gaze.

"Where's Aaron Beth?" Mike demands.

Beth chuckles again, "Who?"

"Don't play with me, Beth. I saw the files in the office," he says.

"Files?" I ask.

"That's what I needed to tell you, Alice," he says, still pointing the gun at Beth. "That day we searched your mother's office, those papers I needed to look into were copies of Aaron's birth records. I saw his birth certificate with your mom's name on it."

I felt like an idiot because Mike was trying to warn me, and I was thinking he was trying to kill me.

"When I returned to Atlanta, I had a friend look into it, and it turns out that your grandparents covered the whole thing up. They made it seem like Beth was the one who gave birth to Aaron," Mike explains, unaware that we've already figured all this out. He's just confirmed what they told us is true.

Beth claps her hands.

"Congratulations, you figured it all out, you're a real detective," she says sarcastically.

"Where's Aaron, Beth?" Mike asks again, steadying the gun on her.

"Oh dear, he's just tampering with the gas lines," she says casually. "You know, making sure this place goes boom."

That's when it hits me that Aaron must be lurking nearby. Beth has stayed calm the whole time, knowing he's probably close by. She's probably just diverting our attention so he can make a move.

Before I can warn Mike, Aaron comes from the other entrance of the dining room and tackles Mike to the floor like a linebacker would in a football game. The gun flies out of Mike's hand and slides across the dining room floor completely out of sight.

The two of them are now wrestling on the floor. Currently, Mike has the upper hand because he is on top of Aaron, pinning him to the floor. With his right fist, Mike throws a powerful jab directly at Aaron's face, causing Aaron's head to jerk sharply to the left. Without hesitation, Mike repeats the move, this time punching with his left fist, making Aaron's head swing to the right. With each punishing strike, Aaron's mouth begins to bleed, blood trickling from his lips as he absorbs the relentless beating.

Aaron finds a way to get out of Mike's trap and jabs him in the ribs several times, causing Mike to tumble over in pain. At this point, Aaron has gained control and has Mike in a headlock, throwing power punches to his face.

Sarah, Lily-Ann, and I must be in shock or too weak to move because we stand there, unsure of what to do in this moment. We should help Mike, but what can we do?

With both hands tightly wrapped around Mike's neck, Aaron refuses to let go; his grip is firm and unrelenting. Mike is struggling to reach for something, but there's nothing to grasp. He tries to press his thumbs into Aaron's eyelids, but it's clear Aaron's hold is too strong—Mike appears to be on the verge of passing out at any moment.

My eyes scan the room for something I can use as a weapon to help him. I peek out of the dining room and spot a small flower vase on the entry table. Without hesitation, I grab it and rush back to the two of them wrestling on the floor. I put all my strength into my swing and hit Aaron as hard as I can on his head. This must have worked because it caused Aaron to loosen his grip and look behind him to see who had hit him.

"I'm gonna kill you," he says through his teeth as he attempts to get up.

Aaron seems off balance, likely from the blow, as he struggles to stand. This gives Mike the upper hand, so he quickly grabs him from behind, causing him to fall backwards onto his chest. Mike then wraps his legs around Aaron's midsection, pulling him close. With his legs locked in place, Aaron can't get up, giving Mike complete control. Mike pulls Aaron even closer, allowing him to wrap his forearm around Aaron's neck and put him in a sleeper hold. I'm not a fan of fighting, but I've seen some of these moves on TikTok from these self-defense coaches.

Mike uses his other hand to grab the arm wrapped around Aaron's neck. He leans back, using all his strength to hold on tight. Aaron swings his arms wildly and kicks his feet, trying to grab anything to hit Mike with, but he's not lucky. He starts swatting at Mike's face, but Mike remains unmoved. He continues to hold his grip, pulling Aaron closer as he leans back.

Aaron's feet are no longer moving, and his arms have dropped to the floor. Mike loosens his grip, but not too much, just in case Aaron is faking. Once he realizes Aaron is out, he pushes his body off of him and lies on the floor trying to catch his breath. *I guess it's tiring trying to put someone to sleep.* They don't show us that part in those TikTok videos.

Lying on the hard floor, Mike slowly lifts his head, his eyes gently shifting upward as if searching for something above him.

"Where did she go?" he leaps up, his eyes darting frantically around the room, his breathless state forgotten. "Did y'all see where she went?"

For a second, I forgot about Beth. I was focused on Mike and Aaron wrestling on the floor; I completely forgot she was in the room. She must have sneaked out during all the commotion.

"Oh God," I say. "I didn't see where she went."

Rushing through the house, I head for the kitchen, recalling the back door—the same back door I saw Mr. Gerald come out of years ago to burn the evidence for our mother. Sadly, it's also the same back door I remember going out of when I discovered what my brothers had done to little Tobby. I shake off those memories and open the door, scanning the area. It's pitch black, I can't see anything. I go back to the dining area, and that's when I'm suddenly taken aback by Mike, Sarah, and Lily-Ann standing there at attention with their hands raised.

Sarah signals with her eyes for me to turn around, and there Beth is standing, pointing Mike's gun at the three of them—and now at me.

"Sit down," she tells us. "Not you," she says, looking at me.

The three of them take a seat, still with their hands raised.

"Take it easy, Beth," Mike says, his eyes laser-focused on her. "Nobody has to get hurt. We can all walk away from this."

"Shut up!" she snarls, spitting a little. "Check my son, Alice. If he's dead, I'm putting a bullet in all your heads.

As I approach Aaron, who is lying still on the floor, I wonder how long someone can stay unconscious after being put in that kind of hold. Right now, I'm praying for a pulse, hoping Mike didn't accidentally kill him when all he meant to do was knock him out.

My heart races as I kneel beside Aaron on the floor. My hands start to sweat and tremble. I glance back over my shoulder at Beth, who is still pointing the gun at the others. I see the determination in her eyes; she will kill us all if her son is dead. I fix my gaze on Mike, who gives me a reassuring nod, indicating it's okay to check him. I'm silently praying that the nod also means that he knows Aaron is not dead. *He would know something like that, right?* Reaching out my arm, I extend my index and middle fingers, like I've seen on those rescue shows, and press them against the side of his neck.

"I feel a pulse! He's alive!"

CHAPTER 75

— • —

With a sudden jolt, I leap to my feet and turn to Beth, assuring her that Aaron is still alive. I plead with her to let us go, since she's already reached the end of the line, informing her that the odds are now against her. Mike has already told her that backup is on the way, but I'm starting to wonder when they'll arrive. She isn't concerned about any of that right now, though. She's ordered Mike to tie Lily-Ann's wrist to the chair, then he'll tie Sarah's wrist down, and I'll be forced to tie his wrist down, leaving her to restrain me once more.

"Beth, come on," Mike interrupts her, likely trying to buy us some time. "You don't have to do this."

It's clear he's trying to pull the whole good cop routine on her, but from what I can see, it's not going to work. Right now, I don't know exactly what it is, but a fire burns inside me because I'll be damned if I go back in that chair. She's just going to have to kill me.

"Beth, please, you don't have to do this," I try to reassure her, echoing Mike's calm tone and steady voice. "Let us go. You can head out now. Maybe you'll get away."

"I'm not going anywhere," she hisses. "This is my town and my inheritance. I won't let another person run me away. I'm taking what's mine."

Beth pulls the slide back on the gun, loading a bullet in the chamber. She steady's the gun and points it in my direction. At this point, we have one of two options: we can do what she's telling us and possibly get burned to death, or we can try our best to get the gun away from her. I ponder for a moment because my mind takes me back to when Aaron got shot. His chances were pretty slim against the intruder who had a gun. *What are my odds?*

Thinking back on some of the TikTok videos I've seen, I realize I'm not going to let myself be a prisoner another day. I vow to stop letting my family's past hold me back from making a change. Another man will not die at the hands of my psychotic family. I also remind myself, it's time to go home to my kids—they need me.

With my hands still in the air, I act like I'm turning around slowly, as if I'm going to do what she told us. I give Mike a look that tells him I'm about to do something either really brave or really stupid. Whatever it is, I quickly spin back around, catching Beth off guard, and I charge at her with all my strength. She drops the gun, and we both crash to the floor.

Wrestling with her, I have the upper hand because I managed to get on top of her, just like Mike did to Aaron. She shoves her hand in my face as hard as possible, trying to push me off. I notice the gun is within our reach, and she sees it too. She reaches for it, but at that moment, I'm faster and kick it away, unsure of its exact location because it's no longer in my sight. Beth growls and strains with all her strength to push me off, but I don't move. I've officially entered fight or flight mode. All I can think about now is the promise I made to Adam when he was born, that I would never leave them.

"Mike, get the—" I'm suddenly caught off guard, frozen from being in shock. Beth has wrestled herself free, pushing me aside with force. Now we're both sprawled on the floor, eyes wide, locked onto what horrifies us. My life flashes before my eyes—every moment rushing past in a dizzying blur—and I can only swallow what feels like a hard lump that's formed in my throat, struggling to breathe as panic grips me.

Lily-Ann has the gun, and she's pointing it in our direction.

Oh God, what have I done?

CHAPTER 76

— · —

R eaching her hand out in front of me, steadying the gun on Beth, Lily-Ann helps me off the floor. I'm not sure whether to be grateful or nervous. Our mother has never helped anyone. She always wanted to get rid of me. Why would she help me now?

As I look at her, still reeling from what just happened, she wraps her arm around my neck. I'm not sure what to make of it, but I flinch instinctively. I'm unsure if she's about to try to choke me, but she does the complete opposite—she hugs me, a genuine hug.

"I'm sorry," she whispers in my ear while I'm in her embrace. "Take care of the kids and your sister."

This feels like a goodbye apology to me, as if she's preparing to do something reckless and irreversible. Deep down, an inexplicable sadness washes over me. Maybe it's because I finally saw the real Lily-Ann while she was restrained and vulnerable. Or perhaps it's because she was controlled just like us, unaware of her own strength or choices. Maybe she was struggling to break free from that cycle. Whatever the reason, I gently hug her back and rest my head on her shoulder, feeling an overwhelming rush of emotion. This moment—this hug—is the first genuine connection I've ever experienced with my mother, and it cuts deep.

Finally, we can hear the sirens. Backup is nearby, but they haven't reached the top of the hill yet. Mike grabs a pair of cuffs out of his back pocket and places them around Aaron's wrist. He taps him in the face a few times, instructing him to wake up. Aaron looks confused at this point, unsure of how he's gotten in this position.

Mike helps him to his feet and begins to guide him towards the door.

"Ma, get out of here," Aaron cries, fighting the best he can with his hands behind his back. He peeks his head around the corner and holds Beth's gaze. "You better not hurt her or I'll—"

"Or you'll what, you piece of crap?" Mike asks, pushing Aaron in the back of the head, continuing to lead him towards the front door. "Ladies, come on, let's get out of here. There's nowhere for her to go now."

I look at my mother and tilt my head, silently pleading with her to come with us. A tear traces down my cheek because I understand what her apology truly signified. She has no plans of leaving this house. Somehow, this must be her way of trying to do the right thing. I suppose she feels like she owes it to Sarah and me.

"I didn't mean it," I cry, shaking my head. "I don't want you dead."

Steadying the gun on Beth, Lily-Ann lifts one finger to her lips, "Shh. I know. Aaron had one thing right: this will be the last gathering we will ever have. You won't have to deal with my family ever again. It ends here."

"Mom?" Sarah cries from behind me, placing her hand on my shoulder. "Please come with us."

Lily-Ann gestures for Sarah and holds her in a tight embrace. She pushes her away as if that was the hardest thing for her to do. I notice what looks like tears forming in our mother's eyes. This must be real because I had no idea that the devil I thought she was could produce tears. She wipes at her cheeks and instructs us to get out of here.

"You're not stupid, sister. You might have them fooled, but I know exactly who you are," Beth says, eyes laser-focused on our mother as if she's not going down without a fight.

"Go on now, get out of here!" Lily-Ann demands us. "You don't know me at all, Beth."

Mike's voice erupts with panic as he yells at Sarah and me, his eyes blazing with urgency. "Get out! Now!" he commands, his tone leaving no room for hesitation. Without warning, he shoves Aaron toward the door with fierce desperation, forcing him into a frantic tuck-and-roll onto the ground. Sarah and I exchange a final, frozen glance with Lily-Ann, our hearts pounding in our chests. Lily-Ann gives a nod of approval, and without a second thought, we bolt towards the door, adrenaline surging through our veins, knowing our lives are about to change forever.

"Mom, don't forget!" I yell as I dash out the front door, running as fast and as far away from the house as possible.

My chest is burning from sprinting, and I'm gasping for air. I place my hands on my knees, leaning forward to catch my breath. Suddenly, red and blue lights flash, and multiple police cars arrive. Aaron is desperately trying to fight his way back to the house to get back to Beth, but Mike has him pinned to the ground.

"Momma! Momma!" Aaron screams frantically. "Momma! No! Momma!"

One of the officers suddenly leaps out of the car, his eyes sharp and commanding. He urgently asks Mike how many suspects are inside the house. Mike hesitates for a moment before replying, "Two. One of them is armed and dangerous." A surge of frustration and anger rises within me at his response. She's the one who just saved us all, but he fails to mention that. If it weren't for her, none of us would be standing here right now.

The scene unfolding before us resembles a tense moment straight out of an action film. The police presence is heavy, with a row of police cars straddling the tree line, as their flashing red and blue lights illuminate the area. Several officers are covered in tactical gear, alert behind the protective barrier of their vehicles, each armed and ready, their weapons aimed steadily at the house. A few officers are launching drones and are prepared to fly them over the scene. A powerful spotlight has been mounted on a tripod, its blinding beam illuminating the entire front part of the house, revealing every crack and crevice in detail. As the tension escalates, Detective Hudson arrives urgently at the scene, stepping out of a sleek black SUV. Clutching a megaphone tightly in one hand, he surveys the area, his expression grave but determined, prepared to give commands.

Detective Hudson stands in front of the row of police cars with his belly protruding. His shirt still looks as if it is too tight, and one of the buttons is ready to pop off at any minute. "We have the area surrounded!" Detective Hudson says into the megaphone. "Come out with your hands up!"

We all wait in silence, wondering if either Beth or Lily-Ann is willing to give themselves up. If Lily-Ann came out, she'd be going to prison, possibly the death penalty for murdering a police officer, forget the rest of the people she's killed. Murdering an officer calls for maximum punishment. Beth, on the other hand, may serve life in prison for kidnapping, assault, and being an accomplice to murder.

"We are prepared to come in!" Detective Hudson instructs through the megaphone. "Come out with your—"

BOOM!

The house explodes in a fiery blast, and everything around me plunges into a deathly silence. I am unable to hear any sounds; all I can do is witness the chaos unfolding before my eyes. Aaron is sprinting with his hands cuffed behind his back towards the blazing house, his face set with determination. Several officers have quickly tackled him to the ground to prevent him from getting any closer. Sarah drops to her knees, her hands trembling as she clasps them over her mouth, her eyes wide with horror. Mike stands nearby, his hands interlocked on top of his head in a stunned gesture, as if he can't believe what just happened.

The other officers have taken cover behind their cars, instinctively shielding themselves from the fierce, flying shards of burning debris that threaten to hit them. And me, well, I remain perfectly still, rooted to the spot, my eyes fixed laser-focused on the house. I am frozen, trying desperately to process what I am seeing. The house—our grandparents' house, the place we grew up in, and the house that holds so many painful memories—is finally going up in flames.

CHAPTER 77

— • —

SIX MONTHS LATER

Time passes quickly when you're not running for your life every day. I can honestly say my bad dreams have gone away. I'm no longer looking over my shoulder. It hurts when I walk outside and look over at the house beside me. It brings back so many bad memories. The poor old lady next door was murdered in that house. Mr. Gerald took over the house, and then he was also murdered. Maybe that house should have gotten burned down as well. Perhaps that's something I'll run by Aaron when I go visit him in prison.

Some may call me crazy, but yes, I visit my oldest brother in prison. I'm learning how to forgive and trying to move forward in life despite my messed-up family history. To me, it's not all Aaron's fault. He was passed off to his aunt without hesitation. Our aunt, who raised him, was hypnotized into believing she gave birth to him. If that doesn't send a person off the hinges, I don't know what will. Honestly, I feel sad that he never got to know his siblings. I really think that if he had been in the picture, things might have been different. Cameron wouldn't have been the oldest, so maybe he wouldn't have felt so entitled. James was nice to us once upon a time, so perhaps with

Aaron around, he wouldn't have had a brother influencing him to kill people's dogs and torture his sisters.

Aaron was pretty cool when he wasn't trying to slit our throats and put bullets in our heads. I honestly felt a connection with him at one point. I really do miss him being around here at times, hearing him and Adam screaming to the top of their lungs about who is winning at Mario Kart.

Adam has his moments of sadness because he can't convince Kandice to play the game with him. As for me, I don't understand the buttons on the controllers, but I do my best to play with him. I've tried to encourage him to get some friends from school to stay over so they can game all night, but at this point, he's ready for a change. If I'm being honest, we all are. I think someone trying to kill us twice now is enough for us to finally say it's time to pack up and head somewhere else.

So I've connected with a realtor and decided to put the house on the market. I was unsure at first who would want to live in this crazy town after everything that has happened here, but surprisingly, many thrill-seekers have become fond of Shelly Grove and its history. I've decided all the thrill-seekers can come as much as they want because soon we'll be heading to Atlanta.

This town has become the talk of all social media apps. A lady reached out to me and asked if I'd be interested in telling my story. I told her I was already two steps ahead of her because I had started writing this book about my life a long time ago, unknowingly, when I would write in my journal. *Thank goodness I kept those journals all these years.* I've just had more to add within the last two and a half years of my life.

We are scheduled to have a potential buyer visit the house today for one more walk-through. I suppose they want to ensure it's everything they've hoped for in a home. Apparently, they are also big fans of my psychotic family and decided they wanted to be closer to feel what the mysterious Mrs. Sally was thinking. *They must be a couple of nut jobs if you ask me.*

Winter is in full effect, so I don't have to worry about cutting the grass or trimming any bushes. I suppose that's one of the advantages of selling your house in the winter. Not too many people care to be outside for too long when it's this cold. The last couple that came for a showing quickly took a peek outside in the backyard and hurried back in. They said it was too cold to be outside. I guess they weren't the right ones, though, because they ended up buying Mr. Gerald's house next door. Maybe my house didn't have enough dead people connected to it.

I'm trying something a little different this time, though. I'm desperate, and we are ready to get out of this town. I watched a video on how to get people interested in buying your house, and the lady mentioned leaving a note and some treats to make the potential buyers feel more at home. "There's nothing like walking into your house and smelling a fresh batch of chocolate chip cookies," the lady on the video said.

So I've made a batch of melt-in-your-mouth chocolate chip cookies and placed a few cups of hot cocoa on the counter in those little to-go cups you can get from the coffee shop. I did happen to take a few from Mr. Brewer's down the street. It's a new coffee shop that's opened up in town. One of those thrill seekers decided we needed another coffee shop, as if Sarah's donut shop didn't already have the best coffee in town. Sarah's okay with Mr. Brewer's being here, though, because she's decided she's ready for a change as well, so she will be tagging along with us and moving to Atlanta as well.

"Mom, can I get one?" Adam asks, reaching his hand out to grab one of my melt-in-your-mouth cookies.

I swat at his hand because if he's trying to get out of this town, no one is going to buy my house with a batch of half-eaten cookies. It's something about a fresh plate of cookies. You have to lay them just right to make them look appealing, and if he takes even one from the batch, that's it, game over, house not sold.

"How about we make a fresh batch of cookies later when Kandice gets home. I saw these Valentine's Day cookies, and I wanted to try making them. Apparently, they come out red if you follow the recipe right," I say, hoping this will help get rid of this cookie monster.

"I guess that does sound kind of cool. Red is my favorite color," he says.

"Okay, well, make sure your room looks good, so we can step out for the potential buyers to come view the house. They will be here in about forty-five minutes," I instruct him.

"Ugh, why are they coming to look at it again? Do they want the house or not?" he asks. "And why are we leaving now if they're coming in forty-five minutes?"

"Well, buying a house is a big deal, and a big purchase, so I'd want to take another look at a house before making a final decision if I were them," I explain. "And I'd like to take a few more items to drop off at the thrift store that we aren't taking with us when we move."

"Alright," he sighs, heading back upstairs.

I continue to set the stage for the potential buyers to view the house one last time before making their final decision. Following the lady's advice from the video, I write a nice note instructing them to take a cookie and feel at home. I tell them that this place will bring nothing but great memories to their family. I fold it neatly in a hamburger style, just as we learned in elementary school, and on the front, I label it "Take One" with a bold arrow pointing to the batch of cookies.

"There, this ought to do it," I say to myself with a smile.

I head to grab my purse from my room so Adam and I can head out, but my cell phone vibrates on the kitchen counter. I pick it up and notice it's Shelly Grove PD calling.

"Hello," I answer, confused as to why I'd be getting a call from them.

"Ms. Alice," a familiar voice says on the other end.

"Detective Hudson, is everything okay?" I ask.

"Sorry to call you, do you have a minute?" he asks.

"Yes, of course," I say, putting the phone on speaker as I walk through the house to get my purse out of my room. "What can I help you with?"

"Do you remember when I told you that I pay close attention to detail?" he says.

I nod my head as if he can see me.

"Well, I've been running through this report and I'm trying to make sense of everything from the night of the house explosion," he says, and then coughs. I can tell he's moved away from the phone because his cough sounds a little distant.

"Yes...what about it?" I ask hesitantly, locating my purse on my ottoman.

"Well, my report states there were only three bodies found in that explosion. From what I understand, y'all told us there would be four. We've identified three of the bodies but…" he pauses.

I pick up my purse and place it on my shoulder. I also grab my boots because I don't want to freeze my toes today by wearing tennis shoes.

"What do you mean, three bodies?" I ask. "And who were the three identified?"

"Mr. Gerald," he clears his throat, moving the phone away from his ear. "Your grandmother, and…" He pauses for a moment, coughs again, and then continues, leaving me on edge from the sudden break in the conversation. "Lily-Beth, the lady who claimed to be y'all's aunt."

My heart is pounding because everyone saw the house go up in flames. Officers on the scene even said there's no way anyone could have survived that explosion. It took the fire department a considerable amount of time to put out the fire, and they were concerned that the nearby trees might catch fire.

"So you're telling me…" I stop because at this moment, I'm not sure I'm understanding what he's saying. Everyone around us saw the fire. That's all we could see was the fire because of how big the house is.

"Yes, ma'am," he coughs again, saying a few curse words this time because he's beginning to have a hard time talking on the phone. "I'm telling you, your mother Lily-Ann did not die in that fire."

EPILOGUE

"So, Alice, we've all seen the social media posts about your hometown," Jade, the television host of All Is Not Forgotten, says. A show that talks about how the past can shape individuals for their good or for their bad. She's been in contact with me for over six months, and she read a few pages of my new best seller, Controlled Through Time. According to the producer, she contacted me immediately after learning that I was the woman from Shelly Grove with the crazy mother. Apparently, she knew she would be inviting me on her show one day.

It took us a little over six months to get to Atlanta, but that's okay. The right couple needed to find our house, and the house needed to touch the right couple. It just so happened that the cookie trick worked, and the note they absolutely loved. They told the realtor that it's an idea they will have to pass along to a friend or family member because they're not going to use it, as they plan on making our house their forever home.

"So, tell us, how do you feel seeing your real-life story constantly on repeat every second of the day on social media?" Jade asks. "I can't imagine going through what you and your sister endured, and God even the kids, and having to see it on socials. That has to be awful."

My cell phone vibrates and I pull it out of my back pocket. I read the message and sent a quick response back.

"Sorry, Jade, kids," I say jokingly. "But to answer your question, it doesn't bother me. I want the world to know what happened in that town. I want people to see that we don't have to become our past or even like our parents. I vowed never to raise my kids the same way my mother raised us. I want Adam and Kandice to know without a shadow of doubt how much their mother loves them."

Jade places her hand to her chest, "This is why we do what we do here on this show. Girl, that was deep."

I chuckle.

"Thanks, Jade," I say.

"So how did it feel having to wait over six months for someone to buy your house? I remember you expressing how desperate you all were for a change," she says, crossing her legs, getting comfortable, I assume, for my next response. "Why did you wait? Isn't your family like super wealthy?"

I nod.

"You know, it was a little nerve-racking. It seems like when you need something in that moment, time always moves slowly. I just tried to keep the faith that one day someone would buy it," I explain, then I chuckle at her next question. "And my family is super wealthy, but I've never been big on living off of my inheritance. I've always wanted to work for what I want and make an honest living. That's what I'm trying to teach my kids, at least."

"Wait, so you're telling me you didn't take the money?" Jade sits straight up and holds my gaze.

I chuckle.

"Oh, I took the money, I just said I want to make an honest living. It's okay to have a rainy day stash set to the side," I say with a chuckle.

Jade laughs.

"That's exactly what a rich person would say," she says with a chuckle.

"So tell us about your brother James. Has he tried to contact you at all now that you're all over TV?"

I shake my head no.

"Does that worry you at all? I mean, wasn't he one of the ones who tried to unalive you and your sister?" she asks. "Sorry, we can't use triggering words on TV anymore."

I think back to the night of the explosion when the house went up in flames and everyone was panicking. Aaron specifically. He was tackled to the ground because he was crazy enough to try to run towards the explosion. When the officers got him off the ground and escorted him back to the police car, I noticed something lying in the same spot he had fallen. I recall thinking to myself that something must have fallen out of his pocket.

Without hesitation, I rushed over to where they had tackled him and picked up what was on the ground. I slipped whatever it was into my pocket, making a mental note to look at it when I wasn't surrounded by a bunch of officers, including Detective Hudson, who always pays attention to detail, according to him.

After being treated at the hospital and released a few days later, I remember noticing the pile of dirty laundry that I'd been meaning to get done before I was taken. I went through my usual routine, checking the pockets of all my pants and hoodies before loading them into the washing machine. As I sifted through the clothes, I recalled the nurse putting my clothes, which I was wearing when the officers took Sarah and me to the hospital, in a small bag. Grabbing the bag, I reach my hand in and pick up each piece, adding it to the washing machine. I pulled my pants out of the bag, and something fell out onto the floor: *a Ziploc bag?* It was the bag I had found on the ground. I picked up the bag and took a closer look at what was inside. I was reminded of what Beth had said that night—that she'd found the instructions and the family inheritance. It was clear to me what I had put in my pocket that night.

I pulled it out and observed it. It's a quart-sized Ziplock bag with about a handful of tablets inside and a folded sheet of paper. I pulled the paper out of the bag and observed what was written down: a *recipe*. But it wasn't just any recipe; it was labeled 'Family Inheritance.' I was holding the recipe for the tablets our grandparents created to hypnotize and keep people hypnotized. I was holding my family's inheritance. It felt wrong. I wanted to burn it. I wanted to call Sarah and tell her what I found, but then something hit me. Something that surprised even me. I was tired of being caught off guard. I had something in my hand that could change my life. I no longer had to worry about whether James was coming back because now I have the power to control him.

I put the bag and the folded piece of paper in a safe place. I told myself I wouldn't use it unless I were in a desperate situation. Well, that desperate situation arose sooner than I expected when I decided to trick the couple interested in our house. I followed the instructions on the paper thoroughly, crushed a few tablets, and added the powder to the cookie dough. I wasn't sure if baking them would weaken the strength of the tablets, so I crushed a few more and added the powder to the cocoa. I made sure they had a note to read, which essentially told them what they were going to do: *take a cookie and feel at home.* This was why I was adamant about Adam not eating the cookies. I would never forgive myself if he ate those.

"Alice?" Jade interrupts my thoughts.

"Sorry," I say with a smile. "To answer your question, no, it doesn't bother me because this time, if he were to come back, I'm prepared for him. Nobody in my family can ever catch me off guard again."

www.ingramcontent.com/pod-product-compliance
Lightning Source LLC
Chambersburg PA
CBHW020549120726
47903CB00001B/189